The Disinherited

100

THE
Disinherited

BY

Michel del Castillo

TRANSLATED FROM THE FRENCH BY

Humphrey Hare

ALFRED A. KNOPF, *New York*

1 9 6 0

c. 2

L. C. Catalog card number: 59–15322
© Rupert Hart-Davis, 1959
THIS IS A BORZOI BOOK, PUBLISHED BY ALFRED A. KNOPF, INC.

FIRST AMERICAN EDITION

Originally published in French as LE COLLEUR D'AFFICHES. *© 1958 by René Julliard. Published in England as* THE BILLSTICKER *by Rupert Hart-Davis, Ltd.*

H R

To Michel Remy-Bieth

these pages are dedicated as
a first stage in our friendship.

Foreword

IN 1936 I was only three years old; I was six when I came to France with the flood of refugees after the Franco victory in 1939. So this book is not a direct account of a war which I obviously could not understand, and of which I have only a few confused memories.

But the Spanish Civil War has scarred me for life. It was on scenes of blood that my eyes first opened. My childhood cradle rocked with the lyric tirades of the Republicans, and with the racket of bombardments. At the age when other children drop off to sleep with Teddy bears in their arms, I was hurrying with my mother down into the cellar of our building, my belly hollow and my throat tight with fear. For many years the conflict that ripped apart the country where I was born made me an exile and an alien.

I am a product of this war, and I see it now with more than merely the eyes of a novelist. Is it surprising, after all, that I should want to understand it better in order to trace my roots within it?

I have not written a book of history. The true chronology, the exact military positions, the actual course of battle matter little to me. All I tell here is what I remember and what has been told me by dozens of witnesses of good faith. And, above all, there was much killing in both camps.

Of course, the Civil War is only a pretext here. Between 1956 and today a good many events have occurred to enrich and occasionally even to modify this book; for what interested me are those still relevant elements in that 1936 revolution.

Nor is this book *engagé* in the leftist sense of the word. I had no intention, in writing it, of instructing or attacking. I have little taste for polemics, and the only commitment I accept is toward myself and toward God. Nonetheless, I have had occasion, in some of these pages, to touch on contemporary questions and especially to speak of Communism and Communists.

I have never belonged to the Party and am thus not a renegade. But neither am I anti-Communist. Communism needs neither apologists nor detractors. It is what it is, and every man must define his position in relation to it. This is what I have done here—I believe, with honesty. The accusations I make against the Communist Party and the crimes for which I hold it responsible can surprise only a few simple souls. We all know that tomorrow's song is made from the tears of today.

Each one of us owes it to himself to assume or reject these crimes. It is a personal matter, and I can easily conceive that a person might, after having read my book, join the Communist Party in all good faith. I say, very simply, that if bloodshed is absolutely necessary in making history, I would rather someone else did the history-making. That's all.

Does this mean that nothing matters to me? *No!* No one can withdraw from the issue that easily. In spite of ourselves, we are plunged into history, and sooner or later we are forced to take sides. But there is a great difference between taking sides and joining a party.

Having said that, I must add that it was never my intention to write a political book. If my characters are sometimes obliged to speak politically, it is merely an accident. On the contrary, I remain convinced that the solution to this problem, a problem that seems fundamental to me—the suffering and the alienation of men by men—must be found elsewhere than in any political program.

Perhaps some readers will be surprised that, after having frequently stressed my atheism or at least my religious indifference, I concern myself so largely now with the religious problem.

I have undergone no spectacular conversion. I have not been visited by the Holy Spirit. But I have always felt an agonizing need for that God to whom I bear witness so badly. To many this avowal will seem a weakness; but what man can boast that he doesn't feel a need so human?

PART ONE

The Way of Hope

"I have heard so many arguments that have almost per-
suaded me and have sufficed to
persuade others to consent to
assassination. . . ."

ALBERT CAMUS
The Plague

The Way of Hope

I

OLNY opened his eyes; his mother was clattering pots and muttering under her breath. Motionless, he watched her out of the corner of his eye as she moved about nervously, her face drawn and her gray hair still uncombed, wearing her eternal black dress and *espadrilles*. She looked older than she was, and the young man thought: "It's the work." She turned toward him, and he closed his eyes, not wanting to talk; she would only start whining again about the way his father treated her. "She probably loves it, down deep," he told himself; but, on second thought, what did he know about it? He had no idea what his parents were like; their lives were apart from him. They had given him nothing but beatings and mistreatment. "The bastards," he thought.

"Up! I told you to *get up!*"

His young brother started to cry. Each morning their mother found some reason to beat the child. She kicked and pummeled him, in the belly, in the head. The boy went on crying.

"You brat! You little stinker! Get the hell out of bed!"

3

Olny did not move. When he had been Francisco's age, she had beat him, too, but he had never cried. He had been able to stand up to her and answer back, which had infuriated Consuelo, but Francisco was weak. Olny disliked people who cried; still, he loved his young brother.

"You finished hitting the kid?"

"Oh, you're up, huh? . . . I do what I want around here, and if you don't like it you can get the hell out. This is my house, and if I want to smack him I smack him! Understand?"

Olny rose slowly from his mattress on the floor. He had slept fully dressed. He ran his bony fingers through his hair, and his mother drew back as he moved toward her.

"Manuel!" she shouted. "Manuel!"

"Go ahead, call him, your man. You know as well as I do he's so drunk he can't see straight."

"That's none of your business. Your father can do what he wants. You've got a lot of nerve!"

Olny approached her slowly, his voice tight. "Listen to me, you bitch. If I ever catch you hitting that kid again, you'll be damned sorry, you hear? I'll leave and I won't come back, and you and your rotten husband can starve here!"

Consuelo stood her ground, her small black eyes burning like coals, her jaws clenched. "You have no right to talk to me that way. I'm your mother, remember? Your mother!"

Olny stared at her with contempt. "My mother? You don't even know what the word means."

4

Consuelo lunged forward and twisted her fingers into his hair. He almost shouted with the pain, then tore himself away. Crazy with rage, he raised his fist and smashed it down again and again. His mother slid to the floor with a dull cry. He kept pounding, and Francisco shrieked: "Kill her, Olny, kill her!"

The young man turned to him, his tone weary. "Go out and play."

"I didn't eat yet."

"It's not time to eat."

"I didn't have anything last night."

Olny looked at his brother with sorrow and started toward him. The child cowered and threw his arms up in front of his face. "Don't get scared, Paco. I'm not going to hurt you." He laid his hand on the trembling boy's black curls. "You afraid of me?"

"No."

"Then why are you shaking?"

"I don't know."

Francisco was ten. His eyes were black, and his short nose turned up slightly over his full lips.

"Paco—what do you do when I'm not here?"

"I play."

"Do the other kids hit you?"

The boy bent his head; his eyes filled, his nose trembled, and his lips tightened.

"A lot?"

Francisco shrugged.

5

"Why don't you hit them back?"

"I'm sick."

"How do you know you're sick?"

"I just know."

"But what do you feel? Where does it hurt?"

"Everyplace."

Olny hugged the boy's head to him, suddenly overcome with disgust. He had to get out, leave everything—the Zone, this shack, his parents. . . . "What do you want to be when you grow up?"

"Like old man Almadon. Play the trumpet and make a lot of dough."

"Don't say 'dough,' Paco. Say 'money.' "

"It's the same thing."

"No, it's not. Dough is slang."

"Everybody around here says 'dough.' "

Olny was quiet for a moment. Then he asked gently: "You want to leave here, Paco?"

"What do you mean, leave?"

"Don't you want to live in a real house, in the city?"

Paco shrugged again. "I don't care."

"Why not?"

"She'd be there, too."

"Who's 'she'?"

"Consuelo."

They were silent again. Olny was tired and found nothing more to say. He closed his eyes. "You don't like her?"

"I hate her! She's a dirty whore!"

6

"Paco, don't say that."

"I know! I saw her out in the empty lots with old man Joyal the day before yesterday. I was hiding and I saw everything."

Olny didn't answer. He reached into his pocket and pulled out a peseta.

"For me?"

"Here—go get something to eat."

Francisco scurried out. His older brother stood for a moment, unmoving, then let himself down on a bench against the wall and looked around him. There were a couple of mats on the ground, a white wooden kitchen table, a stove, and a faded screen that divided the room; behind the screen was the large folding bed his mother and father slept in. Here and there around the walls his mother had stuck religious pictures and holy palm branches.

Olny's face crinkled with disgust. He had never had any home but this filthy, miserable shack. His whole childhood had been surrounded by these same four scabbing walls, and now he had to get out. He cracked his knuckles—where would he go, and how? He earned just enough to keep from starving as it was; he could never pay for a room, too. Besides, no one would hire a man from the Zone. He looked at his hand, closed it, and then ran it through his hair. What a lousy mess. Then he noticed his mother, still writhing on the floor, sobs shaking her skinny shoulders.

Olny wanted to strike out, pour onto her the immense disgust that was in him. He crossed the room, and she cried:

7

"It's not true, Olny! I swear! He's lying! He hates me! I swear to God . . ."

"Get up." There was no sound. He repeated brusquely: "Get up."

Consuelo obeyed. She wiped her nose, twisted her skirt into place, and tried to say something. But Olny was not listening. He was spent, dizzy with lassitude and futile despair, an automaton. He took his mother by the arm and dragged her outside.

They went down the Zone's only road, lined with shanties and makeshift shelters, in the air stinking of garbage, bad wine, and old cigarettes. The neighbors, from the doors of their huts, understood that something was going to happen and followed the young man and his mother, murmuring and signaling.

"What's going on?" someone asked.

"Consuelo."

"Boy, now she'll get it," snickered a third, rubbing his hands.

Olny seemed to hear nothing and see nothing. He crossed the full length of the Zone and stopped before a damp-rotted wooden shack on the Madrid route, the bar near the vacant land. From under a sign at the door a small thin man, with dark eyes and thick hair, watched the group approach without surprise. The two men gazed at each other wordlessly. The silence swelled around them and the spectators drew back. The young man pushed his mother toward the shack and asked in a broken voice: "You know her?"

"Your mother? She's one of my best customers, even if she does owe—"

"Don't get funny." The young man's voice was low, threatening.

"What do you want, anyway?"

"I want to know what happened the night before last."

Joyal smiled vapidly, like a movie Don Juan. "You really want to know?"

"Yes."

"You asked for it, son! . . . Your mother was alone, and bored. . . . She was telling me how your father wasn't strong enough to satisfy her very often. So . . . I'm a good guy. . . ."

Laughter rippled around them. Olny reddened and sweat ran from his forehead. Slowly he pulled his knife from his pocket; only the click of the opening blade broke the silence. With encouraging murmurs the crowd retreated a little more, the women in the front.

"Go ahead, Olny! Cut 'em off!"

"Don't be scared, kid!"

"Remember your mother's honor!"

Joyal pulled his own knife out of his pocket and watched Olny indifferently. "Okay—if that's how you want it!"

Joyal came toward the young man. Olny did not move. He watched every gesture, possessed by a terrible, superhuman desire to kill; a huge hatred gripped him. Joyal must die. The young man's glance had gone cold, metallic, as murderous as the edge of his knife; his jaws were tight, his body iron-springed, ready to lunge. Joyal stalked about him, and he pivoted. Neither dropped his eyes. Each awaited the faintest signal of inattention, of fatigue; each felt the weight of the crowd's eyes, their unbreathed breath. The children stretched on tiptoe to see, and the women gasped. Suddenly Joyal leaped on his enemy. But Olny stepped aside; the older man lost his balance, stumbled, and sprawled on the ground. The knife bounced from his fingers, and Olny covered it with his foot. Then Joyal, white, damp-faced, opened his eyes and gazed up in anguish.

"I'll explain! Let me tell you—"

Olny, unblinking, raised his arm high and plunged it down in rage. The man tried to avert the blow, but could not. He cried out the raw cry of a wounded dog, and a wave of black blood flooded from his mouth. Olny held his victim's body with his right foot and freed the knife. He struck three times more, while his eyes flowed tears and his hands quivered.

Finally the young man rose and moved away silently. The watchers respectfully made way for him. While his mother sobbed quietly in a corner, the children bent to kick at the cadaver. The women laughed uncomfortably, and the men reviewed the fight in low voices, step by step.

His back slightly bent, Olny walked toward home. He was sick to his stomach. He had no regrets about killing Joyal, nor had he been sickened by the sight of the man shaking with fear of death. It was all familiar. He had grown up with this kind of savage brawl, single and collective ones. That was the Zone. No, he didn't regret it—what had he killed, after all? One man, when it was the Zone that needed killing. He had to lie down.

His father was sitting on the bench inside the shanty. He was a medium-sized man, with dark eyes and hair already turned white; he wore black pants, a white shirt, and a filthy beret that he never took off, even to sleep. Olny did not greet him. He opened a drawer in the white table, took out a box full of cigarette stubs, cut some apart, and rolled a new cigarette with the tobacco.

"There's no more tobacco," he told his father. "Go look for some butts."

"I'm sick," the drunk mumbled. "I'm sick. . . ."

Olny stared at his father with contempt, and the old man coughed and spat on the floor. "I'm as tired as you are. But still I go to work every day so you won't forget how to chew and swallow."

The drunkard whimpered: "Nobody cares about me. . . . Nobody loves me. I'm so unhappy."

Split between disgust and pity, Olny said nothing. He wanted to tell the old man that he loved him, that he loved them all, despite their badness and their filth, that he understood their misery. But he said nothing, only closed his eyes and caught his head between his hands, the cigarette dangling from his lip.

"I'll go if you want," his father said.

"Never mind. I'll find some on the Castellana."

The young man rose and left the hut, his father following behind him. Outside children played, screaming at each other and throwing stones. Some old men squatted in the sun, hats jammed down on their heads, taking butts apart. Olny reached the wasteland, where the garbage trucks of the city dropped their cargo, and he strode faster. Once he heard his father's voice calling for help, and when he turned he saw the old drunk sitting in a wet patch of mud. The children had gathered around him, pushing at him, and Olny hesitated. Then he spat on the ground and walked on.

2

WHEN Olny reached the office where he worked, he had to wait a few minutes at the door. The other workers were already there, and he greeted them with a slight nod; then he went and stood with Ramírez.

Ramírez was about thirty; he wore his shining dark hair long and had jet-black eyes and a straight, thin nose. Born in Burgos, he spoke a slow but extremely pure Castilian. Olny knew very little about him, for Ramírez never talked about himself. Nevertheless, the two young men had become friends.

"Hola!"

Ramírez looked up and smiled affectionately. "Hola!"

Olny hesitated a moment and then suddenly made up his mind. "I just killed a man," he said.

His friend seemed not to have heard him. Then he asked abruptly: "From the city?"

"No, a guy in the Zone. He laid my mother."

The two young men spoke in low voices, as if they were in the confessional.

"Did you kill him because he was sleeping with your mother?"

Olny did not answer right away. His forehead was burning hot; he needed to feel a woman's cool, refreshing hands against his face. "No," he replied in a low voice. "I don't know why I killed him. It was as if I went crazy. What I wanted to kill was the Zone. You know what I mean?"

"Vaguely."

They fell silent. Passers-by stared at the two friends. Olny's *espadrilles* were full of holes; his trousers were patched; his shirt was torn.

"Aren't you going to say anything?" Olny asked.

"What do you want me to say?" Ramírez seemed to hesitate, then asked: "Do you think the police'll find out about it?"

Olny smiled bitterly. "Never. What do they care if there's one more or less of us in the Zone? But that's not what I wanted to talk to you about." After a moment he went on. "Can you understand how you can want to kill a man?"

"Yes. But I think it's stupid."

"What's stupid?"

"What you've done."

Olny didn't argue. Ramírez never tried to understand, to

put himself in anyone else's place; he spoke like a judge, pronouncing some infallible, immutable law. He had an absolute, precise answer for everything. Olny felt uncomfortable and would have liked to tell him . . . What exactly did he want to tell him? About hunger, poverty, vice—all the things that are so difficult to talk about.

As if he could read his thoughts, Ramírez said: "So you've killed a man—so what? The Zone's still there, and you'll go on living in it. You haven't changed anything. It was a futile gesture. Every act that doesn't fit into a definite social movement is gratuitous, pointless, without meaning."

Ramírez often said things like that. Olny didn't understand them, but he thought his friend's outlook was too simple, too clear-cut. He felt somehow that reality was infinitely more complex. But he could not translate this feeling into words and so kept silent.

"You should come to Carabanchel," said Ramírez. "You'd understand things better."

"Understand what?"

"Everything. That it's both a filthy and a fine thing to be a man, for instance."

Olny lowered his eyes. Ramírez had been asking him to go with him to Carabanchel for some time. But he had always refused, for he was afraid of politics. What bearing could politics have on his own life? But because this morning he would have welcomed any wisp of hope, he replied: "I'll come if you like."

"Tomorrow?"

14

"Okay."

Ramírez smiled. "You'll become a man!"

"You think so?"

"I'm sure of it!"

A bell rang and the two friends went into a big hall where the walls sweated dampness. For a few moments they stood in line at a counter. A clerk gave them a meal ticket and a five-peseta bill.

"What is it today?" Ramírez asked.

"Calo-Cream."

The men loaded the sandwich boards on their shoulders and left the office one by one.

Above the street and the brightly dressed crowds the sky was blue, the sun warm. Cooking smells rode the air. Well-dressed young men sat on the café terraces, drinking beer with French fries. There was such a hollow pain in Olny's stomach that he felt dizzy. He nearly wept at the sight of the glasses full of beer. He couldn't even remember what beer tasted like; the last time he had drunk it had been October 12, and it was seven months now since he had been able to afford it. How many bottles had those young bourgeois emptied in seven months? There they sat, wearing a different suit each day, having their good shoes polished. They looked casual and proud; their features were refined, their hands well tended. When they laughed they showed white regular teeth. And yet Olny did not hate them. To see them there day after day, not knowing what to do with all their time, did not revolt him. That was what life was like, he thought, and it was not their fault that the Zone existed. He had been born on the wrong side, that was all!

The two friends went down the Gran Via toward Alcalà Street and Cibeles Square. The sandwich boards weighed heavily on their shoulders, and they walked in silence. Passers-by glanced at them absently; one or two stared at Olny insolently and laughed, but he walked on, unembarrassed. He was used to it.

He had been doing this job ever since the age of fourteen because it was the only job a child of the Zone could get. Most people in the Zone lived by begging or stealing. But Olny preferred to work, for the one thing he feared above all else was the reformatory. Friends of his had been sent there; he had seen their ravaged faces and dull eyes. He had guessed that their silence was due to hunger, beatings, atrocious punishments, appalling loneliness, and suppressed hatred, and he had sworn never to suffer that. It was better to carry a sandwich board through the center of the city. The work was not too hard and it gave him an opportunity to enjoy quietly the sights of the city he loved. He glanced sympathetically at the children playing in the squares, gazed at the thousand changing hues of the sky above the roofs, strolled through the richer districts that were redolent of peace, good cooking, and expensive perfume. He could forget about the Zone and its smells.

Olny had reached La Castellana. The trees were fragrant, and the well-to-do were sitting in comfortable chairs, laughing and talking of women and of bulls. But he kept his eyes glued on the ground. From time to time he stooped and picked up a carefully selected cigarette butt.

"Look, Ramírez! A 'Craven A'! It hasn't even been lit! Do you want half?"

"I don't smoke butts."

"But it's not a butt! It's whole. Look."

"You found it on the ground. I don't smoke that kind of thing."

Olny shrugged his shoulders. He could not understand his friend. Which was better: not to smoke at all, or to smoke an English cigarette picked up on La Castellana? He lit the cigarette, smiled, closed his eyes, and inhaled slowly. The odor of rum and honey made him feel giddy. He wished the moment could last forever.

"There are good things in the world after all!" he said in a low voice.

Ramírez smiled bitterly. "For the others!"

"But I'm the one that's smoking."

"Other people's butts."

Olny had no answer, but he felt that Ramírez was a little too concerned with his own dignity.

He walked on in silence through the quiet, elegant streets of the Salamanca district. Pink-cheeked children all dressed in white were playing ball, and Olny thought of his little brother. Francisco was no fool—in fact, he was intelligent. His features were just as refined as those of the children who lived in this district. And yet Francisco would never be a

17

gentleman. And even if Francisco did manage to become one, there would always be other children, poor, starving, ragged, who could never make it. He tried to suppress a mounting feeling of rebellion, but was unable to master it.

Olny was young and his heart was full of loving-kindness; it was not a heart made for revolt. Yet, what else could you do but rebel when day after day you were thrust deliberately further and further into squalor, refused the right to live, even?

He was not asking much: only the right to leave the Zone, forget, and put his strength at the service of no matter whom. But this right was refused him. He was given the choice of prison, total poverty, drunkenness, or this work that did not give him even enough to eat.

He stopped thinking. The word "eat" reminded him that it was nearly time for lunch. He felt a strange, heavy weight in the hollow of his stomach, and his legs were trembling.

The sun was scalding, the air thick with the scent of cooking food. Radios shouted the latest news, and Olny pictured families sitting around their dining-room tables. Mealtimes were the worst for him. He felt even lonelier then, hungrier, and more miserable.

The two friends turned back, stepping painfully on the simmering asphalt. The streets had emptied; traffic had almost died. Olny felt like stopping and sliding gently to the ground, never to get up again. He clenched his fists and swore, hard, to give himself courage. Ramírez said not a word. His eyes were bloodshot and his face had turned livid.

But he clamped his lips tight and went on walking slowly down La Castellana.

When they got there at last, they put down their sandwich boards and went into a huge hall with bare, whitewashed walls. There were long white marble tables and wooden benches screwed to the floor. Fifty or sixty workers were waiting, standing in line against the wall. They were all clothed in rags and unmatched *espadrilles*. They coughed continuously, spat, and scratched themselves, staring insistently at a door that seemed determined to stay shut forever.

It opened at last and two young women came in, carrying a basket filled with slices of black bread and piles of tin bowls. They put them on the floor and waited a few moments. The men crowded together, jostling and insulting each other. There was a sudden silence and the superintendent came in.

She was a woman of about fifty years, short, thin, with blue eyes, very white hair, her face sharply rouged. She was dressed entirely in white and carried a whistle between her lips. She signaled with her hand. The two young women seized the bread basket and walked slowly down the line of workmen, each of whom took a slice and handed over his meal ticket in exchange. Those at the head of the line naturally took the biggest slices. The others protested and swore. The woman with the white hair said curtly: "If you go on whining, you won't get any bread at all!"

The noise stopped at once. Olny watched the basket as it

drew near. By the time the two women came to him, it was almost empty. There was a curious constriction in his throat. He took a piece of bread, then changed it for another. There were mutterings behind him. Olny blushed. He felt ashamed and disgusted with himself; he stared at the piece of bread and dared not raise his eyes.

The whistle sounded. The men went to the tables and stood by their places. They carried their rations of bread in their hands, for it was forbidden to eat them before the superintendent gave permission. The whistle shrilled again in the silence.

"Oh, Lord," began the superintendent, "we thank Thee for Thy infinite mercy. We pray Thee to bless those who help us and forgive us our sins. Amen." She recited the words in a loud voice, and the paupers repeated them after her and at last they could sit down and be served their soup. The superintendent gave each one a ladleful.

Unconsciously Olny rubbed his hands together. He held out his bowl. Three potatoes and a piece of cod floated in boiled water. Smiling with pleasure, he cut his slice of bread in two and made a sandwich of the cod. Then he squashed his three potatoes and ate the mash, slowly, to make the pleasure last longer.

"Swap my soup for your bread."

It was the man on his left. Olny looked up, hesitated, then said: "Let's see."

The other showed him the contents of his bowl—a few potatoes and two pieces of cod. Olny couldn't make up his mind. At last he murmured: "Okay."

He took his bread from his pocket and took out the cod. He was happy. He could always buy bread and he preferred to eat a double ration of soup.

When the meal was over, the superintendent said another prayer, and the paupers left the canteen. They went in silence, walking with their shoulders bowed. Some sold their ration of bread at the door or traded it for cigarettes. Olny was still hungry and wondered if he would ever be able to eat his fill. But he told himself it was better to eat even a little than nothing at all, and went over to Ramírez. The two friends smoked a cigarette before starting their walk through the streets of Madrid again.

They stopped work at seven o'clock in the evening. They had earned a welfare meal and five pesetas—the price of a couple of pounds of bread.

3

WHEN Olny reached the Zone, night was falling. The sky was colorless. One single star, green and twinkling, was already alight. The air was cool, but it smelled of garbage and poverty, and shouts and insults rent the silence. Dirty, ragged children chased each other.

Olny halted, closed his eyes, spat as far as he could, and swore. He hesitated before crossing the wasteland. Then, walking slowly, he came to the first hut.

The Zone was crowded with noises. Prosky was beating his wife, and the woman's unhappy cries drowned out all the others. Prosky was of Polish origin. No one knew or cared whether it was his real name. All that was known of him was that he always beat his wife before making love with her. He made her undress and whipped her with a leather belt. He seemed to do it without pleasure, almost reluctantly.

The children of the Zone peeped through the cracks in the wooden walls of Prosky's hut.

Stealing is a difficult art. There are classes among thieves, and the greatest of these is the pickpockets. And among the pickpockets there are still other classes: those who work with their fingers, and those who use the razor; those who work alone, and those who need lookouts. The art can be learned, but the apprentice must start young. Maestro Piccioni provided training in his "Academy."

Signor Piccioni, of Naples, was the most respected man in the Zone. Tall and slim, with brown hair and pale blue eyes, he could have passed for a Frenchman. He even spoke French with the accent of Tours—and English with an Oxford accent, Italian like a Roman, and German with the accent of Hanover. He knew everything, read Dostoevski and Balzac, and his conversation glinted with quotations from Cicero, Dante, and La Bruyère. He had been in Paris, Rome, London, Bucharest, Istanbul, and knew their prisons as well as he knew his own pockets. The most comfortable prisons, he said, were the Danish ones; the English were the dullest, the Spanish the funniest, and the French the dirtiest. He was the idol of the children of the Zone, and in their daydreams they grew up to be like him.

He lived not in the Zone but in Madrid itself, journeying each day to the edge of the city, dressed elegantly as a gentleman, his shoes gleaming, his tie and gray gloves spotless, his head crowned with a brown derby. He looked like a real schoolmaster. Piccioni spoke with pride of the two generations of pickpockets he had sent into the world, and the walls of the Academy were spotted with photographs of those of his students who had made names for themselves—Oe-the-Mexican, Smiling Ramon (Pretty Teeth Ramon). They served as examples to the class. "You could be another Oe-the-Mexican. You're deft, decisive, quick. You need only a touch more suppleness to your fingers, a shade more *savoir-faire*," he would tell a student encouragingly.

When the seven-year-old apprentices began to study, Signor Piccioni would start them on what he called their "scales"—a series of exercises designed to limber their fingers, make them longer, stronger, capable of working separately. After four or five months they were permitted to practice on a dummy. The first finesse was to develop "the touch"—discover which pocket carried the billfold. Then came the real work. Students with long supple fingers would work with the hands alone, while others learned to slash pockets and untie purses. Only after six months more did the professor allow a good student to go into the field. The first time the student would go with a professional and watch him work; sometimes it was even Piccioni himself.

The maestro worked the public transport during rush hour. After a brief survey he would spot his quarry and stand close. In the crush he would lose his balance and jostle the victim, excusing himself with a disarming smile and "I'm so sorry—it's terribly crowded."

Now he knew where to find the billfold, and the maestro set to work. His two fingers, index and middle, moved steady as pincers, and in seconds the button was undone and the wallet in his own pocket. All that was left to do was get off at the next stop, calmly, without haste.

Thievery was not an immoral act in the Zone; it was a profession. Everyone did it, one way or another: the least enterprising were shoplifters; others did armed robbery. They were the big shots. People listened to them, admired them, dreamed of living the way they did. They would gather around a bottle and talk freely about the jobs they pulled off; anyone could go hear them. If there was one thing everyone shared in the Zone, it was hatred for the police.

Still, it wasn't easy. Most of the young robbers were picked up and sent to the reformatory. They would disappear for a while, six months or a year, and suddenly reappear one day with their heads shaved, their bodies terrifyingly thin and striped with scars. Depending on the charges, they might have been at Carabanchel, at Alcalá de Henares, or at Barcelona. Those who went to Barcelona came back different people.

24

Poor people throughout Spain spoke low when they spoke of the Asile Duran. It was worse than prison; young people dreamed of becoming twenty-one and beyond its reach. No one really knew what life there was like, because those who came back never talked about it. But their manner of not talking about it was worse than the darkest tales. It was their black, hating silence, their cold gaze, their hunched shoulders. These were enough.

Olny had needed all his will and strength to keep from joining his companions. But he dreaded the Asile Duran, and its fearful name alone had kept him from the life of vice and crime which is the last revolt of the poor. Olny had been the closest friend of José-Antonio.

He was a thin dark boy, with the deep, shadowed eyes and long features of an El Greco. And he was good. He loved dogs, and flowers, and longed to go to America—anywhere that had no Zone. His mother and her lover, who lived with them, beat him black and blue, and finally he decided to leave. But he needed money. He made his plans and, without telling even Olny, his sole friend, he broke into a villa he thought was empty. He was caught and sent to Barcelona, and it was two years before he returned.

It was a Sunday. Olny was out in the wasteland and he saw a face he dared not recognize. José-Antonio had lost almost all his hair; he was bald at nineteen. In his eyes was something so terrible, so atrocious that Olny could not speak. They clasped hands silently.

"How are you?" Olny said.

"Okay."

The next day they found the shredded body of José-Antonio on the tracks. And from that day Olny was afraid. He understood that all there was ahead of him was to be taken someday by the police and sent to Barcelona. He was probably the only one to mourn the lost boy.

Olny closed his eyes. Why was he remembering those things again? Because of the Prosky woman's screams. He tried vainly to black out his childhood, that ugly time of filth, vice, blows, and fear. The cloying, indefinable smell of the Zone was enough to thrust him back into a past he wanted to forget. He clenched his fists and silently swore at all the gods. It was all he could do—blaspheme. It released him. But as he was not too sure of the existence of God, it was not much consolation.

He walked on slowly. The women were cooking in front of their huts, blowing on their *braseros* and concocting the strange dishes found only in the Zone: rice with carrots, potatoes boiled in wine.

There was an area of pain in Olny's mind—all those screams and insults resounding through his childhood. That was why he so much loved to walk through the richer districts of the capital: because there all was silence. A silence that contrasted with this hell of abuse that went on the whole day long. He ran his long, bony fingers through his long, fair, curly hair, which a few paler locks made even lighter. His eyes were green; his eyelashes too long; his nose

26

thin and long, very slightly curved. His lips were thick and heavy, like overripe figs, and his teeth were large, regular, and white. There was a strange look in his eyes—a look made up of weariness and disgust, but also of love. Tall, thin, narrow-shouldered, and stooping, he wore an expression of perpetual apology: apology for having been born, for existing. Shy and resigned, he talked very little, yet he had the makings of a leader: he was a man. As a boy, he had won respect and obedience from his companions. Though he had fought rarely, he had done it well. He had left Toni —a talkative, conceited Italian—stretched out on the ground, half dead. After the fight, he had gone off quietly to wash his hands. Gestures like this had won him the admiration of the other boys.

He stopped in front of his hut, found his key, and opened the door; he placed the bag of rice and potatoes he had bought on the table and, sitting down on a bench, burrowed his head in his hands. He was exhausted; he had crossed the Zone like an automaton, seeing and greeting no one. He had reached the end of his strength. He heard his mother's raucous, inhuman voice outside. "I could have been rich. . . . The police sergeant wanted to marry me! . . . I could be living like a queen! If only it hadn't been for the kids! Because I come from a good family . . . yes, sir! I can read and write, you know. Did you know that? I even took piano lessons when I was young! Yes, sir, my father was a gentleman! Not like yours, who was a pimp! We had moral standards in my family! We used to say grace before meals!

. . . Yes . . . I even know the prayers by heart! You want to hear me recite them? You don't? I'm no liar, I want you to know! *'Turris davidica ora pro nobis, Turris eburnea ora pro nobis . . .'* And the Mass, too! *'Introibo ad altare dei, ad deum qui . . .'* "

"I don't give a damn."

"Well, you're wrong! Damn wrong! Because if you'd had the faith, we wouldn't be here today! You ruined my life, that's what you did! I should have married my sergeant!"

"Well, why didn't you marry your lousy cop? If you knew how little I care!"

"You lousy bastard! You queer!"

Olny shook his head, and his lip twisted in disgust. He knew these quarrels by heart.

His parents came in, holding each other up. Their eyes were red, their noses purple. Olny stared at them without moving a muscle of his face.

His mother tripped and kept herself from falling by grabbing the table. "You here?"

Olny did not reply. He looked from one to the other.

His mother hiccuped. "We weren't drinking, you know! Weren't drinking! Just a drop to wet our throats a little."

His father began whimpering: "I'm a bum, son. I know it. I'm a no-good. Nobody loves me. No one."

Olny said nothing and looked down at his big hands. He remembered José-Antonio. The two friends used to go in the evening to the wasteland hand in hand and dream of leaving. Brazil, Argentina, Australia—how those magic names sang awake their hopes of a better life, a juster one!

"We'll get some kind of a job, all right," José-Antonio used to say. "We've both got guts. We're men. We're not afraid, eh? We'll go into the jungle if we have to. It'll be better than here, anyway. Then we'll come back with our pockets full of money, with suits on, and wearing ties. We'll just say how do you do to them, eh? We'll always be together, the two of us. . . ."

They forgot reality, imagining they had already left, no longer aware of the reeking, clinging smell of the Zone. It was with José-Antonio that Olny first understood that in the poorest man hope is still immense; and that it grows greater the worse life is.

Francisco came in and sat down quietly by his brother. "Did you bring anything?"

"Yes."

"Potatoes?"

"Yes."

"Good!" The boy rubbed his hands, and his eyes grew brighter. He looked at his parents, spat on the ground, and said: "You'll have to fix them."

"What?"

"The potatoes."

Olny looked at his brother in amusement. "What about Mother?"

"Her, she is drunk. She burned them the other day. You

do all right. You get something at noon. But us . . ."

Olny hesitated; then he got to his feet, took a knife and a saucepan, and began peeling the potatoes.

Francisco came over and started to help. "Olny?"

"Yes?"

"Could we really go away without Consuelo?"

"Maybe."

"You won't go without me, will you?"

"No."

"I could help you. Like now."

"Sure you could."

"That'd be good. Maybe I could even learn to play the trumpet. Do you think someone can earn a living playing the trumpet?"

"Why not?"

"I don't want to go to the Duran. So I'd like to earn my living the right way. But first I have to learn to read, of course. Do you think you have to know how to read to play the trumpet?"

"I don't know. I don't see the connection."

Francisco stopped talking. He drew close to his brother, putting his small curly head on Olny's chest, and said in a low voice: "I like you a lot. I'm proud of you. You're stronger than anybody. I mean you can even kill a man, but you never hit me. You're good."

Olny put his knife down and kissed the boy tenderly. "I'm not good, Paco. It's hard to be good, maybe even impossible. If I were good, I wouldn't have killed Joyal. It's ugly to kill someone."

"You are good. If Consuelo and the old man were like you, we wouldn't be here. And I'd be able to read. I'd be learning how to play the trumpet."

Olny fell silent. He, too, at Francisco's age, had blamed his parents for their worthless life. He had often sworn that one day he would spit his hatred and contempt in their faces, or kill them. But now he understood that it was practically impossible for a poor man to escape from the Zone; that life took hold of him and put him there. He guessed that his parents also must have dreamed once of a better life; they must have had their hopes. Weary and sickened, they had tried to forget them. For, if it is true that hope is always fresh in the human heart, it is no less true that when hope is useless, a man grows weary of it.

4

IN THE middle of the night Consuelo came awake sharply and sat up in the creaking bed. Her mouth felt furry; her head ached; there was a humming in her ears. With a trembling hand she searched for her shawl, spread it over her shoulders, and got up. She left the hut silently, carrying a spade, and went and crouched outside. The sky was heavy with stars and the air was cool. The Zone had sunk into the shadows; the crooked huts and hovels were asleep. Consuelo coughed, spat, got up, and filled in the hole she had dug.

When she went back into the hut, she realized her elder son was not there and she wondered what he could be doing outside. Then she shrugged her shoulders: after all, he did as he liked; it was nothing to her. Olny hated her, she knew. Perhaps he was right. And if he were wrong, he had his own reasons for doing so, which amounted to the same thing. She lit a candle and looked to see if her sons had left her anything to eat. The pan was empty. Consuelo felt tears sting her eyes and she ached with hunger. She had fallen asleep—but when? She wasn't sure. Olny had been peeling potatoes and talking to Francisco. How she hated that boy!

Consuelo went back to bed, and it creaked again. Francisco was asleep beyond the screen. He moaned a little in his sleep. She felt suddenly she wanted to touch him and smiled at the thought. "Little brat!" she muttered.

Consuelo did not understand life, neither her own nor other people's. Perhaps there was nothing to understand. But why and how had she become the drunkard she was? How had she landed in the Zone? Why did she hate her children?

Lying on her back, her eyes wide open, Consuelo stared into the darkness, and shivered. She had gone to bed fully dressed, but the cold was inside her; shouting thoughts tumbled through her tired mind. She felt as if she were living a nightmare. Everything was blurred, imprecise. She wanted to understand—but understand *what?*

Consuelo had been born near Valencia, in the Huerta. Her parents were honest peasants living in a white thatched cottage in a forest of orange and lemon groves. The Mediterranean lapped a few yards away.

Consuelo's mother was a little woman, prematurely aged and inured to labor. She sewed for the ladies of the town, and though she worked at her sewing machine twelve hours a day, a complaint never slipped through her lips. Dolores was religious, but not devout. Always happy, smiling, she was well known to the poor people in the district; for if someone was ill, she hurried to nurse him, and if he was in trouble, she gave help so discreetly that people almost forgot to thank her. Dolores was charity itself. She lived for others; her first thought was always for her neighbor, and she seemed to see beyond his surface somehow to his essence. To her, people were neither good nor bad—they were, that was all. She saw in them what they might be. "If only there were not so much poverty and suffering, how wonderful the world would be!" she said.

She was never disappointed in people, because evil itself was part of what she had accepted. If someone she had helped played her false, she only murmured: "I don't know what I would have done in his place. And even if I had not behaved as he has, I would certainly have thought of it. It comes to the same thing."

She loved the unfortunate, most of all when they had done wrong. She often went to the town prison to visit criminals and take them parcels. She hated people to talk about them as if they were exceptional in any way. For Dolores crime was not a calamity, but the consequence of calamity. She understood these people's unexpressed rebellion, their suppressed hatred. She never talked to them of God, but listened silently to their pathetic stories, asking a few discreet questions, but never permitting herself to pry into their consciences. She did not blame them; she blamed herself, for she felt indirectly responsible for their fall. The soul's trouble could not frighten her, for she knew that all souls were troubled and that the problem is not so much to be good as to be able to admit that one is not. She hated bigots, religious processions, and organized charity; and she often said: "Doing charity work is like making love: a cheat. One must *become* charity, *become* love."

Dolores was not good, she was more than that: she was Christian. She lived the Gospel as others live their businesses or their vices. The sufferings and problems of other people kept her awake at night. She had the strange faculty of being able to enter another's person, to live his tragedy. She never condemned, for she never judged, having understood once and for all that one cannot judge a man by either his words or his acts; that what a man does cannot defile him, for within every human being, submerged and jealously concealed, there lies an immense goodness, made up of hope and love.

Consuelo had had a happy childhood. She had not loved her mother much, although Dolores had cherished her. But the little girl could not understand this angelic mother who never grew angry, never raised her voice, never condemned. Anything would have been better than her infinite patience, her inexhaustible smile. At night she wept sometimes with

34

rage. She insulted her mother in her thoughts, called her a fanatic, a fool. And this was followed by remorse.

"I'm wicked," she would admit. "I don't love you, Mama. I'm jealous because you're better than I am. I'm ugly and bad inside."

Dolores would smile. "Really, my child, how do you know what you're like? Only God knows what is in your heart. He alone can read your soul. We humans know nothing. Perhaps I'm not very clever and haven't been able to find the best way of helping you. All human beings are complex. But for a mother, her child is even more so. You must forgive me."

Consuelo would begin to weep again. She did not want her mother to be wrong. It was she who was wicked. Already she *could not understand* and suffered from not understanding. All her efforts to become like her mother foundered on the badness within her. And yet she knew that she was not really bad—that this was not the problem.

Her father was a typical Valencian peasant—tall, thin, with deep-set eyes and a prudent manner. He talked little. He spent his days working in the fields, wearing black corduroy trousers, a white collarless shirt, a straw hat, and *espadrilles*. Most of the time he went to the rice fields. When he came home, he would sit down to his meal without washing his hands, to eat in silence and ask no questions. It was as if he had been born to work as Dolores was born to charity. Husband and wife never disagreed and needed no words to understand each other.

Consuelo's father was a believer—in his own way. He said grace before meals and went to Mass every Sunday, but his Catholicism ended there. Apart from that, he was violently anticlerical. He despised the priests for living without working; he called them "God's pimps." But Dolores said nothing. She loved her husband as much for his faults as for his qualities. She cherished him, respected his silences, and admired the amount of work he did without complaint.

Consuelo wanted to be the center of her world. But her mother talked all day of the poor of the district and their troubles, which were always the same. They weren't even good stories! It was not that her mother took no interest in her—far from it; but Consuelo accused her of loving too many people at once. The accusation was without basis, for Dolores looked after her daughter as few mothers do.

Consuelo did not know what it was that she lacked. She dreamed of a man who would live for her alone, who would buy her the most expensive dresses and the most exotic bouquets of flowers. She spent her days watching the sun's glitter on the waters of the rice fields. She loved the rice fields when they lay still in the sunset, looking like huge pools of blood. To her the oranges were enormous rubies, the lemons gold nuggets in the hot sunlight. She spent long hours at her window, gazing out at the white cottages that lay among the orange groves, and the cross above them. She watched the laborers going to and fro, sockless in their *espadrilles*, their skins darkened by the sun, their hair gleaming, their smiles radiant. Consuelo, who was no more than seventeen, was afraid of the tumultuous sexuality she felt within her. She knew she could never resist the call of one of these bronze-skinned boys, and wondered in anguish whether this was not the source of that wickedness she hated in herself. But was it her fault if she could not look at one of these male bodies without feeling an urgent need to caress the hard outlines? Was it her fault if she felt the need to love and be loved?

On Sundays her parents took her to church. To Consuelo the Mass seemed endless. Black-clothed women sang out of tune; a priest with a hoarse voice commented on a text he did not understand; poor peasants put a few pence in the plate. And then everyone came out of church.

The gossips whispered snidely about those who had missed the service; the men tried not to look bored and went to refresh themselves in the nearest bar. Dolores had her poor; but Consuelo's father liked playing a game of cards before lunch. Consuelo joined a band of young girls.

Young men laughed and gesticulated to attract their attention. They stood under the shade of the plane trees, which made a rectangle on the round square. A band played a *paso doble*. The flower sellers cried out the price of carnations. The dancing began at noon.

That Sunday Consuelo had put on her best dress and let her hair hang loose to accent the whiteness of her neck. Her parents had gone off, and she remained with her friends.

37

Her heart was beating to burst; her face was pale; the blood hammered at her temples. She at once longed and feared the young man would turn. He stood with his back to her. Consuelo could see nothing of him but wide shoulders, wild hair, and a tall, slender figure. He was standing with his legs apart, his hands on his hips. From where she was, Consuelo could hear his frank, gay laugh. Suddenly what she had dared not hope for happened: the stranger turned and looked her straight in the eyes. His own were small, bright, and lively; his nose was short and straight; his lips were thin; his teeth, when he showed them in a smile, were small, sharp, and very white. Consuelo smiled, and the young man smiled back. Then he came over to her. He had a peculiarly individual way of walking: he took short little steps, practically on tiptoe. He asked her shyly for a dance. Consuelo accepted.

Soon she forgot her parents and her friends. They danced in silence, finding nothing to say. Their hearts beat to the same measure; their bodies trembled, tense with the same intimate desire; their mouths smiled with the same secret hope. Suddenly he broke the silence to ask her first name and repeated it after her. Consuelo blushed. Then he told her his: Manuel.

The band stopped playing, and, in silent agreement, they went and sat on a bench. Consuelo's friends giggled significantly. But she was not aware of them, any more than she was aware of the implacable sun beating down on her head. She listened to his talk. He was telling her he had been born at Vallcarca, near Barcelona; that his parents were laborers; that he had left the factory because he couldn't earn enough to live on there; that he had no liking for the land and wanted to go to Madrid. He talked to her of life in the big cities, of advertisements in lights that went on and off, of air-conditioned theaters, of restaurants where bands played the popular tunes of the day, of broad avenues lined with tall blocks of apartments. Consuelo listened to his talk and was already prepared to follow him, to leave all for him. They talked for a long time. The last of the crowd had left the square but they were still sitting there on the bench. Manuel was dreaming aloud, and Consuelo moved into his dreams. She believed everything he said: that he would find a good job in Madrid and be able to buy a house. She could see the house already, its red curtains and white shutters.

Manuel took her to the Grao[1] for lunch. They ate a *paella*, watching the too-blue sea and the too-white sails. She laid her head against his chest and listened to the beating of his heart; then she closed her eyes: nothing existed any more but his voice. She wanted to console him, give him back his confidence, embrace him. She could feel how shy Manuel was, how he lacked self-assurance. She talked to him of *their* house in Madrid. He smiled in joy and lived the fairy tale she created fresh for him. For Manuel, dreams were the only escape from a life he did not understand. He was like a child, stunned by a reality in which he could find

[1] The Grao is the Port of Valencia.

no place. He had done everything he could to slip away from his poverty, but all his efforts had come to nothing: what could he do but dream? For, otherwise, he would have had to understand that there were people condemned to poverty as others were condemned to disease.

Night fell. One by one the stars came alight in the sky; a gentle breeze blew in from the sea; steamboats hooted as they left the harbor. The prodigal moon strewed white diamonds on the dark waters. There was a huge silence. They walked over the soft sand of the beach, which crunched beneath their feet, and looked out across the infinite sea. There were no waves, only a delicate rippling. They were alone in the world. She looked at his wild hair that stood straight up all over his head and wanted to fall on her knees before him and tell him she loved him because he was what he was: a shy, awkward, dreamy child. She would have liked to kiss his hands and tell him he was good, too good to understand life or face it with anything but dreams. Yet Consuelo said nothing and, as she watched the sparkling sea, found the silence of happiness.

They lay down on the sand, warm as a marriage bed, scented as a linen sheet. She clung to him and forgot the world. She knew suddenly that what she had believed to be her wickedness was, in reality, but a longing to love. This was what she had been waiting for throughout her adolescence: a body to caress, a glance that brought tears to her eyes, a happiness that made her tremble. The words

40

she spoke were the same as thousands of women had uttered before her, yet it was impossible that they could have been said as she said them. Lying on the beach, she felt the soft warmth of a honey-tasting tongue in her mouth. Tears of happiness pricked at her eyes. She was afraid of what would happen afterward, guessing that human beings must weep long for the rare moments of happiness granted them. The scents of orange and lemon trees and of the sea reached her there.

The sky was already pale when Consuelo went home. She had made up her mind to leave with Manuel, and wanted to fight for the right to do it. Her mother was waiting for her in the one room that served as dining room, sitting room, and kitchen. She was sitting by the stove, bent over a piece of embroidery. She raised her head as Consuelo came into the room, and her eyes smiled. She signed to her daughter to come near. Consuelo did not know what attitude to assume and went to her, holding herself very straight, her expression cold. Dolores smiled again, took off her spectacles, and asked gently: "Are you happy, my child?"

Consuelo did not know what to say. She had foreseen everything but that. She hesitated a moment, then replied: "I have sinned, Mama."

"No, my child! You have loved. It is not the same thing at all. Come and sit by me and tell me what he's like."

Conseulo wanted to cry. Could her mother know where she had been, what she had done?

"I too have loved, Consuelo. It may seem strange to you. I am old now, but I have not always been."

Consuelo lowered her eyes. Then she fell to her knees, burst into sobs, and discovered that she loved her mother beyond words, beyond thought even; that she had never not loved her.

The two women talked for a long time. Dolores put no difficulties in her daughter's way. She understood everything and knew above all that every human being must find his own path to God; that this path always, or nearly always, passes through sin and human love; and that man can become good only through tears.

Her father accepted his wife's decision, for he knew her to be good and had confidence in her.

It was a working-class wedding. There was a good meal, and singing and dancing. Then it was time to leave. Consuelo wept as she said good-by to her mother and asked her forgiveness; but Dolores saw nothing to forgive, since she had already forgiven everything to everyone once and for all. The train left. Sitting in the corner by the window, Consuelo looked out at the white houses, hidden among the orange groves, as they faded in the summer haze, and saw the blue sea strewn with white sails for the last time. She did not weep, but rested her head on her husband's chest and let the monotonous jolting of the train rock her to sleep.

Madrid was a disaster. Consuelo was not surprised, for she had learned to know her husband. She bore him no grudge, loving him; she resigned herself to it.

They spent the first months in a hotel in the Lavapiés district. They had taken a little room on the sixth floor, and there she waited for him all day. In the evenings she could hear him coming up the damp, sweating staircase and hesitating outside the door. He entered with his head bowed, like a child bringing home a bad report card, and sat down on the bed. His small eyes were veiled. He twisted his hands in a nervous gesture, sought for something to say, but was unable to find it. Consuelo smiled, took his head in her hands, stroked his wild hair, consoled him, told him you couldn't expect to find work right away, that you had to be patient. Manuel smiled. He told her about his day: long hours spent going from one employment office to another, turned away everywhere. He spoke in a low, sad voice, blaming himself for having led her into so uncertain an adventure. Consuelo kissed his damp forehead. Their situation was not yet desperate. They still had a few small things to sell. Besides, he was bound to find work; good jobs were never easy to come by. Manuel became hopeful again, smiled, got into the game. They were in love, and wasn't that the most important thing?

One by one they sold all their possessions down to the engagement ring. One day they had nothing left to sell and no more money. Every morning the manageress of the hotel waited for Manuel at the bottom of the stairs. "Well, when are you going to pay me for the eight days you're overdue?"

Manuel smiled and tried to be polite. He had been promised a job as an accountant by a very important man. It wouldn't be long now. Then he would pay her everything he owed and make her a present besides.

"You needn't bother about the present! And you can save that story about an accountant's job for your wife! All I know is that if you haven't paid me within three days from now, I'll call the police. And that's all there is to it!"

Manuel trudged all over the town. He was sweating from every pore. His legs trembled; he was tortured with thirst. He stopped at every public fountain to drink some water and hurried from employment agency to employment agency. But at each one he found thirty or forty people waiting on benches. Tears of disappointment welled up in his little eyes; he twisted his hands, and waited for hours. At last a clerk would put up a notice: No More Today. He swallowed his impotent hatred and ran to another address, where other poor people were already waiting, coughing, spitting, unwrapping cigarette butts. And so it was from morning till night.

He had discovered a big restaurant in Carmen Street where he was allowed to help wash up from time to time. On those days he had a right to a hot meal and ten pesetas. Of his meal he ate only the soup and the vegetables. He put the bread, meat, and fruit into a newspaper and went

44

happily home to give Consuelo his parcel with a tender smile.

At these moments she loved him, clasped him in her arms, and burst into tears. She called him "my little man," pitying him because she knew that life would kill their love in the end, as well as the hope that kept him going. She was afraid.

They had to leave the hotel empty-handed, hiding from the manageress, not knowing where to go to find a refuge. They walked for days on end, and slept under a bridge by the North Station, clasped in each other's arms against cold and despair.

Manuel had lost all confidence in himself. His eyes had grown dull; his back was stooped. He no longer washed, no longer shaved, or sought work. He stood in the Puerta del Sol for three hours a day, begging. Sometimes he brought home enough to buy food; then Consuelo would boil a few potatoes and a handful of rice in an empty tin can. They ate with their fingers in silence, no longer daring to look at each other. Neither of them could find the words they needed.

Winter came. The temperature fell below freezing under the bridge. Consuelo took refuge in a hole far back under the arch, and Manuel lay close up against her, but at night they shivered and their teeth chattered. Consuelo had been pregnant for three months. When the cold came, Manuel had made a last attempt to find work—nothing. Consuelo had written to her mother and waited, puzzled, for an answer. Each morning she dragged herself as far as the Central Post Office and left her last illusions there. One day a letter came, edged in black. The mayor had written that Dolores had died in the hospital at Valencia.

Consuelo did not weep. She had come to the end of her strength. She went back to the bridge and waited for Manuel's return.

It was a Tuesday. As the hours passed slowly in cold and despair and Manuel did not come back, she grew afraid and in frenzy saw herself abandoned. She zigzagged through the city, looking for him, and walked for thirteen hours on end. She was giddy from hunger; sweat ran thinly from her forehead, and her legs felt numb; her eyes were blind with tears. She walked like an automaton knowing neither where to go nor where to stop. She thought of committing suicide, but lacked the courage. No one asked her what was the matter with her, why she was weeping. People looked at her oddly because she was dirty and unkempt. When she stopped for a moment too long in front of a café in the center of the city, a man in a white coat came out to her and pushed her away. "Move on, keep moving!"

She was picked up unconscious.

Consuelo spent three days in a social-assistance center. Two nuns shaved her head, made her take a shower, and put her to bed on straw. Consuelo was able at last to explain her circumstances. A few days later she learned that Manuel was in prison and she was allowed to go and see him. They barely recognized each other. They pressed each other's fingers through the bars in the visiting hall and found nothing to say to each other any more. And it was that day they realized they were conquered for good.

Manuel had a cell mate who lived in the Zone. It was he who suggested to Consuelo that she should go there and that his wife would certainly take her in while she was waiting.

And then . . . When Manuel came out of prison he built a hut in the Zone. He swore that it was only temporary, that he would find work in the end, that he would rebuild their lives. But Consuelo knew already that a life cannot be rebuilt.

To forget their circumstances, they manufactured anger against each other; but soon the flashes of anger were no longer false, and bitter quarrels killed or blacked out their love. Manuel went back to prison twice again, and their downfall went on.

Consuelo caught hold of herself; she did not want to think of the past. Indeed, she had no wish to think at all. She hated herself and she hated everyone else. Without exception. Except, perhaps, for a certain Manuel whom she had met one Sunday in Valencia as she came out of church. Of all her life of misery and suffering, one memory alone subsisted with power and tenacity: the memory of a certain night beside the sea. This was the memory she wanted to take with her when she died. Was it enough to justify the life that came after it? Consuelo was uncertain;

she was not used to asking herself questions. But one thing was sure: had she been able to turn back and choose her life again, she would have chosen her present fate, ugly and poor as it was, because somewhere in that fate was a night of stars and love. And the rest? They had been defeated; and it was not entirely their fault. Inside of the alcoholic she had become there was another woman, who had once been young and had passionately loved a man who was shy and poor and a dreamer.

5

OLNY left the hut and went toward the wasteland. The night was dark and the sky brilliant with stars. He pulled up the collar of his coat. Rebellion churned inside him once more, so that his hands trembled and his teeth clamped tight. He could have killed again, anyone. Even when he was a child, this sudden urge to do evil had sometimes assailed him. Then he would hurl himself on the first one who came along and fight him.

Olny reached the wasteland and sat on the ground in the shadow.

"Is that you? Do you like the night, too?"

Olny turned. Marianita was standing behind him. She was dressed in a dirty, colorless skirt and a green blouse. Marianita was nineteen, with big gray eyes, long chestnut hair that fell to her shoulders, small round lips, and a sad smile. She had been one of the victims Olny used to need from time to time.

But Olny was only fourteen then. He was leader of a band of six of the Zone boys. One evening he had suddenly felt that need to do someone harm. He had seized Marianita, prevented her from crying out, and, with the help of his band, had taken her to the wasteland. There he had compelled the other boys to rape her before his eyes. Marianita had stared at him with wide eyes and said nothing. When it was over, she had gone away weeping.

"I like the night. It's the silence at night that's so nice. Can I sit down?"

Olny assented. They sat side by side, looking straight ahead of them at the sky glowing purple from the city lights; behind them the Zone was asleep. Olny looked furtively at Marianita. "Marianita," he began in a low voice.

"Yes?"

"What I did was filthy and disgusting. We were only kids then. You have to understand. . . ."

"I'm not mad any more. It wasn't you."

"It wasn't me?"

"No. I think there are moments in the Zone when you go mad. You're just not the same person. I guess it's the whole filthiness of the place that does it."

Olny looked down. Then he took Marianita's hand in his, and she did not resist. They sat hand in hand in the silence, and peace fell on them.

"You killed old Joyal. But it wasn't you who killed him.

There are two different people in each of us: the one belonging to the Zone, who's ugly, and the other, who's good. Maybe it's the same for people in the city, too. You'd like to be decent, but life's like it is and it's sad. Then you turn rotten. Do you think I'm crazy?"

Olny shrugged his shoulders. "I don't know. You may be right."

"But you're good. Even if the others say you're a fool, I know it's not foolish. There are just times when you'd go mad if you didn't have someone to hit. . . ."

Olny smiled and kissed Marianita's hand. "I'm not good."

"Yes, you are. Especially when you do rotten things. Because somehow it's not really you. Do you understand?" Marianita lowered her voice. "I'm not good, either. I'm vicious even. But I know what I'd like—to have someone I could love. Deep down I'm bad only because there's no chance to be good. That's what life's like. I think it's easier to be good in the city. There's not so much yelling or so much filth. If I could, I'd leave the Zone and the old woman and go and live in the city. I'd have an apartment and a kitchen full of faucets that ran all day. Wouldn't you like to leave the Zone yourself?"

"Yes." He pulled Marianita to him and began stroking her hair. He felt happy with her, the way he had felt with José-Antonio when he was young. She wanted to leave, too. She came to the wasteland at night to watch the magic lights of the great city on the horizon. He felt suddenly like weeping. Why couldn't one leave the Zone? Why wasn't there any escape but crime or suicide? He closed his eyes and felt the warmth of Marianita's frail and delicate body against his own. He would have liked to take her with him to a far country where she could have a white kitchen full of taps that never stopped running. He leaned down to her and kissed her, then covered her face, her neck, her hands, her whole body with kisses and caresses. She smiled and nestled against him. Olny took her in his arms. There was a feeling in his breast that was different from anything he had ever felt before. He wanted to become good, tender, generous; he wanted to give Marianita everything she had never had.

The hours passed. It turned cold; the wind from the Guadarrama had risen. Olny had taken off his coat and put it around Marianita's shoulders. She was leaning against him, and he sat still for fear of disturbing her. And there, on a piece of empty land where the city of Madrid dumped its garbage, they found the silence of happiness. Beneath a sky reddened by the neon lights of the capital they discovered the hidden meaning of unsaid words and, leaning one against the other, with their shy and silent love they atoned for all the cruelty and baseness of the world.

6

THE next morning Olny reached the office happy, ready to smile at everyone. There was a long day of hard work before him. But in the evening he would go home and see Marianita again. Then nothing would matter any more.

Ramírez was standing in the doorway. "So you're in love?"

Olny smiled. "How do you know I'm in love?"

"At your age one is always in love."

"Well, you're wrong! I wasn't in love yesterday."

"So it's the bolt from the blue, is it?"

"It's better than that, you old idiot. It's happiness."

Ramírez slapped him amicably on the back. "Is she pretty?".

"The girl you're in love with is always perfect."

"You're right."

They took their sandwich boards, loaded them on their shoulders, and began their perambulation of the streets of Madrid. They walked in silence, one behind the other.

It was a warm day. The air was full of the scent of limes. The young city boys were sitting as usual on the terraces of the cafés. Olny was happy; he wanted to stop every passer-by and tell him he was in love with a girl whose like did not exist. He whistled a popular tune and forgot to pick up butts.

"Do you know what she said, Ramírez?"

"Who?"

"Her, of course!"

"No."

"She wants an apartment!—an apartment with a white kitchen full of taps. Can you imagine it? You could come on Sundays and eat with us. In the afternoon we'd go to the movies or a bullfight. Not bad, huh?"

"Dreams are always wonderful."

"But why should it be only a dream? After all, I could have an apartment."

"On five pesetas a day?"

Olny fell silent. He knew Ramírez was right, but he felt so happy that he didn't want to become depressed. "I'll find another job," he said finally.

"Where?"

"No matter where."

"You've never tried before?"

"Yes."

"And what happened?"

"It wasn't the same before. I was alone."

"Just you go and tell one of those little bourgeois bastards, who spend their days drinking lemonade, that you're in love and want to make money to spend on your sweetheart. What the hell do they care about you and your love! You're less than a dog to them."

"After all, it's not their fault I was born in the Zone."

"But it's their parents' fault the Zone exists."

Olny could think of nothing to answer. Ramírez was

probably right. An inhabitant of the Zone was just that and could never be anything else. "You've got to be in love to think you could have an apartment!" he thought.

"You'll see tonight," Ramírez said. "They'll explain to you about those people who spend their days drinking. Then you'll understand."

"You think so?"

"You're no stupider than the next man."

It was an old abandoned building in the Carabanchel district. The walls of the hall were oozing dampness. A few school benches faced a platform with a chair and a table for the speaker. Above the platform, on the wall, was a picture of a bearded man. His face looked like the holy pictures of the Apostles.

"Who's that guy?" Olny asked.

"Marx."

"Oh!"

Olny did not pursue the matter. He was utterly ignorant of who this Marx could be and what bearing he could possibly have on the Zone. Then he shrugged his shoulders and looked about him with curiosity. There were some thirty men sitting on the benches. They sat in silence. Their faces were grave, their complexions drawn, their eyes surrounded with dark circles, and their lips pale. They were poorly dressed; some wore berets or caps, and Olny concluded they must be workmen.

A door opened suddenly and the speaker came in. Olny

was astonished at his youth. He was tall and thin, his hair black and curly, and his eyes deep and liquid. The young speaker climbed onto the platform. He was dressed in a black suit with white pin-stripes, a white shirt, and a black tie. Olny found him very elegant. The speaker stood behind the table, raised his clenched fist, and began singing:

> *"Agrupemonos todos*
> *En la lucha final . . ."*

The workmen sang gravely, standing straight, their heads held high, their expressions determined. Olny hesitated at first, but then raised his clenched fist and sang too in order not to be conspicuous. He leaned toward Ramírez and asked in a low voice: "What are they singing?"

"The '*Internationale.*'"

"Oh!"

Olny no more knew what the "*Internationale*" was than he knew who Marx was. The voices fell silent and everyone sat down. The speaker took some notes from a leather brief case, which he placed on the table, and began speaking. His voice was grave, warm, and expressive; his delivery was slow and regular. Olny began to feel impatient. What the speaker was saying was not for him. He did not understand a single word of what the elegant young man was talking about. It was all as much a closed book to him as Chinese. He would have done better to go back to the Zone and find Marianita. But he had promised to come and he always kept his promises. There was silence all around him; the workers listened with concentrated attention. Olny wondered whether they understood what it was all about, then blushed at the thought. These men looked as if they were not only understanding, but really *feeling* the speaker's words. Olny began to pay attention to what the young man in the black suit was saying. He was talking about men. He spoke seriously and with gravity. He was saying that peasants, workmen, tramps, or even people from the Zone were men similar in every respect to the bourgeois. Olny opened his eyes wide. This directly concerned him, and what the intellectual with the boyish face was saying was not, after all, so difficult to understand. He was expressing himself in simple, direct terms, using popular phrases, often repeating a difficult sentence. Proletarians were those who had not realized their possibilities; the proletariat consisted of the sold, the exploited, the ignored, the trampled underfoot. The capitalist system had made slaves of them. They sold their strength, but their labor was in its very essence a degradation, as it had no meaning for those who sold it. There were tears in Olny's eyes, yet he was smiling with happiness. He was a man, and Marianita was a woman. It was merely that their birthright had been kept from them. But they could free themselves and win their dignity as human beings. The Revolution would set them free.

"The Revolution," said the speaker's slow voice, "is not a question of eating better, drinking more, or working less. The Revolution is the liberation of man. What we are fighting for is the reconciliation of man with himself. There must be no more masters and no more slaves. Simply men, equal in dignity, who will build together a better world. Those who join us merely to eat better are half fooling themselves. They must give their strength, their sweat, and, if necessary, their lives to create a more just society. It is not just two social classes that are in opposition, but two kinds of man: the possessor and the dispossessed, the master and the slave. Our struggle is for the abolition of these opposites."

When the lecturer ended his talk, Olny was grinning with joy. What he had just learned was so important, so *essential,* that it seemed impossible it should have been unknown to him until this moment. He wanted to embrace these men and call them "comrade," for he had only just learned that word, too.

"Did you enjoy it?" Ramírez asked.

Olny nodded. "How have I been able to live without knowing all that?" he murmured. He asked what the speaker's name was.

"Santiago de Leyes. We don't really know why he's on our side. He's an aristocrat and has odd ideas. He's not very trustworthy. You've got to watch out for him. The Revolution will liquidate him."

Olny looked up in surprise, thinking he must have misunderstood. "Liquidate him? Why?"

"I've just told you. He's an aristocrat, and you can't trust them."

"So what?"

"The Revolution will do away with them."

"But why, when he's on our side?"

"We'll give him a fine funeral."

Olny fell silent, sickened. Ramírez had a discouraging way of talking. To Ramírez everything was perfectly clear; he seemed to have decided once and for all what was right and what was not. He sat in judgment and pontificated with assurance.

"But it's not as simple as all that!" Olny cried.

"What's not so simple?"

"Killing a man. I can understand liquidating the bastards, but why the good ones?"

"Do you call him good? He's an aristocrat. He's not class-conscious. He's not a trustworthy element."

"What do you mean? Do you think you've got to be born in the sewer to be good? I know men in the Zone who are a lot worse bastards than he is."

Olny wanted to hit Ramírez, with his smug assurance. Who was he to judge men from a pedestal and divide them into the good and the bad? Who had made him judge of others?

"People in the Zone are not bastards. They're unlucky."

"What the hell do you mean, 'unlucky'?" Olny's eyes glittered, his nostrils quivering with fury. "There are all kinds there! Good, bad, and bastards! What do you know about the Zone? Besides, who made you God to decide who the bastards are?"

"The Revolution."

58

"The Revolution is Santiago, too. That's what he said: it's all men who work together to create a new world."

"Not all. The proletariat."

"Then the hell with *your* Revolution!"

Ramírez smiled sarcastically. "You kill a pauper and stand up for an aristocrat. Bravo!"

"Bravo, nothing! I killed a rat in the Zone because he was scum like you, and I'd kill a bourgeois who smelled of lavender if I had to. Right now I'm defending an aristocrat who's a good man."

"Oh, now you're Justice, huh? Blind but sure."

"I'm nothing at all—just mud, like everyone else. I just don't dirty beautiful things, that's all. I killed a man, sure, and maybe it's not the nicest thing I've ever done. But to kill in the name of the Revolution—that's even worse. It's sabotage."

"Look who's talking about the Revolution! You heard of it for the first time in the last hour. I learned it with my mother's milk."

"Then it must have been poisoned!"

They stared at each other in silence. Ramírez was pale; there was a bitter smile at the corners of his mouth. "You poor fool," he said in a low voice. "You've sold out."

Olny smiled and spat on the ground at the feet of his friend. "Say that again, you scum! You're vomiting all your anger and weakness into the Revolution. You're not out to serve it, only to use it. Now we can fight it out, if you want."

"We'll fight it out soon enough, don't worry."

"That's it. In the Revolution."

"Why not?"

7

AS HE went home alone, Ramírez wondered why he felt this hatred rising in him against Olny. He breathed deep the odors of the street and his memory turned back toward his past.

He saw his parents' little house, standing by a grade crossing. His father was the gatekeeper.

The house was built of red brick, with narrow windows decorated with pots of geraniums and ridiculous curtains that were always dirty. Dark furniture, heavy with poverty, filled the three rooms.

Ramírez's father was a small thin man with gray hair and cold eyes; he was dressed always in patched black corduroy trousers and a blue striped shirt. He spoke little and never kissed his son or showed him any affection. By nature sarcastic and misanthropic, he hated the whole human race and blamed it unconsciously for his accident.

Before becoming a gatekeeper, Antonio Ramírez had been

60

a conductor for many years. He enjoyed the work, for he loved traveling. Moreover, he earned a good living and owned a five-room flat in a modern worker's block at Saragossa. Though an atheist himself, he had sent his son to the Brothers of the Christian School, with children of the middle and lower-middle classes.

"Why shouldn't my son go to the Brothers?" he would say, a contemptuous smile curling his lip. "My money's as good as anyone else's. And my son is certainly as good as the son of a notary or a businessman."

Luis Ramírez worked hard and well with the Brothers of the Christian School. He was a brilliant, gifted boy and extremely proud. One day, because he had not been awarded the first prize for geography, which he thought his due, Luis rose in the middle of class and insulted the master. He was nearly expelled.

But the Superior liked young Luis. He summoned him to his study, a small, ill-lit room, its walls covered with books. In the corner was a *prie-dieu;* just above it a crucifix hung on the wall.

Brother André, the Superior, had come from Lisieux. He was a man of some seventy years of age, with very white, very fine hair, which he wore long and never combed. His triangular face, with its wide brow and snowshoe chin, was cut by deep wrinkles and illuminated by blue eyes of a piercing warmth. His dignified bearing reflected the peace of his spirit. He had great lucidity of mind and rare psychological insight; and he had become interested in this boy

61

born in such humble circumstances, who was intellectually so well endowed, because he was fearful of where his pride and sensitivity might lead him.

Luis, then twelve years old, had big dark eyes, curly hair, and that olive skin which is so common among Castilians.

Brother André took off his spectacles, rubbed his eyes, and was silent for a few moments. At last he said in a gentle voice: "You must know, Luis, that your offense is very grave. My duty should be to send you home."

The priest paused for a moment and gazed at the child with a mixture of tenderness and anxiety. "And yet you're one of our best pupils, Luis. So I shall not expel you, but I shall have to punish you severely. And since I know your pride and conceit, I know the proper punishment to inflict on you."

Young Luis raised his eyes and tightened his lips. Brother André held out his gnarled hand to the child, smiled affectionately, and said: "You will go and find your geography master and apologize to him publicly."

The boy's eyes glittered.

"You will do it for me and for Him," he added, indicating the crucifix.

Luis hung his head, his jaws clenched.

Brother André rose to his feet, went to the boy, and clasped him to him. "You will have to give a strict account of your abilities, my child. And I am afraid for you. I fear your pride will win in the end." The Superior added still more gently: "You must be humble and pray. Pray a great deal."

There was a silence. Luis Ramírez had leaned his head against the priest's chest and was crying quietly.

"My mother was a washerwoman and I had no father," Brother André continued. "I was often tempted by the pride that lies in wait for those who are gifted and yet have to suffer social injustice. My primary education was at the communal school, and I was able to complete a secondary education only through a scholarship from the Ministry of National Education. To keep it I had to achieve a very high average in every subject, which obliged me to work very hard."

Little Luis was crying more violently yet, till his shoulders shook with sobs.

The Superior went on. "I had only one suit. A rich woman had given it to my mother, for it had become too small for her own son. My mother spent many hours repairing it." The old priest was talking very low. "I suffered a great deal because of that suit. I was ashamed of it. My schoolfellows were always properly dressed. And I had no money for vacations. So, my friends, who knew how difficult my position was, invited me to spend a few weeks with them."

In a different tone, as if the avowal he was about to make were peculiarly painful to him, Brother André said: "I had to make great efforts not to resent their invitation. In my heart of hearts I was not grateful to them for their generosity. To accept as charity what seems to you your due is one of the hardest things in the world, my child."

There was a long silence as Brother André stroked the hair of this boy, his young other self. Then he murmured: "Today, though, I am proud of my poverty. For it has brought me closer to Christ. It is not in vain that He was born poor, my child. You may be one of the elect, and you have no right to disappoint Him." Then in a fatherly voice he added: "Do not estrange yourself from Him, my child. He is your surest friend."

Young Luis stayed with the Brothers till he was fourteen. It was then that his father had his accident.

Antonio Ramírez got out of the Barcelona express at the Madrid Station and, to save time, slipped between two cars of a freight train standing in a siding. The train moved backward suddenly and crushed his right leg.

He spent long weeks in the ward of a hospital. His leg was amputated.

Luis went with his mother to visit his father every Thursday. His mother was a little woman, with gray hair and a colorless, wrinkled face; her eyes were blue and full of a shy kindliness. She stood a little apart always, her head bowed, her hands held flat against her black skirt. She never complained or grew angry, but, humble and simple, lived for her husband and her son, serving them in silence and doing her best to satisfy their wants. It was difficult to know what her thoughts were or even to know if she thought at all. Her husband treated her gruffly. Sometimes he lost his temper, insulted her, even went so far as to hit her. But Isabelle never turned on him. She went back to her kitchen and wept silent tears as she did her daily work.

She was accustomed to loneliness. Antonio Ramírez was seldom at home, as his job involved constant traveling. She spent her days in her kitchen, sitting on a chair, but her thick, small, red hands were never idle.

When Luis was a child and his father had punished him or hit him, his mother would come to him in the middle of the night, sit on his bed, and kiss his forehead protectively, murmuring: "Don't be angry with him, Luis. He's not a bad man. He loves you, you know. But he's got a bad temper. You mustn't bear him a grudge for it."

Before the accident, Luis and his mother had led a quiet life. Isabelle was proud of her son, who was handsome and worked hard. Sometimes, on afternoons when Luis was playing in the street with his friends, she would secretly look through his school brief case and steal a furtive, awed glance at the complicated signs that filled his notebooks.

Yet Luis had but little affection for his mother. He reproached her above all with her resignation. He would have liked her to be able to stand up for herself.

"Why don't you shout, too? Why do you just submit? How can you allow him to hit you?"

Isabelle, in her plain dress, lowered her head and seemed to retreat into herself. "He's not wicked," she murmured. "He didn't want to hurt me. He's not a bad man. It's just his nature, that's all."

Luis shrugged his shoulders and left his mother alone in

her submission. Besides, he was embarrassed by her admiration for him and her naïve respect for books and writing.

One day—and he never forgot this scene—he was alone in the dining room doing his homework. His mother came in, smiled, and sat down beside him. She was wearing a blue apron over her black dress. She gazed at her son a long time and then asked timidly: "What are you doing, my child?"

"My homework, Mama. You can see I am."

Isabelle nodded her head and then asked again: "What sort of homework, darling?"

"Arithmetic. It's a problem. Rule of three."

She nodded her head again and then cried: "What a lot you know, darling! I'm sure none of the other boys knows as much as you do."

"But, Mama, any boy of my age knows how to solve a problem by the rule of three."

She seemed unconvinced and said: "But not as well as you, I'm sure."

Luis got to his feet in exasperation. "You're absurd, Mama. That's nothing, don't you understand? Nothing at all. And you annoy me with your questions. Why can't you leave me alone when I'm working?"

His mother bowed her head, got slowly to her feet, and left the dining room without another word.

A few moments later Luis found her in the kitchen, standing by the stove. She was weeping.

"Don't cry, Mama. I didn't mean to hurt you. Don't cry."

"It's nothing, Luis. Only you're so clever! I'm an ignorant

woman. I can't even talk to you. You never tell me anything. I'm not worthy of you."

And that day, at the sight of his ignorant mother's tears, he was ashamed.

After the accident, Antonio Ramírez was out of work. Life in the apartment became intolerable. The cripple spent his days complaining, cursing, jeering at his son, punishing or beating him. Luis had to leave the Brothers, even though the Superior went so far as to suggest to his father, in order to keep him, that he should become a free boarder.

"Your son's gifted. You'll have nothing to pay, neither his food nor his teaching. Will you accept?"

"Do you think my son's going to lead an easy life, while his father's out of work? We're not millionaires. Besides, I might as well tell you, you seem to be a little too interested in my son and I don't like it. I know you priests! None of that around here! I'd rather see him dead."

"I have no ulterior motives. I am merely thinking of the boy's future. That's all."

And it was thus that Luis had to interrupt his secondary schooling at fourteen.

His parents left the apartment they had lived in since his birth and took a dreary, dirty lodging in a working-class district. It consisted of three narrow rooms facing a dark courtyard. The house had damp-corroded walls and was filled with factory workers, unemployed laborers, and prostitutes. The staircase smelled of dirt and poverty. Dirty

67

underwear hung from the windows. The tenants spent their days insulting each other from landing to landing.

Luis found it difficult to accustom himself to this new life. He regretted the school, Brother André, his masters, and his friends. He often cried at night. Then, little by little, he got used to it.

The children of the district lived in the street. They went neither to primary nor secondary schools, and few of them found jobs before the age of sixteen. Luis was rarely at home, only at mealtimes. He was always dirty, and his clothes were ragged. He answered his mother back rudely and fought with his father, who went from bar to bar, not drinking, but growing drunk on the attention of men who were even worse off than he was. His father loved to boast, telling of his travels, and the poor devils, most of whom had never left their native town—some not even the neighborhood—listened to him in amazement.

"What are sleeping cars like?" one would ask.

"And the dining car—what's that like? Do they really serve champagne in it?"

"Champagne?" cried a drunkard, opening his eyes wide.

"I once went from Madrid to Malaga in a sleeping car," said Antonio casually.

"Malaga? Where's that?"

"Which is bigger, Madrid or Malaga?"

"Is it far from Madrid to Malaga?"

"Unless you keep quiet, you fools, I'll tell you nothing at all. It was like this. I was going from Madrid to Malaga.

Madrid, as you all know, is the capital of Spain. It's so big that no one, not even those born there, knows it really well. There are skyscrapers on the Gran Via. . . ."

For hours, days, and months Antonio talked to a delighted and astonished audience.

Isabelle grew anxious. She didn't like her son wandering about the streets in the company of boys she mistrusted. She was sad, too, that he had left the Brothers' School, and had tried vainly to oppose her husband, who had become more sullen than ever since the accident. Hardly had he come home when he began complaining; he seemed to blame his wife for what had happened to him. Isabelle said nothing and never rebelled. At a quarter to seven every morning she set off with a big basket on her arm to collect linen to repair, for she earned their living by taking in sewing. The light in their flat was bad, and Isabelle soon had to wear glasses. Sitting by the window that looked out on the courtyard, leaning over the sewing, her back bowed and her spectacles on her nose, she already looked like an old woman. From time to time she would raise her eyes, glance sadly into the courtyard, utter a sigh, and then take up her work again. This continued from morning till night.

Neither her husband nor her son worked. They stayed in bed till eleven o'clock, drank their coffee, and then each went off his separate way: one to a bar, the other into the streets. They returned for lunch and then went right out again. So, Isabelle was always alone. At night she had her supper in the kitchen, laid the table, and went to bed, exhausted. She would not go to sleep, though; and when her son came in, she would get up, put a worn coat over her nightdress, and keep him company while he ate.

Luis had grown. He was only fifteen, but looked eighteen. Isabelle gazed at him in admiration. Sometimes she said in a timid voice: "You oughtn't to spend your time in the streets, Luis. It's not good for a boy of your age. Why don't you stay at home and try to do a few lessons?"

Luis either didn't reply at all or answered roughly: "Do you call this a home? I prefer the streets."

His mother bowed her head. "It's not your father's fault that he's had an accident. You must realize he's hurt and unhappy, too. He's put in an application to become a grade-crossing guard—he has a right to the job. We won't stay here always, you know."

Thirteen months later Antonio Ramírez got his job. They left Saragossa and went to live in the neighborhood of Burgos. Isabelle was delighted to return to her native province, where her son had been born.

The grade crossing was about forty kilometers from the town, in a dry desert region. Life there was hard and monotonous. Antonio, with no audience to amaze, was bored, railed continually at fate and mankind, and bullied his wife and son. Luis answered back. Now sixteen years old, he was strong and was not afraid of his father, whom he despised. They looked at each other with hostility and rarely exchanged a word. Isabelle had grown older still. Her legs ached and she found it difficult to walk; her eyes were worse.

Luis thought he was going mad. He had no one to talk to, and his days were empty. Desert stretched before him and around him, endless, stony. Four times a day a train slashed across it, rattling the windows of their house.

The boy watched the trains go by. The passengers sat comfortably in first-class carriages; they did not even notice the gatekeeper's house surrounded by its absurd garden. Luis did not hate these men who were able to travel and buy books. He despised them. He, too, dreamed of traveling. Awakened every night by the midnight express, he got up, went to the window, and watched the long luminous ribbon tearing full speed across the sleeping desert.

Luis was not naturally a hater, but the injustice of the world had hardened him. He loathed false sentimentality, useless tears. He looked coldly and uncompromisingly at the world. He had grasped the fact that there were two kinds of men in the world: those who could travel, and those who were doomed to poverty. The first clung avidly to their privileges and prevented the poor from living like humans. Luis considered that two dangers lay in wait for the disinherited: on the one hand, resignation, and on the other, individual revolt, which was dangerous and bound to fail. He was thus already, without knowing it, looking for communism. He felt the need to belong to an organized party that embodied the aspirations of men born to poverty. That party must be strong and disciplined in order to struggle effectively against the rich. Naturally Luis dreamed of playing a leading role in it.

Isabelle was sitting alone in the dining room. Her husband had gone to shop in Burgos and would not return till evening, by the ten o'clock bus. She looked out at the red earth, which stretched to where, in the far distance, the Sierra was screened with a purple veil. A harsh sunlight lay across the earth and made the stones gleam. Luis was in his room. Isabelle was thinking of nothing. She accepted life as it was and no longer tried to find an explanation. She sat there dreaming, thinking that the land was beautiful and that the Madrid express would pass at any moment.

Suddenly the door opened and Luis came in, carrying a suitcase. She realized at once that he was leaving for good, but she neither moved nor wept. She suffered, of course, but from a secret pain to which she had been long accustomed. Isabelle looked sadly at her son and managed a smile. She felt weary and thought that to weep would do her good, but she shed not a tear.

Luis tried vainly to smile, his eyes large, dark, and glowing, and said: "I'm leaving, Mama."

Isabelle was silent for a moment. "Perhaps you're right," she said. "Life is dull here, and you're seventeen now. You're a man. Where are you going?"

"To Madrid. We'll stop the express. Then I won't have to argue with Father."

His mother nodded her head and rose painfully to her feet. "You're right," she repeated.

Luis bowed his head.

She went to the sideboard and opened a drawer, lifted up a pile of soup plates, took a few carefully folded bills from under them, and handed them to her son. "Take these. You'll need them in Madrid."

He realized suddenly the immensity of his mother's love for him, and was ashamed. He kissed the poor work-worn hands, clasped the thin tired body to his chest, and said only: "Thank you, Mama."

A bell rang: the express had left the last station. They went out together. He took a red flag and stood in the middle of the track while she slowly lowered the barrier.

The train came in sight, and Luis waved the flag. When the express stopped, Luis ran forward to the engine. "Will you take me with you? I'm going to Madrid."

"Get in," the engineer said. His face was black with soot.

Luis kissed his mother tenderly. She murmured: "Look after yourself. Don't catch cold. Eat at regular hours. Watch out for women. Write to me."

He nodded and climbed up into the cabin. The train whistled and started again as Luis watched his mother standing lost in the Castilian desert. She was waving a handkerchief. He turned his head away.

Isabelle continued waving, even after the train had disappeared.

At first Luis had a variety of jobs in Madrid. Then he worked for long years as a simple laborer in a textile factory. He lived in an attic room, small, but clean and sunny, in Tetuan.[2] He wrote long letters regularly to his mother, who replied in her awkward, uneducated hand.

It was while working in the factory that he had his first contact with the Communists. Luis was a Communist already without realizing it; he had need of this theory at once simple and complex, like all living things, and of the strong, united Party, which was struggling for the liberation of the proletariat. He threw his whole soul into it and became a complete militant. He served the Party faithfully, not through fanaticism or ambition, but because he was convinced that the Communist Party alone could lead the proletariat to victory.

The leaders of the Party trusted this sober, reticent, competent, and devoted Castilian. Ramírez soon held an important position in his cell.

Nor was his task an easy one. There were different tendencies within the Party itself. This was a normal and salutary situation. But what was less so was that a number of the comrades refused to accept the overruling of their policies, and when these were rejected by the majority, they carried the debate on in public. These vain discussions were dangerous to unity, and for Ramírez unity was the very foundation of all action. He devoted all his powers, therefore, to reintroducing discipline within his cell.

Years passed. In January 1936 Ramírez organized a strike in his factory. On the tenth day the Socialists and the Anarchists accepted the employers' proposals and went back to

2 Tetuan de las Victorias, a district of Madrid.

work. The strike failed, in spite of the U.G.T.'s decision to continue it. Ramírez and five of his comrades were fired.

For many weeks he was without work; then, to avoid dying of starvation, he became a sandwich man and walked the streets of the capital. This was how he met Olny in the month of April of that same year, 1936.

Ramírez had quickly felt a certain friendliness toward the young man from the Zone and wanted to take him to Carabanchel. It was not very easy to do.

Having agreed to go with him, Olny had developed a lively admiration for Santiago de Leyes. Ramírez distrusted the young aristocrat, and not only because he was a noble. Santiago was one of those unhappy, tormented people on whom it was difficult to rely. And for Ramírez only one thing was important—the advent of socialism.

8

SANTIAGO DE LEYES staggered and caught himself against the wall of a building on Velasquez Street; he had nearly fallen. The silence was absolute, and singly the stars died in the paling sky. A cool wind was blowing from the Sierra and shaking the trees in the Salamanca district; the leaves quivered, whispering. Santiago closed his heavy eyes and was grateful for the cool caress of the breeze against his burning cheeks. He was exhausted. He had been wandering through the city for nearly eight hours, never daring to stop for fear of meeting himself head-on. Now, though, he could go no farther. "If only I could stop thinking!" he screamed silently.

Santiago thought as others breathe; his mind was so constructed that it could not stop working even for a second. He had always asked himself questions that led to further questions that led finally to other question marks. Thought was torment to him, and now, at the edge of madness, his whole being howled for a moment of thoughtlessness. He needed peace, needed even a brief respite, but he knew all respite would be denied him. He knew he was fated to see everything, live everything, through the always glinting prism of his intellect. He would reason till the day of his death—and indeed at this very moment was he not reasoning out his death? His own and that of many others who had joined the Revolution for the same causes as himself? He was not frightened; what should he fear? Death? Santiago had never had a personal destiny, and therefore personal feelings had no grip on him. He felt things only in relation to other people. In Santiago lived the fullest embodiment of the principle that each man has in him the whole of the human condition. And this he knew, for he had never been able to love or suffer purely on his own account without at the same time feeling the love and pain of others.

His ailment was the agony of the philosopher. He had tried to be honest to himself all his life, never to take his footing on falsehood, even when falsehood wore the aspect of truth. And he had kept his word. It was his love of truth that had led him to socialism, and it was this same necessity that, this evening, was compelling him to call socialism into question. He was suffering. He was like a child who had been told to throw his marbles away, gazing at the last and best before it, too, was gone. When he had abandoned this last hope, what would be left to him and where could he go? He had no idea. He felt like falling to his knees and bursting into tears, but he knew God was too often the refuge of cowards, and he was determined not to sin through cowardice. The greatest homage that could be paid God, if He existed, was to prefer truth to falsehood always, and to remain till the end one of the men of goodwill to whom peace was promised. Santiago had burned all his ships one after the other. Tonight was his night of sorrow; he wanted to weep, but had never known how. He felt cold and weary. He remembered a phrase of Nietzsche's which had much impressed him in his boyhood: "The most terrible thing at sea is to die of thirst. Salt your truth, therefore, till even that will not suffice you." And now he was dying of thirst.

Today Santiago felt more than ever alone. Everything appeared strange to him: the big city with its long avenues; the thousands of people, sleeping, dreaming, or making love; the sick in their hospital beds, watching in anguish for the new day that might be their last; the priests praying in the silence of their retreat. He was "the man apart," the "man different from others." No one was concerned for him, whereas he was concerned for the whole world. And even if some bethought themselves to love him, Santiago would still feel lonely and lost in face of the immensity and diversity of a world he loved passionately and for which he was prepared to give his life.

Santiago de Leyes was born at Valladolid on an estate that had belonged to his family for generations. It was a vast manor house lying in a wooded park. As a child, Santiago loved walking among the dark cypresses of the gardens and sitting long hours by the lake, watching the swans glide majestically over the still water. He sat quiet for fear of disturbing the tranquillity of the time and the place; from time to time he would throw a few bread crumbs into the lake for the pleasure of seeing the swans bend and raise their necks with regal indifference.

Santiago was a handsome, dark-complexioned child, with bright eyes and black, curly hair. His parents and tutors loved him because he was sweet and gentle, though a little melancholy. He was never noisy or insolent. The servants looked on him almost as their own child, so affectionate was he, and Miss Bentson, his governess, never had to punish him. It was enough for her to say: "Santiago, you grieve me. You don't know your lesson." The child would lower his head and begin to cry. Miss Bentson noticed that on the days she had reprimanded him, he did not go down to look at the swans and thus deprived himself voluntarily of his only amusement.

Santiago's father was a just man. With great simplicity he saw that everyone got his due. Tall, slender, with gray hair, dark eyes, and a straight nose, the Marquis de Leyes was respected and beloved by all the people of the district. He never left his estate. The country was his universe. He ran the great estate he had inherited from his father with prudence and justice.

The Marquis de Leyes knew the Christian names and the families of every man working on his land, and he watched over them like a father over his children. He visited the sick, was godfather to the children born on his estate, and attended the weddings of all his employees. They admired him. They came to him to settle their disagreements or to ask his advice about their children's futures. Santiago's father knew how to talk to them. He looked on himself merely as the trustee of his possessions, which belonged to God alone, and tried to make the best use possible of them. He had paid for the education of several of the more intelligent of his farmers' sons and had spent a great deal of money on constructing model cottages for his laborers. The *hacienda* was, moreover, a little world in itself, with its school, its hospital, its small movie theater, and its church.

The Marquis de Leyes took his meals in the kitchen with his servants, who were unembarrassed by his familiarity;

they were accustomed to it and felt in no way inferior. The master was to them what the manager of a factory is to the workers: the most competent employee. His trade was to give orders, theirs to obey. Their responsibilities were different, but just as great.

Santiago's mother was a little woman with dark eyes, a slightly curved nose, and brilliantly white teeth. It was impossible to look at her without admiring her almost too perfect beauty. No single defect impaired the harmony of the astonishing purity of her features, and her intelligence was lively. Victoria de Leyes talked easily, expressed her opinions with moderation, knew everything, had read everything, and traveled widely. Santiago loved her as the angels must love God in paradise—beyond words.

Santiago had a happy childhood with a mother he loved and a father he admired. His days were filled with study, for Santiago loved books passionately and spent long hours reading at his desk. From time to time he went to church alone. There was a fifteenth-century monastery not far from the town, where he loved to go in the evenings to hear the Benedictine monks chanting Vespers. As their voices rose in the empty, solitary church, mingling, flowing over the arching stones, and dying away in a sigh, the boy felt an intangible longing. Sometimes he wept—tears not of sorrow, but of tenderness and love. He wanted to be just and kind, and he asked God to give him strength to love his fellow men always. It was in this lonely church, to the sound of the melodies of prayer, that he had asked himself the first great questions, those he was to continue asking himself for the rest of his life: "How can one be good? How can one avoid foundering in hatred?"

By the time Santiago was twelve, he had grasped the fact that the world was vast and that one had to establish a personal relationship with it. The boy was seeking his path: that of abnegation and self-giving. He thought he had found it in Christ and in charity, but soon realized that charity alone could not suffice to quench the thirst devouring him. He discovered that the Church had made of charity an end in itself, whereas it was but a means. For charity was love; and love was an attitude that consisted in forgiving everything to everyone, being ready always to give all, even one's life, and in understanding the incomprehensible. Charity was not generosity. Real charity was a sort of grace, a total transformation of self, a rebirth. To be charitable was to become a new man.

But the new man must take his place in the world of action, must somehow put his love of humanity to use. Where? That was the problem. Santiago sought eagerly for a solution. He felt a need to give himself, to lose himself among his fellow beings. It was then he discovered an idea that was to alter his whole life: justice.

At that time he was living in Madrid and studying law. He had a flat in Goya Street, but took his meals in the university restaurant, near the Moncloa. It was there he met Carlos Ozcuna.

Carlos was about twenty years old, a boy with mischievous eyes in a freckled face, and chestnut hair. He came and sat at the same table and at once began looking Santiago up and down with unconcealed amusement. Santiago was embarrassed; he felt himself blushing and thought how silly it was to blush just because someone was looking at you. He tried to think about something else, but his neighbor continued staring at him. It occurred to Santiago to leave the restaurant, but he angrily decided against it.

"You're studying law, I suppose. All rich men's sons study law. Oh, don't mind me! My name's Carlos Ozcuna." He seemed to be considering what to say next.

Santiago felt more and more embarrassed and wondered how anyone dared talk to a stranger like this. "What nerve!" he thought. "I could never have done that myself."

"What was I saying? Oh, yes! I was talking of rich men's sons. You're obviously one of them. . . . It's odd—I use *tu* with everyone usually, but somehow with you it keeps coming out formal. Strange, isn't it?"

Santiago felt like getting up and leaving without a word. But he was curiously attracted by this talkative boy with the mischievous face.

"It wouldn't surprise me if you told me you were an aristocrat."

Santiago smiled.

"I've guessed right, haven't I? Were you brought up in England? I see. Will you shake hands? You will? You know, you look congenial!"

82

The two boys shook hands. They smiled at each other. The ice was broken.

"I'm glad to have met you. I hate this damned town. Everything's false about it. The whole town seems unreal, set down in the middle of a desert like a dare. You cross arid plains and hot, sun-loaded valleys, and there, suddenly, the skyscrapers of Madrid shoot up in front of you. I wonder who on earth could have thought of building it?"

"Philip II, they say."

"I'm not surprised. Only the absurd appealed to him. It was his peculiar way of teasing God."

There was another silence. In tacit agreement they got to their feet and left the university restaurant.

"What's funny is that one loves it all the same," Carlos murmured.

"What?" Santiago asked.

"Madrid. It's like a whore. You know that what she gives you is fake, packaged love, so to speak, but you can't help giving her a little real love all the same. Do you get me?"

Santiago blushed. Was it the word "whore" that made him blush? Or was it the expression "packaged love"?

Carlos looked at his new friend with suspicion. "Are you homosexual?" he asked.

The young aristocrat was completely bewildered. "Are you crazy?" he stammered.

"Then it's even worse." Carlos Ozcuna stared up at the sky and shrugged his shoulders with an expression of stupefaction. "Another virgin! Am I wrong?"

Santiago smiled. "No."

"I knew it! Well, then! As for me, I love women and I'm a Communist." Santiago glanced at his companion with an expression of such distress that Carlos burst out laughing. "I obviously can't say the right thing." Changing his tone, he asked: "Where do you come from?"

"Valladolid. Why?"

"The city of priests and nuns! That explains things a little. But not everything. Is your father religious? Very religious? Communion every day? I can see it a mile off! That's why you don't go with the whores. You don't want to sin, eh?"

"That's my business," Santiago replied curtly. The young Communist's questions were beginning to annoy him.

Carlos flushed, and dropped his eyes, then took him by the hand and led him to a bench.

"Listen, Santiago, I scarcely know you. I like you because I see in your eyes qualities I like seeing in the eyes of young people: seriousness and integrity. I've been talking a bit at random. It wasn't easy to approach you, believe me. I'm very shy. Don't laugh! Talk is the refuge of the shy as heroism is that of cowards."

Carlos paused, smiled, and went on. "I've been joking, mostly. Now I want to say something important. I'm exaggerating. Let's say I want to talk sensibly. I've a bit more experience than you have. Not much. A little. I'm no longer a virgin and you are, for one thing. So I can give you a bit of advice about that. It's rather difficult. But try to understand me: you must never be ashamed of your body. There's no shadow of moral or religious concern in what I'm saying. Nor is there any reason you should believe me or follow my advice. No, I'm wrong. There is a reason: I'm speaking in good faith and with complete honesty. I'm advising you as a doctor. It's a question of health and balance."

Carlos fell silent. He released Santiago's hand, which he had held in his throughout the conversation. "Are you angry with me for having talked like this? I wouldn't upset you for anything in the world."

Santiago smiled and shook his head. "On the contrary. It's the first time in my life anyone has dared talk so frankly to me. I must admit I'd never thought of it from that angle."

"Good. I'm reassured. Then we can stay friends?"

"Of course."

No doubt it was this simple, direct approach to the problems of life that had attracted Santiago. He saw, as yet, no connection between communism and the love of truth. He thought Carlos was simply being frank, just as other people were liars; he did not begin to understand until much later that the particular need to posit problems clearly and resolve them rationally was essentially a Marxist quality. He had believed sincerely that to be a Marxist meant that one wished to take everything away from everyone in order to redistribute it differently.

Carlos and he met often. The young Communist avoided

talking politics, or mentioned it only in passing. What he said was based always on concrete facts. Carlos seemed to see both things and people with different eyes. His reasoning was astonishingly precise, and Santiago was surprised by the workings of his mind, which seemed to him of great quality.

It was a summer night, thick with heat and approaching storm. Carlos lay on his bed, reading a work by Engels. Santiago sat by the window, looking at the multicolored neon lights firing the sky and thinking that Carlos's revolutionary enthusiasm was rather similar to his own early religious fervor. But then he thought better of it. Carlos maintained, after all, that mystical fervor was the negation of thought.

Suddenly Santiago felt a need to talk to Carlos of his childhood, of his aspirations, of the thirst devouring him, of the overflowing love he had vowed to the world and to all men living in it. Dawn was breaking over the city roofs by the time he stopped talking.

Carlos got up, smiled, and put his hand on Santiago's shoulder. "Thank you for talking to me like this. I knew you would one day. You know, you have the smell of honesty. I had guessed almost everything you've told me. The one thing that surprises me is your separating yourself from the Church. With a father like yours, it's almost unbelievable. What drove you to it?"

"I don't know. The self-satisfaction of Catholic circles, their overready answers, their hypocrisy. Above all, perhaps, the contempt they have for man. You see, Carlos, as far as I'm concerned, every man is sacred. I love the man in the street as I would love Christ if He appeared to me. I don't mean by that that I love my neighbor through Christ. The opposite is the truth. You see the difference?"

"Yes."

"A man is a big thing; he has wept, loved, hoped, despaired. How can you fail to respect such a sum of love and suffering?"

Carlos nodded, his eyes thoughtful. "Your charity is all very fine. But it's ineffective. The essential is to transform human relationships by transforming the conditions of men's lives. Without this revolution all the rest is futile."

They talked on for a long time. Santiago wanted to know everything: what the class war and the dictatorship of the proletariat were, how this dictatorship was to be reconciled with liberty. Carlos explained it all in simple terms. His words went home. The young aristocrat drank it all in. That night decided his future.

Santiago learned about Marxism. He read the essential books, attended the meetings of Party cells. He felt more and more astonished. At last he was being given a scientific explanation of the world. There were no more "mysteries," no question now of "Providence!" There were dialectical relationships, and that was all. He was dazzled, and threw himself into communism with all the enthusiasm of his eighteen years. And when fifteen months later he decided to join the Party, he went to visit his father to tell him of his decision.

He journeyed home in a state of great emotion. His eyes devoured the bare and desolate countryside with eagerness, were intoxicated by the light, and followed the curves of the hills and the line of the horizon with an almost voluptuous pleasure. When at last he arrived, he hesitated before opening the gate into the garden. Someone saw him and began calling for the Marquis, shouting: "Señor Santiago has arrived! He's in the park!"

He walked slowly through the old garden. He gazed nostalgically at the lake, whose waters still were disturbed only by the silent gliding of the swans. Nothing had changed.

Some children came to meet him, greeting him with joy. Santiago stroked their heads and distributed a few pesetas. When he reached the house, he saw that his father was waiting for him on the steps. The Marquis de Leyes was dressed in a black corduroy coat and gray trousers. Santiago kissed his father tenderly, thinking how much older he seemed. He stood less upright, his hair had grown white, his voice was less firm and less assured.

"To what do I owe this unexpected visit? Are you in trouble? No? Good! Tell me what's the matter, then."

"I've come to talk to you, Father. I've taken an important decision and want to tell you about it myself."

The Marquis de Leyes gazed at his son attentively, then

murmured: "I am grateful to you for your trust. Let us go into the library where we will be alone and can talk without being interrupted."

The Louis XIII furniture was still in the same positions; the walls, as in the past, were lined with books in rich bindings; two El Greco's caught and drew the eye. As a child, Santiago had loved this room. In winter, when a log fire burned on the hearth, the bindings of the books shone brightly, and the glow of the flames was reflected in their gilt. He closed his eyes and breathed deeply of the odor of the past. It was in this room one night that he had been told of his mother's death.

"I'm listening, Santiago."

There was an emotional note in Santiago's voice. When he had finished, he looked at his father anxiously. The Marquis de Leyes appeared to be thinking, his eyes half closed. Slowly he raised his head and looked at his son sadly. At last he said: "What can I answer you? If you had come to ask advice, I would have given you an old man's counsel: I would have told you to wait. But you're announcing a decision. What can I do? The reasons you have given me are perfectly sound and, taken by and large, justify the position you have adopted. Besides, you're no longer a child. Nevertheless, I should like to say this to you: beware of oversimple ideologies. Our need to *understand* often leads us to rely on certain truths as self-evident, when they are not at all. Your reasoning is too clear-cut. I'm suspicious of things that are too clear-cut. You will find in the Communist Party what you blame the Church for so much: its self-satisfaction, its ready-made answers. It is true that good and evil are not so easy to delimit as many believers think. And yet the Church is not that alone. It is also a bank in which the suffering of the innocents is placed on deposit for the salvation of the world. There is a good deal of self-satisfaction in what you have just told me. You have given me to understand that some of your assertions are self-evident, but nothing in life is self-evident. You imagine that those who do not see things as you do are fools, because what you are saying is reason itself. But, believe me, your elders are not all necessarily fools. They have thought and reflected. They even had aspirations similar to yours once, and your generous longings, but they did not adopt your conclusions, and for valid reasons, too."

The old man rose with difficulty and went to one of the library windows which looked out on the modern quarters of his employees.

"Look, Santiago. Can you say honestly that what I am defending is my own interest? Of course, I'm defending the estate because that does not belong to me. It belongs to you, too, and you'll inherit it. You will have the responsibility of these men and women who work the land. You will make of this inheritance what you will. That is no one's business but yours. But think of this: will those men and women and children be any happier working for a community? I wonder. For the community will be blind to their interests and dumb in support of them. Man, you see, has a need to have recourse to someone, to cling to someone. Loneliness waits for all of you—the most tragic loneliness."

The Marquis de Leyes smiled bitterly, shrugged his shoulders, and continued. "I know what you're going to say: 'That is not the problem.' It is not. But where is it? It is not so easy to know precisely where the problem does lie." The old man lowered his voice still further and seemed now to be talking to himself. "For twenty centuries men have been trying to achieve justice and have struggled to better the lot of their children. And now, suddenly, you are certain you possess the answer to all our ills. . . . Can you do away with ugliness, disease, and death? Can you change the way men love? What can your Revolution do against suffering and despair? Can it suppress jealousy and envy? If man no longer has his neighbor's goods to covet, he will covet his wife, or his intelligence, or his job. Cain did not kill his brother to seize his goods. And we are all potential Cains. How will you keep the Revolution out of reach of the Cains?"

The Marquis de Leyes fell silent. His eyes were wet with tears; his hands trembled; his face, lit by the last rays of the setting sun, had turned crimson. Santiago dared not break the silence. He thought about what his father had said. The Marquis added in a weary voice: "I, too, wanted justice. I have tried to realize it on this estate because it was *only* here that I could realize it. Do you really think, my son, that you are alone in having a heart oppressed by the sufferings of humanity? But I cannot agree with you.

Transforming the conditions of life will not change the fundamental problem, which is evil. For evil exists. It is here, within reach of your hand, all about us. You cannot really claim that capitalism invented it!"

There was another silence, longer than before.

"No, Santiago, your Revolution is not an open-sesame. It will fail as Christianity has half failed: because it must rely on men to bring it about. For a revolution to succeed, man must be protected from himself. But that's enough! Perhaps, after all, I'm too old to see these matters clearly. An 'old reactionary' is, I believe, the expression. But I am grateful to you for having come to talk to me like this. Perhaps you will find peace, that peace Christ promised to men of goodwill. In any case, I hope you may."

There were tears in Santiago's eyes. He knew there was something he wanted to say, but words no longer seemed to make sense. He took his father's hand and kissed it. Then, in a strangled voice, he murmured: "Father . . . I wanted to tell you . . ."

"I know, my son. I know . . ."

"You have been the best of fathers. Often, when I was a child, I prayed God that I might resemble you one day. . . . Give me your blessing, Father."

The old Marquis placed his hands on Santiago's head and blessed him in the name of the Holy Trinity. The sun had set behind the hills. The sky was green and rose. All was peace.

. . .

For two years he led a dangerous, but intoxicating, clandestine life. Santiago traveled about Spain and taught dirty, half-starved men in ill-lit halls what the Revolution was and what they were themselves. The workers listened to him attentively. Santiago loved to see the glow of hope he made light up in their eyes. They discovered Marxism with the delight with which other men discover love. It was in the deep light in their eyes that Santiago found his recompense. Face to face with these poor men who gathered to listen to him, he knew he was on the right path.

Then the Party got organized. It emerged from the shadows and became a strong, disciplined army that had to be taken into account. The walls of Spanish towns were covered with white posters with a slogan in red letters: WORKERS OF THE WORLD—UNITE! The Party led the proletariat. It was the Party that expressed its demands and aspirations; it was through the Party that the workers became aware of their own strength. Big strikes were organized. The streets of Barcelona, Madrid, and Valencia were invaded by crowds of marching men and women singing the *"Internationale,"* their fists raised, their heads held high. The class struggle reached its climax. The moment seemed near when the great dream of every revolutionary must be realized: all power in the hands of the workers and peasants.

But then a change came over the Party. It ceased to be the vanguard of the proletariat and became the refuge of conformists and opportunists. Marxism ceased to be dialectic; the Secretary General of the Russian Communist

Party became the pope of a church that soon began to burn its heretics and persecute its deviationists. The meetings of the Central Committee became touching ceremonies at which the various resolutions were passed unanimously but for a single vote, and the name of Stalin was greeted with thunderous applause. No real free discussion was possible. The ambitious, the vengeful, and the faithless began to occupy all the posts of importance and set aside anyone not prepared to grovel to their idiocies. Dialectic was replaced by auto-criticism. Any member of the Party might be called a Trotskyite, and trembled at the thought of seeing his name on the list of suspects. Certain members of the Central Committee were pleased to make no distinction between their personal enemies and the enemies of the Revolution. The best elements left the Party. Some members committed suicide; others survived to be insulted continually in the Party pamphlets. Everyone was afraid, lived in terror, dared not think, even.

Santiago found difficulty in understanding what was happening around him or in grasping its real significance. For him the Revolution was still that anonymous and silent mass whose aspirations the Party should interpret. But he had to see that the Party was ceasing to be the instrument of the Revolution and was becoming the Revolution itself; that it was no longer the conscience of the proletariat, but its caricature. Then he started asking himself a series of questions, all of which led to further questions of a more general nature. In this way he was led to a serious reconsideration of the problem of the relation of men to ideas. In other words, were there true Communists? What did it mean to be a Communist? Did the mere fact of joining the Party and reading its newspaper every morning make you a Communist? Was there not a Socialist morality? Did one not have to die and be reborn to become a revolutionary? Were ideas simply labels you could stick on your back? And could those labels transform a man? Could the Party card make a jealous man cease to be jealous, or a liar cease to lie? Santiago remembered the conversation he had had two years before with his father and once again weighed carefully what had been said. But the problem became more difficult when he thought of the mass of the workers, the whole of the proletariat. For, after all, the proletariat was not the Party. Its values and aspirations were not false. Had one the right to abandon those millions of human beings for whom the Revolution was much more than a mere alteration in their living conditions—was a rebirth? On the other hand, it was only through the Party that you could work actively for the proletariat. What then? But suppose the Party, as it was now organized, was in reality a counterrevolutionary movement. Suppose, historically speaking, it was a step backward. These problems obsessed Santiago, who lived like a monk while he tried to find the answers. Of the monthly allowance his father sent him, he kept only enough for the absolute neccessities of life; the rest he gave to the poor. He had left the two-room flat he had owned in Goya Street and had taken a servant's room on the seventh floor. But if this self-denial brought Santiago a certain peace, he knew very well that it was only a drop in the ocean. The sufferings of the world could not be abolished by gestures of this kind; nor was the poverty of the proletariat diminished because Santiago de Leyes ate less than usual. How could he leave the Party without betraying the proletariat? And, above all, how was the Party to be prevented from taking over the Revolution and making it its own?

Santiago continued to be busy with the affairs of his cell. Each week he went to Carabanchel and talked to the workers; he spoke to them of socialism, trying to avoid confusing communism and socialism in their minds. The rest of the time he spent taking part in various meetings and editing the newspaper, and continued to spend himself, carrying deep inside him the secret feeling that he was the dupe of a handful of opportunists who had cashed in on the greatest and most noble of ideas.

One evening, on his way to Carabanchel, he learned from the newspapers that Article XII of the Constitution was to come into effect and that the Assembly was to be dissolved. There would be a general election in Spain. Santiago shivered. What he had feared so much was bound to happen: the election was certain to be a victory for the Left. But neither the Church nor the Army would let so good an opportunity to crush the democratic forces pass. Civil war was coming. In face of the danger of fascism his duty was clear: he must defend liberty. But there were dark days ahead. The Communist Party would try to seize power and set aside the other Left Wing parties. He knew that civil war would be the knell of the hope that had begun to shake the Spanish workers into life.

Santiago reached Carabanchel with a heavy heart. He noticed a new face in the front of the room. Two wide green eyes lit up as Santiago spoke, and, when he had finished, the newcomer applauded frantically. Santiago smiled. No, the Revolution would not die. Men would rediscover it sooner or later; and these men of the future would draw, perhaps, a lesson from the errors the Party was about to commit.

9

OLNY came away from Carabanchel like a schoolboy from his first rendezvous—so happy he wanted to sing. But when he had left the last houses of the city behind him, he was assailed by that feeling of disgust and weariness the Zone always gave him. He crossed the road and reached the wasteland. Children were playing there, running barefoot with a ball made of old rags. One of them came up to Olny and said: "I'll sell you a clock. It works. I'll give it to you for a pack of cigarettes. Want it?"

Olny shrugged his shoulders. "What the hell do I want a clock for?"

"You can use it when you get married, can't you?

Do you want it?" He was a handsome boy of about four-teen, with dark, deep-set eyes, at once cunning and good-humored, a long straight nose, and curly hair. He looked strong and was clearly the leader of the band. Olny smiled. "I'll give you a cigarette if you stop bothering me. Keep your clock for someone in the city. You can sell it at the Rastro." [3]

The boy broke into a laugh, and his white, regular teeth sparkled. "I can't. I stole it there!" The other boys had come up and joined in his laughter.

Olny took out a cigarette and gave it to the boy. "Here."

"Thank you," he said in English.

"You speak English?"

"Yes, sir. I go up and down La Castellana and when I see an Englishman alone I go up to him. I say: 'Hullo, Mister. How do you do? Have you a cigarette? I am not so young? If you give me a cigarette, I give you everything you want. . . .' "

Olny smiled. "What's your name?"

"Loto."

"Loto? That's not a name."

"My old lady's idea. Anything to make me different!"

"Have you been in the Zone long?"

"Three months. We come from Murcia. My mother had a little trouble with the tax collector."

"Where do you live?"

"Next to Marianita." Loto winked, and the other boys

[3] The Madrid flea market.

began laughing. "Look at those jerks! What a bunch! They like to think they're men and then they go into hysterics every time you mention a girl's name. They've never even come close to one, the idiots!" Loto stood with his head held high, his legs apart, and his hands on his hips. He wore a piece of rope for a belt. His face and knees were filthy.

"Will you do something for me, Loto?"

"Sure."

"Go and find Marianita. I'll be here."

The young Murcian smiled knowingly and went off, having first issued his orders. "Wait here, you kids. I'll be back."

Olny sat down on a stone. The land stretched away in front of him as far as the eye could see, cut only by the road. There was not a tree. Behind him lay the Zone with its smells and its shouts. He was thinking of what he had just heard at Carabanchel: was it possible that all this filth might disappear, that this stinking heap could be replaced by real houses? He remembered the speaker's words: "Men, equal in dignity, who will build together a better world." Olny tried to remember Santiago de Leyes's face. He repeated the sonorous name to himself and smiled. He would have liked to talk to Santiago and ask him questions. Without quite knowing why, he felt attracted to the young intellectual. "It would be wonderful to have a friend like that and be able to tell him everything," he thought.

Marianita stood before him, smiling. She was still wearing her black skirt and green blouse; but she must have washed them, for in Olny's eyes her clothes seemed new. She had done her hair and had bought a pair of *espadrilles*. Her feet were clean. Her skin smelled of soap and water and youth. He looked at her and took her hand. They sat down side by side.

Olny began talking to her about the Revolution, the proletariat, and Santiago. "Then we could have a kitchen full of running water. We could even have a bedroom and a sitting room, like rich people."

Marianita smiled. She believed in the Revolution, but she could not have said whether she believed in it because it was he who was talking about it or because she needed to believe in it. She put her head on her lover's knees. Then, tenderly, in the infinite desire of her heart to love, she began covering his hands with quiet, confident kisses.

Olny smiled and stroked Marianita's silken hair. "Why are you doing that?" he asked in a gentle voice.

"I don't know. Maybe it's love. It's funny—I've never loved anyone before you. I've made love because I was crazy, but I wept with rage while I was doing it. But with you it's different. I feel happy. I feel as if I'd like to stay like this forever. I read a book once. It was a serious book where everything was explained. There was an engineer— you know, those men who build bridges? He was in love with a girl who was a maid and he said to her: 'I should like to die holding you in my arms, so that you would know that you have been loved and be saved by this love. . . .' It's good, isn't it?"

"Do you know it all by heart?"

"Not all. Just that. I liked that."

There was a silence. Suddenly Marianita went on, her voice tender. "That's the way I love you. I even wonder how a person can be so happy. Life's really not so bad, is it? Do you love life?"

"Yes, of course."

"I'd like to live a hundred years! There are wonderful things in the world, you know. I saw the sea once. I couldn't tell you what it did to me. Have you ever seen the sea?"

"No."

"It's enormous and changes color. Like your eyes. They say it's the sky that does it."

They fell silent. Night had come and the stars were bright. On the horizon the city had lit all its magic lanterns. Through the cool air the round white moon illuminated the plain.

Olny leaned down to Marianita and kissed her neck. Suddenly he started up. "What's that?"

"What?"

"Your back."

"Nothing, Olny. Forget it. Don't be angry."

"Who did that?"

"My mother and Pepe."

"Is Pepe your mother's lover?"

"Yes. He beats her, too, but she likes it. Olny, promise you won't do anything silly. Swear, Olny."

The young man stared at Marianita and muttered finally:

"I swear I won't kill your mother's man. Don't worry. Come with me."

They reached the Zone. Most of the people, still out of doors, looked with sharp interest and fell in behind them.

"What is it now?"

"Where are they going?"

"Probably after Marianita's mother!"

"That'll teach her, the bitch. She'll go with anyone who wants it. She even lets the little boys feel her boobies."

"She's a whore, that's what she is!"

"Go on, Olny! Give it to her!"

"Kick her in the rear end!"

"Throw her out!"

Marianita was walking behind Olny, her eyes full of tears; some fifty people were following behind them.

Olny stopped in front of a wooden shack, much like his own. The shouting died as he knocked on the door. A woman opened it. She was about fifty years old, but looked sixty. Her hair was no real color, just strands of red, blond, and white around a rouged face. She was wrapped in a black kimono. She looked at Olny coldly. Her eyes were gray, her nose long and slightly curved, her lips thick and too heavily painted. She could have been taken for an old dancer in a second-rate music hall; she claimed to have been a singer and to have done *Tosca* at La Scala in Milan; actually she was an old prostitute who had had trouble with the police and had sought refuge in the Zone.

"What do you want?" Her voice was hoarse with alcohol. "Are you going out with my daughter again? I forbid you to go out with her. She's a good girl, she is. We're respectable people. We've got education. I'm not going to allow the first man who comes along to get Marianita! I don't want to see you with her again, understand? If ever I catch you hanging around her again, I'll go and find your whore of a mother and pull her hair out. Yes, a whore! Do you think we don't know what she does with your little brother? A mother like that ought to be ashamed of herself!"

The people who had followed Olny and urged him to "kick her in the rear end" were now laughing and egging the woman on. They had no stake in the matter; they just loved to jeer at the one who looked the weaker, wanting something to happen, some unexpected event to distract them from their wretched, hungry lives. Their laughter was at once cruel and obscene; their eyes glittered like the eyes of wild beasts at the sight of their prey. Even the old had gathered around.

"Besides, where do you come from, eh? Valencia? The land of the clap-ridden. And where does your father come from? Handy, the Zone, isn't it? People from everywhere come to hide here. . . ."

La Remedios was shouting louder and louder, enjoying her act, intoxicated with the presence of her delighted audience. Her gestures grew violent as she pretended; she threw herself into the part and succeeded in turning herself into an outraged mother defending her daughter's virtue.

Marianita was weeping. But suddenly, unable to bear it any longer, she began shouting back. "Shut up, you filthy whore! Do you think people don't know about you? Has it ever embarrassed you to sleep with Pepe in front of me, or ask him for 'a few kicks'? Has that ever bothered you? I've had enough of him and of you, enough of the whole bunch of you! You disgust me! Look how delighted they are! They love a quarrel, they love to hear people saying revolting things to each other! It excites them, these bums! . . . And you, an opera singer? A brothel singer, that's more like it! Why don't you tell them what my childhood was like? Why not, eh? You'd be afraid, wouldn't you? It'd embarrass you, wouldn't it? From hotel room to hotel room! And the men you slept with in front of me! And your drunkenness! Slut! Bitch! Whore! I spit on you!"

Marianita had turned pale; there was sweat on her forehead, and tears of disgust filled her eyes. She drew up close to her mother, looked her hard in the eyes, and, without a word, spat in her face. Shouts came from the onlookers. The situation was reversed. The crowd applauded, demanding blood.

La Remedios hurled herself on her daughter and seized her by the hair. In the struggle, the woman's kimono fell open; the boys screamed their joy at seeing her naked. Her heavy, hanging breasts shook. Olny, who had stood quiet till then, took a step forward and separated the mother and daughter. His face was pale. He took La Remedios by the wrist and twisted it in fury; she uttered a cry and fell to her knees, looking up at him fearfully.

"Now ask your daughter's forgiveness. Say: 'I'm a whore, I ask your pardon, I'm not worthy of you.' Repeat."

La Remedios did as he told her. He dropped her wrist and said, his voice quavering with emotion: "Marianita, go get your things. I'm taking you away."

Then, turning to the mother, he asked: "Where's your man?"

La Remedios was sobbing. "I don't know. I don't know where he is. . . ."

"I don't suppose your brave pimp is hiding inside. . . ."

Olny took a step forward to go into La Remedio's hut. But Pepe appeared on the threshold, his eyes imploring. Olny looked him up and down in silence, then smacked his face five times. Pepe only whimpered, making no attempt to defend himself. Then, when Olny finished hitting him, he hid his head in his arms and burst into sobs.

Silence had fallen around them. The spectators said not a word. Marianita came out of the hut, a bundle under her arm, and passed by her mother without even looking at her. Then she took Olny's arm, and they went off together as they had come—sadly, shyly almost.

"What are we going to do now?" Marianita put into words what Olny was wondering himself.

He shrugged his shoulders. "Don't worry," he said. "We'll find something. Are you cold?" He took his coat off and put it around her shoulders. Then they sat down side by side and were silent for a while. "Life's really not easy! It's enough to drive you crazy!"

Marianita made no reply. She was afraid and felt very

much alone face to face with the great city full of well-dressed women and men wearing ties. What was to become of them? She leaned against him. What had she to offer him?

"I don't know what the hell we're doing in the world," Olny went on. "If I could, I'd get hold of God and put Him in a hut in the Zone. That'd teach Him, all right! There's nothing for us to do on earth!"

"Yes there is—love each other."

"Love doesn't get you anything to eat."

"It helps you put up with the muck!"

"You're right. I've got only one thing in the whole world —you. And I can't even talk right to you. I don't know how to say things like you read in books." He kissed her tenderly. Yes, he had that at least: the certainty of their small love born on the wasteland of the Zone. As long as he had that, nothing could be altogether lost.

"That's what happiness is," Marianita murmured. "To be together."

"Yes, maybe that's what it is."

They got to their feet and took the road to Madrid. Suddenly Olny thought of his little brother. How could he abandon him? "Marianita, do you mind if we take Francisco with us?"

"Of course not."

Olny made a detour around the Zone in order not to meet anyone, reached his hut, and went in. Francisco was alone, sitting in a corner. Olny went up to him silently, knelt, and asked in a low voice: "What's the matter, Paco? Are you ill?"

The boy raised his head, tried to smile, but could not manage it. He murmured: "She hit me. When I'm grown up, I'll kill her."

Olny smiled bitterly and said in a gentle voice: "No, Paco. You won't kill your mother. You'll be better than she is. You'll become a good man and learn to play the trumpet."

Francisco shrugged his shoulders. "How can I? You need money for that!"

"We'll find it. But now listen: I'm leaving the family and the Zone. Are you coming with us?"

"Are you taking Marianita?"

"How do you know I'm with her?"

"How do you think? All the whole Zone knows! And that you hit Pepe." Francisco smiled with childish pride. "They say he didn't even try to defend himself, the fag! Is that true, Olny, he didn't even try to defend himself?"

"Yes."

The boy looked at his elder brother in admiration. "You're stronger than any of them. I bet you're the strongest man in the world. There's no one stronger than you, is there? Tell me, Olny, is anyone stronger than you?"

"I don't know, Paco. But now answer me: are you coming or not?"

"Are we going right now?"

"Yes."

"I'm coming. But where are we going?"

"We'll have to see."

Francisco took a shirt and a pair of trousers. They were all he owned and he didn't want to leave them behind.

10

THE sky was green in the cool dawn. Municipal trucks were watering the streets, and early servant girls, in blue and white, slipped from doorways to buy milk for breakfast; other women, in black, walked quietly to church, prayer books in hand. The clock struck six.

Santiago de Leyes reached his door, hesitated a moment, then went in. He walked on tiptoe for fear of awakening the concierge, a fat Andalusian woman, curious and gossipy. Since he had given up his flat on the third floor to move up into a servant's room on the seventh, she had decided he was mad or, at least, extremely eccentric. Whenever she saw him, she shook her head and said in a meaningful voice: "Good day, Señor *de* Leyes."

As long as she let him alone, he did not mind how mad she thought him. However, he had no luck that morning, for she was already up and sweeping the landing on the first floor. He lowered his head as he passed her and said in a neutral voice: "Good morning, Dona Maria."

"Good *morning?* You're right! If that isn't a shame, a

young fellow like you coming in at this hour! And for what, I ask you? If it were because of a girl, I'd understand. But of course it's all those lousy bums again! Let them starve! What have they got to do with you?"

Santiago made an irritated gesture of dismissal.

"All right, all right! I'm just telling you for your own good!" But, as he reached the next floor, she called after him: "There are people upstairs waiting for you! Three of them! And a pretty sorry-looking bunch, too, I'll tell you that. Anyway, it's your business! They must have slept on the landing. Gypsies or something—terrible!"

Santiago stopped listening and ran upstairs, wondering who they could be. When he reached the seventh floor, he turned into the long dark passage that led to his room, then stopped, astonished. Sitting on the floor, a young couple were sleeping clasped in each other's arms, while a boy of ten or eleven was leaning against them. Santiago approached them silently and examined them carefully.

Suddenly Olny woke up and scrambled to his feet, embarrassed. "I'm so sorry," he stammered. "I know it's not right to wait for someone like this. We didn't know where to go. You're not angry with me?"

"No, not at all. Weren't you at Carabanchel last night?"

"Yes. I thought you looked good—you know, kind. And we were in a mess, so I thought . . ."

Santiago looked Olny straight in the eyes, then blushed and lowered his own. How could he look into the very face of misfortune and not die of shame? How could he bear a gaze made up of suffering and hunger? "Who is he?" Santiago asked, pointing to Francisco.

"My little brother. I couldn't leave him behind, could I?"

"No, of course not. But where do you come from?"

"From the Zone."

"Oh," said Santiago, who felt as if some distant and inaccessible place had been mentioned. Then he asked: "And who is she?"

"My wife—or practically, you know."

"I see."

Santiago stood silent for a few moments, then said in a weary voice: "What's your name?"

"Olny."

"Listen to me, Olny. I'm going to help you as much as I can. I ask you only one thing: be sensible about it. Believe me, it's very difficult to give. And I want you to understand this: whatever I give you or do for you, you owe me nothing. Do you understand? *Nothing*."

"Yes, Señor."

"Call me Santiago, will you?"

"Yes."

"Shall we shake hands on it?"

"Yes."

The two young men shook hands in silence. It was Olny's turn to lower his eyes. He had never met anyone like this before.

"For the time being I'll lend you my room. I'll go and take one at a hotel and I'll send you food. Get some sleep.

You can come with me, Olny, and tell me your story. Who gave you my address?"

"Ramírez."

"Good. We'll carry Francisco as gently as we can and put him to bed. Has he spent the whole night here? I'm so sorry I kept you waiting. I didn't feel well and have spent the whole night walking about. If I'd known . . ."

"Oh, we're used to it!"

Santiago blushed. Why had Olny said that? Perhaps he didn't realize how bitter the remark was, but it sounded like a reproach.

"Let's go."

Marianita woke up and stared at Santiago, her eyes sad, but trusting. Uncomfortable, he tried to smile; he shook the girl's hand and helped her put the child to bed. Francisco did not wake up.

The room was quite big and furnished with a certain sober refinement. In a corner was a divan covered with a tartan bedspread. By the little window, which looked out across the roofs of the city, were two large armchairs. There was a Louis XV chest, covered with books and papers, and English sporting prints on the walls. Against the wall opposite the divan was a piano.

Marianita stood with her hands crossed over her skirt, as if trying to hide her poverty. She seemed ill at ease.

"I generally call everyone '*tu*,'" Santiago said. "I hope you don't mind."

"No, Señor."

"Then call me Santiago?"

"Yes, Señor."

"Lie down beside Francisco. I'm sorry to take your husband away, but I must talk to him. He'll come back very soon. You don't mind, do you?"

Marianita smiled and shook her head. Santiago left the room and waited in the passage till Olny joined him; then the two young men went down into the street.

The sun was already high in the sky, and the street was busy again with happy-looking people coming and going. A few laughed when they caught sight of the two young men. Olny lowered his eyes in shame, looking down at his worn *espadrilles* and patched trousers next to his friend's elegant clothes. Santiago hailed a taxi and gave the address of a big shop.

When they were in the taxi, he took some bank notes from his notecase and gave them to Olny. "Take these, go into the shop, and buy a suit, a shirt, and socks. All you need, in fact. Get a dress for Marianita, too. Don't be taken in by the salesman. He'll try and palm all sorts of things off on you." He paused, smiled, and added shyly: "Forgive me. But I know what they're like. I'll wait for you in the taxi. All right?"

"It's wonderful. It'll be the first I've ever had in my life!"

"The first suit?"

"Yes. Crazy, isn't it? But it's true. I've never had a suit of my own. We bought everything at the Rastro."

The taxi stopped. Olny got out. Making himself as comfortable as possible, Santiago closed his eyes and rubbed the lids. It was a habit he had. He was not sure of what was happening to him, but simply accepted it as it came. A feeling of shame gave him a lump in the throat. During the years he had worked for the Revolution, Santiago had often addressed audiences of workers and small peasants, but he had never before been face to face with complete social disaster. And that was what Olny was: a human disaster, an inhabitant of the Zone. In his voice, eyes, and gestures there was so much real distress, such a habit of misery that one hardly dared look at him. And Santiago knew that Olny was no exception. There were hundreds of thousands who had never eaten their fill, who had never worn a suit of their own; thousands of faces like Olny's betrayed the same weariness of life, the same degradation. Santiago could help one here and there, a dozen, perhaps, but what of the others? The Party would make mistakes. But what did those mistakes matter when you thought of all the thousands of human beings whose lives had been a mistake? The world might lose a little of its freedom; but millions of human beings would acquire a deep and essential liberty they had never known before and of which they had never dared even dream. For whatever the faults of the Party, one thing was sure: it incarnated the hopes of the proletariat. The Revolution was less of a change of its living conditions—at least in the immediate future—than a change of *perspective*. For five, ten, or even twenty years the proletariat would have to work in poorer conditions than those of American workmen, for instance. But their work would have *meaning*. It would become the tool, not of their subsistence, but of their liberation. It was through work that these hundreds of thousands of men inured to misfortune would one day gain the dignity of the human condition.

Santiago stopped thinking. The heat had become stifling; the sun was melting the tar of the street. The café terraces were shaded by colored awnings, and the passers-by kept to the walls to avoid the sunlight. Olny came out of the shop, wearing a dark blue striped suit and smiling shyly and happily. Santiago smiled back and took him to his boot-maker.

"You look different," said Santiago as they came out. "Whatever the proverb may say, it's amazing how much the habit makes the monk."

Olny looked mistrustfully at his companion. "Anyone looking beyond my new clothes would be stopped short. It's not the clothes that make you suffer. It's something else that's destroyed. And it can't be fixed with money."

Santiago reddened again. He didn't know what to say. "I'm sorry if I hurt your feelings," he murmured. "I didn't mean to. I was only joking."

There was a silence. The two young men walked down Carmen Street toward the Puerta del Sol.

"I haven't been to work. They're sure to fire me."

"What did you do?"

"Sandwich man. Calo-Cream—do you know it? It's apparently the best toothpaste. Do you brush your teeth? I don't."

Again Santiago flushed. Why did everything the young man said put him so ill at ease? "I can find you work, if you like. One of my friends owns a garage at Cuatro Caminos. He'll certainly take you on."

"I have no papers." Olny's voice sounded hoarse.

Santiago had to make an effort to understand what he said. "We can apply for an identity card. You can get one with two witnesses."

"But you've got to have papers to ask for it."

"No. Only a birth certificate."

"I haven't got one."

"You must have a birth certificate. Everyone has!"

"Maybe. But there's no municipal office in the Zone, so . . . After all, what do they care whether there's one more or less in the Zone, eh?"

Santiago made no reply. He did not understand. These things existed, as Olny existed. But how could one believe it?

"You're kind. I don't know why you're doing this."

"I'd have done it for anyone."

"That makes no difference. Why are you on our side?"

Santiago felt weary. He replied slowly: "I don't know, Olny. I love justice. Perhaps that's it. I've read the Gospels. And perhaps I wanted to buy myself a good conscience— who knows?"

"What does that mean: 'buy a good conscience'?"

"Trying not to feel responsible."

"Don't you feel responsible any more?"

"Yes."

"So, what?"

"Nothing."

There was a pause.

"Shall we have a drink?" Santiago asked.

"I'd like one."

They went and sat on a café terrace. A waiter came up and took their order, and Olny asked for a beer and a plate of fried potatoes.

"It's funny—it's the first time I've been in a place like this. It was the dream of my life, practically, to sit on a café terrace and quietly sip a drink."

Santiago felt his heart constrict. His eyelids were heavy. He said nothing, asked no questions, but little by little Olny relaxed and began to talk. He spoke of his wretched child-hood, his unending hunger, his status as a pariah, but in a simple way, without ever raising his voice. From time to time Santiago thought Olny would cry, but he did not. It was he himself who had tears in his eyes by the time Olny stopped speaking. But he did not want to show his emotion.

"All right, Olny, I've got to leave you. I'm going to try to find you a room, an identity card, and a job. Go back to your wife and your little brother. Here's some money—you can buy what food you need. I'll see you again this evening. *Adiós!*"

Olny took the money and blushed. Santiago's face was

ashen. His companion's embarrassment made things still more difficult. He was on the point of leaving when Olny asked: "Are you giving me money to buy yourself a good conscience?"

Santiago hesitated for a moment. "Even if I wanted one, I could never have a good conscience now. Because now *I know.*"

"I said that to hurt you, you know. It's because I like you. I just want to say that you're fine—there aren't many like you. You don't have to have a bad conscience. You're not like the others. I respect you."

Santiago smiled wearily and shook Olny's hand. "Thank you. I respect you, too. You're a man."

II

SANTIAGO crossed the Puerta del Sol with a preoccupied air, glanced at the clock, and walked slowly toward the Plaza Mayor.

Carlos Ozcuna lived in the old quarter of Madrid. Santiago felt a need to see the man who had shown him the way to Marxism. They had not met for nearly two years.

There was nothing of the didactic, self-assured Communist about Carlos. He loved flowers, music, old books, and women, and had come to Marxism merely through a desire for logic and truth. He liked simple ideas well expressed and was curt with pretentious arguments, but never avoided difficult questions. His mind worked like a calculating machine, with speed and precision. Carlos was a person with whom one might have difficult moments, but his influence on everyone who came near him was salutary. His expression, at once intelligent and a little mocking, inspired confidence and liking. People felt they could let themselves go when talking to him, and he listened invariably with attention, though he might say finally: "That's a lot of nonsense. The essence of what you're saying is . . ." That was Carlo's way. He wanted always to reach, to discover the essence of things.

Would he have changed? Santiago wondered. Then he shrugged his shoulders: men like Carlos did not change.

Santiago stopped on the Plaza Mayor. A long procession was coming down Mayor Street toward the Puerta del Sol. About six hundred people were marching with banners and shouting slogans in unison: "Popular front! Popular front! Unite! Unite! The Left to power! Socialists join us!" Santiago watched them go by. Faced with these men wearing *espadrilles* and dressed in rags, he felt terribly isolated. He would have liked to run away, forget, and start all over again; the memory of his childhood obsessed him. He thought of the great solitary park, the wind hitting the cypress row, the dark waters of the lake, over which glided his beloved swans; the little church where he had prayed to God with all his might, kneeling between his parents; the

118

quiet sunsets lighting great fires in the blue sky. He felt suddenly like a child again, afraid of the occult powers that run the world and set man against man.

He climbed a damp, dirty staircase and came to a door on which was tacked a visiting card: CARLOS OZCUNA. He knocked and listened.

"Come in!"

Carlos was wearing pajamas and sitting on a divan bed. The room's furnishings were poor. There were portraits of Marx and Lenin on the walls; in a corner was a kitchen table covered with books, periodicals, and newspapers. Carlos gazed affectionately at his friend. The two young men embraced. "Well, you old bastard, how are you? Just the same, I see. With your movie star's profile, you're the pin-up of the Revolution."

Santiago's smile suddenly turned into a frown. He had noticed one of Carlos's trouser legs. It was empty. Santiago opened his mouth to say something, changed his mind, and bowed his head. Carlos surprised his glance, laughed, and said mockingly: "Are you looking at my amputated leg? It's nothing. Just a present from the Fascists. They left me standing for four days and nights in an ice bath. It was winter. I don't mind telling you, it wasn't funny at all. The bastards wanted to get some names out of me. They were convinced the Communists were going to blow up the Chamber. It'll blow up without bombs, I told them. But they didn't believe me. They're stubborn! They wouldn't give up. And this is the result!"

Santiago was appalled. He could think of nothing to say. At last he murmured: "I'm terribly sorry. There simply aren't any words."

"You mustn't be sorry. Luckily I'm neither a bicycle racer nor am I thinking of winning the hundred-yard sprint. I'd have been much more concerned if they'd cut something else off."

Santiago smiled. No, Carlos had not changed. He had the same smile, the same good humor, the same frankness. Santiago felt happier; he could find with Carlos some of that peace he was so avid for. Without quite knowing why, he began talking about his day and about Olny.

"And what are you going to do now?" Carlos asked when his friend fell silent.

"Find him work and somewhere to live. Before coming here, I telephoned my father. He's sending me a rather large sum of money."

"Excellent. You see, one of the advantages of being rich is that you can do good. It's a luxury I can't indulge in."

Santiago made no answer. He got to his feet and went across to a window looking out on an interior courtyard; it was somber and melancholy.

"But what of all the others? The ones who can find no one to help them out of the mess?"

"Yes. They'll find the Party."

There was a long silence. Someone in one of the rooms which opened on to the courtyard turned on a radio, which began shrieking *paso dobles*. Santiago took a cigarette from a pack on the table and lit it. Then he said: "Carlos, I'm thinking seriously of leaving the Party."

There was no reply. He went on. "I cannot be an accomplice of what is going to happen. I can't. I became a Marxist to serve justice, not to be a murderer."

He had never admitted these things, even to himself. Perhaps the desire to leave the Party had been dormant within him a long time, but he had never been able to define it clearly. Now he felt relieved of too heavy a burden. He was grateful for Carlos's silence. Santiago had no desire to argue. His need was to talk, to free himself, to weep.

"I'm in sort of the same state of mind as people who are still Christians, but indeed because of their Christianity have found themselves forced to leave the Church and to denounce it." There was a pause. He lit another cigarette and went on, talking slowly. "It's no fun being a heretic. No fun at all."

He stopped talking and smiled. Carlos thought of how much he liked Santiago's smile. It was a strange smile that seemed to come from a long way off and to illuminate his whole face.

"Never in my life have I felt so much a Socialist as I do at this moment, Carlos. Nor so alone."

Carlos coughed and lit a cigarette in his turn. He was sitting on the bed, his single foot touching on the floor.

"Have you nothing to say? Do you disapprove? Are you one of those who accept things, applaud at meetings, and stand up when Stalin's name's mentioned?"

"I try to understand, that's all."

"To understand what?"

Carlos put his cigarette down in an ash tray and looked into his friend's eyes. "Are you leaving the Party because you don't approve of it, or because you think that by leaving it you'll be able to serve the workers better?"

"That's not the point."

"Yes, it's precisely the point. After all, we joined the Revolution for the purpose of serving the workers."

"I can't explain it to you, Carlos. You're not being honest. You're deliberately confusing the proletariat and the Party. They're two very different things."

"Is the Party with the workers—yes or no?"

"Yes, of course. Because the workers think they can express themselves only through the Party. But suppose in the long run the Party, as it is now organized, fatally betrays the interests of the proletariat. You must understand me. The workers can't see the danger, but I see it. And if you're honest, you must see it, too. We're going to hand over the workers and leave the fate of the Revolution to a handful of men who aren't Communists at all. We have no right to keep silent."

There was a long pause. Carlos looked concerned. In fact, he was largely indifferent and did not understand Santiago's scruples, although his position did not surprise him. He had always suspected that his young friend would leave the Party for one reason or another. Not that Carlos altogether approved of what was happening. But he could not follow

Santiago, who confused his own problems with those of the Revolution. He was a mystic, one of those natures that thirst for the infinite, for absolute love. "A victim," thought Carlos, and looked sadly at his friend.

"Do you know what Lenin said about Leftism?"

"Yes," Santiago replied.

"I think the time for words has passed. When one's lost a leg in the service of the proletariat, these problems don't look quite the same any more. You seem to be confusing your own anxieties with those of the Party, which is going through a difficult period. You adopted communism to appease your own conscience, hoping to find peace in it. But the spreading of socialism is, above all, a practical problem. It's a struggle against hunger and want, not against metaphysical anxieties."

Carlos expressed himself with difficulty and felt he was not being understood. The two friends were speaking different languages. How could they agree?

"You see, what appealed to you in Marxism was a philosophical theory. I mean an idea and a correspondence of ideas. But Marxism, above all and before everything else, is a dialectic between ideas and facts. It's not a bridge from the particular to the universal, but from the general to the particular. A worker in a Catalan textile factory must *feel* his liberation profoundly. . . ."

Carlos closed his eyes and went on in a level voice. "We can have neither consciences nor valid artists before all men have achieved dignity and liberty. You wonder whether it would not be possible to save the individual conscience and construct socialism at the same time. I don't know. But I do know that it's a dangerous experiment. As far as I'm concerned, the Revolution is too important to allow it to run risks."

Carlos paused again, then added with a smile: "Anyway, the problem's different now. What matters is to defeat fascism. On that point the interests of the Party are identical with those of the proletariat."

"You're talking in the abstract, Carlos. You've forgotten that we're not *the* Left. There's the C.N.T., the F.A.I., the Socialists, and how many more? They, too, are Marxist and want a classless society. By what right do we take possession of what is also their Revolution? For you know, Carlos, the Party's prepared to do anything to seize power. It will massacre its brothers-in-arms, hunt them down, annihilate them. Do you accept that?"

Carlos did not reply.

"In fact, do you or do you not feel capable of killing a member of the C.N.T. on the pretext that his views on how to achieve socialism differ from yours? Could you or could you not fire at a worker who was convinced that the Russian brand of socialism is not the only valid one? That's the whole problem. For their Left, Carlos, is one of liberty. If we fight it, we are fighting liberty itself."

"The liberty of the proletariat consists, in the first place, of its economic liberation. And only the Party can assure that effectively."

"No. You're lying to yourself. Why? You know very well that one of the conditions for successful and rapid liberation is that there should be a Left opposition. It's necessary to the evolution of socialism. It's the dialectical element. If we allow that opposition to be suppressed, we're condemning the proletariat to an emancipation dictated by the Party. Where's dialectic then?"

Carlos seemed tired and remained silent. His eyes were dull. Finally he murmured: "I've lost a leg and sacrificed the whole of my youth to the Party. I cannot have doubts. I'd go mad."

Santiago went to him, placed a hand on his shoulder, and asked in a sad, almost broken voice: "Carlitos, you are really with them?"

"I'm tired, Santiago. I fear the whole cause may be lost anyway. But I understand you."

"Thank you."

12

CONSUELO was drunk. But she was not so drunk that she did not realize she had drunk too much. Her legs felt numb; her head felt like bursting. The sharp, cold air of the night seemed to kiss her burning cheek with the kisses of death. There was a deep silence. In the sleeping Zone an emaciated dog bayed at the moon. A man's voice cried hoarsely: "Filthy bitch!" Consuelo stopped. Could she reach her hut? She hesitated, staggered a little, then went on, through a rising nausea and the weight of repressed tears. Everything seemed in a state of flux in her tired brain. She saw the world as in a nightmare: everything seemed real and unreal. At last she reached the hut door and found it open. With the premonition that something had happened, something serious, she hurried in, and was relieved to hear her husband's irregular breathing. Then she began listening for other sounds. Things seemed to be swaying around her. She wanted to cry out, but could not manage to do so; a low groan was all that issued from her throat. With a shaking hand, she lit a candle end on the table. She knew what the note contained before she read it, but one phrase etched itself on her mind: "We are leaving." She reread the three words, repeated them aloud, then collapsed onto a bench.

She felt cold. Shudders shook her thin back and ran up to her hair. Her eyelids felt heavy. She listened: only the silence of the night answered her despair. Consuelo asked herself no questions. She sat there not knowing what to do or where to go. She suddenly felt her loneliness, grew fearful, and went to wake up Manuel. He was deeply asleep and, though he turned over on the bed, did not open his eyes. She went back and sat on the bench by the cold stove. The two mattresses on which her sons slept had not been unrolled. Consuelo gazed at the empty space. She had never imagined that loneliness was like this: silence. The silence became obsessive and seemed to bear heavily down on her head. Olny had gone—Francisco, too. They had written: "We are leaving." Consuelo tried to gather her thoughts. But what thoughts? Their departure might have been foreseen for a long time. Besides, she did not love her children, had never loved them—good riddance! But there was this emptiness, and above all, this silence. They had left without understanding her suffering. But what was there to understand? Consuelo herself did not understand. Had she ever really been alive? How was she to know? Her life had been a failure. Were there lives that were not half-admitted failures? Now everything was finished; there was nothing left to save. Absurdity had reached its limits; beyond those limits, there was only death.

Consuelo got to her feet, put a shawl around her shoulders, left the hut, and walked across the Zone as if she were walking in her sleep. Was she mad? Why should she be mad? Was suffering madness?

There was a clear, high sky covered with stars. The night was cold, and Consuelo shivered. She went down the slope that led to the wasteland, and nearly fell. She reached the road and, like an automaton, set out for the city.

In the still countryside the stones shone under the moon. The air smelled of thyme, and a majestic peace seemed to rise from the sleeping earth. Consuelo saw nothing, heard nothing. Her eyes were wet with tears; her lower lip quivered. She reached the city and began walking through the long, straight streets at random. She skirted the circles of light cast by the lamps and kept close to the walls till, without knowing how she got there, she reached Atocha.[4] She followed the fence that overhung the railway line, and slowed her pace. The station was lost in shadow. Here and there lights cut through the darkness, and a train whistled. A few seconds later it left the platform and passed below Consuelo, who for a moment or two was enveloped in damp gray smoke.

Consuelo gazed after the train in agony. It was leaving, too. In life everyone and everything departed, even dreams. She wiped away the sweat that was running down her forehead, and tidied her hair. She felt suddenly afraid. The police arrested people clothed in rags and took them to the Paseo del Rey. The women there were shaved, bullied, and beaten by sadistic nuns. Consuelo did not want to be arrested and taken there; she hadn't done anything wrong. She must flee, but where could she go? One must have somewhere to go in life. Consuelo shivered. The cold was inside her; and yet she was sweating, and her worn, ragged dress was sticking to her skin. Perhaps she had a fever; the thought frightened her. She was afraid of illness and terrified of death. Steps sounded behind her; was it the police? Perhaps they had followed her and had waited till she was exhausted to arrest her. The *policías armadas* were quite capable of it! She knew them. They had come to the Zone, and her back still bore the marks of their heavy clubs. But they wouldn't get her! Consuelo began running and felt she was being fol-

[4] One of the main railway stations of Madrid.

lowed. She ran faster still, bathed in sweat now, and her legs began to give way. She realized suddenly, inexplicably, that she was inside the station area near the locomotive shed. There were isolated cars standing in the sidings. A train whistled in the distance. Consuelo heard the sound of voices and cowered in the shadows. Two railwaymen passed close to her, each with a lantern in his hand, waving it in the night. They went off laughing, and Consuelo heard "Damn well-stacked"; and it was some seconds before she realized they were talking about a woman. The silence fell again. Consuelo looked at her dress, blushed, and tried to arrange it. But her hands were trembling. "I can't fall asleep here. . . . I must keep moving! Moving!" She left her hiding place with regret. Her excitement had disappeared. She only felt cold, and walked with bowed shoulders. She was so tired. Consuelo stepped over the rails, which all seemed to be mixed up with each other. She was alone in the middle of a forest of steel. At last she turned her back on the station and began walking between two parallel lines, which disappeared into the distance before her. "This thing must lead somewhere! It must go somewhere!"

Consuelo began to cry. She did not know why she wept, nor did she try to find the reason. She was weeping the way children do at night: from exhaustion and nerves. She walked on, bent double, her black shawl across her shoulders. A train whistled behind her; the noise seemed to come from a long way off. She stumbled onward and remembered her mother's handsome, grave face. It was a fine, calm face, engraved with peace. Then Consuelo saw again in her imagination the orange groves under the setting sun, the long beach with its golden sand, and remembered the day she had met Manuel. She remembered the shy, smiling face of the man she loved, and her tears fell faster. "Manuel! My Manuel!" She saw that loved face so clearly that she stretched her hands toward it in a caress. A noise behind her made her start. The train was coming nearer; the noise was growing louder and louder. Consuelo shook with a great shuddering. She knew she must escape, but escape where? She was too tired to escape. Besides, she *did not understand.* The train whistled twice. It was a few yards behind her. Consuelo fell to her knees; she burst into tears, but she did not move. Nor did she pray.

PART TWO

... *And of Despair*

"That is why I have decided
to deny whatever, from near or
far, for good or bad reasons, kill
or justify killing."

ALBERT CAMUS
The Plague

... *And of Despair*

I

OLNY was now living in a three-room flat not far from the Retiro. He could see from his window the century-old trees in the ancient Madrid garden. In the morning when he got up to go to work, municipal workmen were watering the lawns and rose beds along Alfonso XII Street. He loved this cool hour, with its fresh smells, when the city was still asleep and the sky over the roofs showed pale green and pink and gray. Sometimes he stopped and breathed the scented air, hard, for a few moments. Sometimes he wanted never to move again. This morning hour was made up of nostalgia.

He lit a cigarette slowly and carefully. Since he had been working, he no longer smoked butts, and the lighting of a cigarette had become a symbolic and significant gesture: the symbol of his liberation.

It was warm outside. A heavy, stifling heat pressed against one's skin. A few people in white walked along the park railing, protecting themselves as best they could from the sun. The children's clothes were blue or pink. Seen from above, they might have been beautiful dolls. Their mothers dragged them along tyrannically. They were probably going to church; it was Sunday.

Olny was waiting. In the kitchen Marianita was preparing the breakfast they would eat together like the old married couple they were. For now they were really married. Santiago had been a witness, and after the ceremony they had gone to have lunch in the country. Santiago had done things well: he had even hired a car, and afterward they had all three gone to the Escorial. Olny had never seen anything so beautiful before. Gazing at the bare gray walls, so austere in their majesty, he had felt his breast swell with pride; face to face with this expression of eternal Spain, he had understood that his country was great. Then they had gone to an expensive hotel full of attentive waiters, smiling servant girls, and ironical young pages. Olny had felt embarrassed, but Santiago had known how to put him at his ease. It had been a fine wedding, the kind people have in films. Moreover, his whole life was now from a dream, like this comfortable, modern, sunny flat, which Santiago had called "my wedding gift" and then, as usual, had blushed.

Olny loved his friend and protector as he had never loved anyone before and had never imagined that one could love. It was a bond made up of esteem and admiration. When he was with his friend, he could barely open his mouth. Everything he would have liked to say, the words of devoted friendship he dreamed of uttering, died in his throat. He stood there, awkwardly dumb, timidly smiling, for Santiago had become more and more sad. His eyes, which had been so bright and glowing, had gone dull; his cheeks were hollow. Olny, himself born in misfortune, wished Santiago would pour out to him those tears he restrained and those sobs he smothered. He felt intuitively that Santiago was less strong than he tried to appear. But Olny had never dared make a real gesture of tenderness, though he had said one day, his voice full of emotion: "I don't know how a man should love another, but I love you."

Santiago had stammered: "Thank you. Thank you from my heart. I love you, too. You're honest, loyal, and generous. You're a man. I should be happy to think that in the world of tomorrow, the world we shall perhaps never see, there will be men like you. Because as long as their race goes on, nothing will be altogether lost."

"Why shouldn't we see that world? That's what we're making the Revolution for—to see it."

Santiago smiled. "I see nothing but shadows everywhere, Olny. A long, dark night is going to cover us all. I do not know how many of us will see the dawn, or what sort of day will follow it. Perhaps it will be a still darker and deeper night, a night without a dawn. Then everything will have to begin all over again."

"What'll have to begin all over again? Tell me."

"The Revolution."

"Do you think we're going to have to make two revolutions? Why? We'll win the first one. After all, we're stronger, aren't we?"

"No. We're not the stronger, only the more numerous."

There was a silence. The two friends were near Cibeles. They were sitting on a bench in the Paseo del Prado. Santiago dropped his head onto his hands. "How tired I am!" he murmured. "How I should like it all to end!"

"All what?"

"Everything. Life, suffering, fear."

"But I'm here with you!"

"Yes, Olny, you're here. And I thank you for being here. The only thing is, you see, it's not easy to live." And then, dropping his voice still lower, Santiago added: "Not easy at all."

Olny could not forget these words. He wanted to help his friend; but how can you help someone? All you can do is give—but give what?

Marianita called. He shouted back: "I'm coming."

He owed everything he had to Santiago de Leyes: his flat, his clothes, his work, his wife. But the most valuable thing Santiago had given him was hope. Hope for a more just, a more fraternal, a more human world. And now his friend doubted. But what did he doubt? The Zone still existed. Men were still dying of hunger, silently, discreetly. The Revolution was necessary. Then, what was Santiago afraid of? Was he afraid of dying? But why and by whom would he be killed? Ramírez? Olny could take care of that. It was wrong to fear men like Ramírez, who had nothing to do with the Revolution. The real face of socialism was Santiago's.

"Olny? Aren't you coming?"

He smiled, kissed his wife, and sat down across from her. In her simple dressing gown, her face fresh from sleep, she seemed happy. Olny glanced about him. He could not yet quite convince himself that this flat was his and that the furniture belonged to him. The sudden change in his circumstances had left him a little confused; he couldn't quite fit himself into this new life. He thought again of Santiago. Why had he helped him? But perhaps there was no *why*. He just did, that's all. Olny would have liked to understand his friend better, so that he might love him the better. "But I have no education. . . . I don't know how to talk," he thought. "I can't even manage to thank him."

"Are you going out?" Marianita asked. She was smiling, her face young under her silky hair. He got up, walked around the table, and kissed her slowly, carefully, without saying a word. He emptied his heart of the infinite tenderness lying hidden in it; he put into each kiss all the passion of the words he would never know how to utter, of the phrases he would never be able to construct.

"Yes," he finally replied.

"More posters?" She looked at him anxiously.

"Yes."

"Why don't you stay at home? Francisco's coming. We could go to the movies. Wouldn't you like to?"

"I've got to help the other guys. If there's any trouble, I should be there. I'll come home early. We'll go to the movies this evening, I promise."

137

Marianita got up slowly and clung to him, her head on his chest, stroking his back. She wanted to weep, but knew she would not. "What I'm going to say's silly," she began in a low voice. "I know it's not right"—she clung closer to him —"but don't go, Olny. We've got a home. We're all right here. Let well enough alone."

He felt Marianita's warmth against his body, and stroked her hair with an automatic gesture of love. He said nothing. His wife's words echoed his own doubts, his own anxieties. There was a long silence. "I haven't the right, Marianita. You can't leave your comrades alone like that. We've got to think of the people who want to get out of the Zone and can't. We have no right to forget them."

She was weeping. Silent tears slid down her cheeks. She was afraid, but could not have said of what; she felt she ought to prevent Olny from going out. The atmosphere in Madrid was tense. Gangs of young Fascists patrolled the streets of the capital and attacked isolated workmen, men who sold Socialist newspapers, and those who hung posters. Riots broke out everywhere; every morning the Madrid press reported deaths. The day before, a young Falingist, seventeen, had been killed during a fight in the suburbs, and his comrades had sworn to avenge his death.

Marianita had been pregnant for four months. The heat made her nervous; she was terrified of being left alone. She needed Olny's presence today. "You're not a coward. You've been every day. Your wife's pregnant. There's nothing they can say. You know you're not a coward."

"It's not so much that, Marianita. We mustn't forget, just because we have enough to eat, those who haven't anything at all. We can't betray the Zone. You must understand."

She worked hard to hold back her sobs, wanting him to stay, there against her body. She had nothing but him. He was her reason for living. She could not, had not the right to let him run the risk of being killed. Her throat was tight. She took one of his long, slender hands with its bony fingers and pressed a kiss on it.

"You mustn't cry, Marianita. You mustn't. I never get hurt. I'll come back. We'll go to the movies.

"I'm not crying. I'm afraid."

"Of what?"

"I don't know."

"I'll come back. I've always come back, haven't I?"

"Yes."

There was a long pause. She was tired and her head ached. "We've always lived in the gutter, you and I. We've had our share of trouble. Now we've got the right to be happy, Olny. We've got a flat and work and we're going to have a son. I know it'll be a boy. Surely we've got a right to be happy. We've had enough misery."

Olny closed his eyes. He, too, wanted to sink into a chair and stay there. But he thought of the Zone, of Loto, Consuelo, and La Remedios. How could he forget his past? He had no right to do so. It was hard, of course, to give up happiness. But how could you live happy when those you loved were still sunk in misfortune?

139

"I can't, Marianita. I can't." He hesitated and murmured finally: "You mustn't make a bastard of me. You mustn't."

She had lost, she knew. She made no answer. Olny was moved, and Marianita knew that she had no right to take advantage of a man's emotions. She smiled resignedly. "I'm being silly. I shouldn't have. Forgive me."

He was grateful to her for her tact. She pretended to be the only one who was moved, the only one who was afraid. He kissed her with tenderness and anguish. He hated the world, money, life: everything that was opposed to love. He wanted there to be nothing in the world but this flat of theirs, this warm tenderness uniting them. "I'll come back."

"Yes."

"I'll be back before eight. There's an American film on at the Salamanca. It's set in Brazil, a musical. It'll be good."

"Yes."

"Don't get too tired."

She tried to smile; he avoided looking at her. He went without turning back. She was suddenly afraid again and ran out to the landing, where she heard the echo of his steps. "Olny?"

"Yes?"

He was on the first floor; Marianita was on the fifth. He could not see the tears pouring silently from her eyes.

She leaned over the well of the staircase, parted her lips, thought better of it, and finally murmured: "Don't do anything foolish."

2

THERE was a holiday atmosphere about Madrid; the streets were full of idlers and strollers; the café terraces were crowded. The young bourgeois, who had filled them two months before, were gone, and their place had been taken by people from the workers' suburbs. They seemed neither embarrassed nor impressed; they laughed aloud and whistled as the girls passed by. They were simply dressed; their talk was picturesque and thick with argot; their accents were lower-class. For the most part, they were very young and had come to fight, but there was no one to fight; the city belonged to them. They had no idea of what to do with it and wanted only to return to their own districts. The shoe-shine boys lounged by their boxes.

Olny watched the spectacle with curiosity. Events had moved quickly. When Santiago had talked to him of the Revolution, he had believed it was still a distant, an almost inaccessible event. But now it was here, within reach. This was the Revolution: young men from the suburbs beginning to grasp the fact that the center of Madrid was not a reserved area. Of course, this was not enough; the real Revolution had not yet taken place. The elections had given the Left Wing parties a large majority; this was only the beginning. But there was a threatening tension in the air.

Young Fascists were sowing terror and attacking the sellers of *The Workers' World;* the militant Communists were retaliating. The silence of the summer nights was broken by the noise of gunfire. There was talk of a Fascist *coup d'état;* it was even said that part of the army might rise against the Government of the Republic. Olny placed little stock in all these rumors; but today he was anxious. Was it the damp, oppressive heat that weighed on his nerves? Or was it Marianita's anguished forebodings? He did not know.

He reached Tetuán de las Victorias within half an hour of leaving home. His comrades were waiting for him, checking the magazines of their submachine guns as they stood around a wooden table. Ramírez was among them. Olny had not seen him since the day they had quarreled as they left the meeting at Carabanchel, and he did not know how to treat him. He had heard that his old companion had an important position on the Central Committee of the Party. Ramírez came over to him, a smile on his lips. "Hello. Do we shake hands?"

"All right."

"Anyway," Ramírez said, "he wasn't worth quarreling about. He has betrayed us. It was easy to foresee. Those bastards always let you down."

Olny looked up. He did not understand what Ramírez was driving at, but guessed that he had something important to tell him. He waited patiently, and Ramírez glanced at him with amusement. "Don't you know your friend has left the Party?"

"No."

"Don't you see him these days? You're right not to. He's a bastard. A coward."

"Santiago is not a coward."

"No? He's a hero, is he? He resigns as soon as the first riots break out and sends us back his card, and you think that's just swell, don't you?"

Olny felt ill at ease. It was no doubt true, since Ramírez said so, but it was difficult to believe. How could Santiago have left the Party just when the first riots were starting? That was a betrayal, and Santiago was incapable of betraying.

"Don't you believe me?"

Olny shrugged his shoulders. It was Santiago who had first talked to him of the Revolution; it was through him that he had discovered the Party. How could he have dared abandon his friend, deny all he had said, everything he had taught hundreds, thousands of proletarians?

"Read this." Ramírez unfolded an important daily newspaper. On the front page under a big headline was the following:

Santiago de Leyes accuses the Spanish Communist Party of betraying the interests of the proletariat and of having become a reactionary movement with Fascist tendencies.

Olny glanced through the long article. He did not understand his friend's argument justifying his action. Only one thing was clear: Santiago had betrayed the Party and had betrayed him—Olny. For was it not a betrayal of their friendship to have said nothing about it to him?

"Well, are you convinced? Wasn't I right?"

Olny made no reply. His teeth were clenched and his eyes had grown hard. He picked up a pistol and, hiding it in an inside pocket of his coat, left the room without a word.

The streets stretched away in front of him, long and straight. Olny hurried on. "Santiago's a rotten bastard. He had no right to make me join the Party and then leave it himself. I'll kill him. . . ."

He began working automatically. Each street he passed through was soon full of red-and-white posters: WORKERS OF THE WORLD—UNITE. JOIN THE SPANISH COMMUNIST PARTY FOR BREAD, PEACE, SOCIAL JUSTICE, AND PROSPERITY.

Olny worked well and quickly. He had become something of a specialist in putting up Party posters. His comrades had nicknamed him "the billposter," and he was flattered and amused by the name. He was concentrating on his work and paid no attention to a black Peugeot that drove up, slowed, and stopped. Four young men got out of it and surrounded him. By the time he recognized the danger, it was too late.

"Don't move."

They searched him quickly, disarmed him, and pushed him into the car, which was waiting with its engine still running. One of the young men punched him, and his nose began bleeding; a second blow in the kidneys nearly made him shout with pain.

The car drove off, crossed Madrid at full speed, and made for the open country. Olny felt numb. Would they kill him? he suddenly wondered; horribly mutilated bodies were continually being found on the outskirts of the capital. He thought sadly of Marianita and then tried to think of nothing.

3

SANTIAGO was anxious. He was not concerned about his own future, but about those he loved, those whom he had tried to protect. What would become of Olny, Marianita, and Francisco? How would his father live through the dark days ahead. He lit a cigarette and went to the little window; the roofs and terraces of Madrid stretched away into the distance. Santiago was in shirt sleeves, for the heat was oppressive; the air was heavy, still, without a breath of wind, and a strange silence lay over the capital. The people of Madrid had closed themselves in their houses, hiding from the heat—or from their fear.

Santiago lit another cigarette and looked around the room in search of comfort. His eyes came to rest on a little crucifix on the wall above the head of his bed. He wanted to pray, but could find no words; he fell to his knees, but remained silent. It was all he had to offer God: the sad silence of his loneliness and his anguish.

145

At last he got to his feet and started to dress. He had made his decision: he would go to Valladolid.

From a corner seat by the window, Santiago watched the landscape speed by. The compartment was empty; the light outside was hard as steel, slicing through the air, almost as if the train had difficulty in forcing its way through. He placed his burning forehead against the cool glass, and it did him good. He gazed despairingly at the desolate fields of Castile which stretched away to the horizon. The land was red and arid; in some places it was parceled into fields of gilded wheat.

Santiago could not restrain his tears. He had fought long against loneliness and despair, but now nothing mattered any more. He sought a *reason* for his sobs, but could find none. His nerves were shot. He felt a need to go back to the house in which he had been born and to see his father again. He had no idea what he would say to him, or even if he would say anything at all.

He crossed the town. Like the streets of Madrid, Barcelona, and Valencia, those of Valladolid were full of crowds marching in procession, singing the *"Internationale"* and shouting slogans: "The land for the peasants! Down with tyranny! Down with the Church! Death to the priests!"

He gazed at it all with sadness in his heart, and hurried on. He was surprised that his father had sent no one to meet him at the station, for he had sent him a telegram telling him of his arrival. Could anything have happened to him? Santiago took a taxi and gave his address. The driver had a kindly face, and finally Santiago made up his mind to question him.

"Are you a native of Valladolid?"

"Of course."

"Do you happen to know the Marquis de Leyes?"

"Your father? Everyone knows him."

"Has anything happened to him?"

"We're making the Revolution, but we're not assassins. What did you think had happened to him?"

Santiago sighed with relief. "Nothing, of course. I was just surprised to find no one at the station, that's all."

"Oh, well, that's something else again. He sent no one because he's alone."

"Alone?"

"Well, yes! Things are different now. That's what the Revolution's all about. No more masters, no more slaves. Your father's tenants are now masters of the lands they cultivate. They've set up a co-operative and are running the estate in association. Of course, they're giving your father a good pension. But things aren't like they were before."

Santiago closed his eyes. He was delighted that the peasants should own the land, but could not help worrying about his father.

The taxi turned into the park gates and drove up the avenue leading to the house. The garden was overgrown, deserted. The swans, indifferent to human drama, were still gliding over the dark waters of the lake, and the proud, still cypresses stood in high silhouette against the blue sky. An anxious silence lay over the park. The children who normally played hide-and-seek there had disappeared. Santiago tried to imagine what his father's life was like in this vast, silent, deserted domain. The taxi stopped at the porch, and Santiago entered the house. Javier came to meet him.

He was an old servant, about seventy-five. He had been born in the house and had never left it. He had bright blue eyes and a bald pink skull. He walked with difficulty and seemed to make a considerable effort to hold himself upright. Santiago looked at him in astonishment. He was wearing an old livery with the family arms. He smiled shyly and bowed with ceremony.

"Good day, Señor Santiago. I hope the journey was not too tiring. I have made ready the room next to the Marquis's. You will be company for him." The old servant's voice sounded weary. "I am sorry not to have met you at the station, but, as you know, I have never learned to drive a car. It's tiresome, very tiresome."

Santiago took off his overcoat and handed it to him, then asked with a smile: "My dear Javier, what's all this about? Aren't you going to embrace me? And what do your clothes mean? Is there a costume ball on or something?"

"Times have changed, Santiago. Everything is upside-down. No one is satisfied with the station God gave him any more. Everyone wants to be God's equal. It'll all end badly."

"Very possibly, Javier. But that doesn't explain why

you're wearing those clothes, which, I may say in passing, don't suit you at all."

The old butler gazed at Santiago with his blue eyes and went on, as if he had not heard the remark. "They've lost all respect. No one wants to obey any more. And what happens when no one will obey? Chaos. The Marquis was too kind. I've often told him so. Well, times have changed. The Marquis had to make his own bed this morning. It's not right!"

Santiago suddenly understood why the faithful old servant had put on a livery he had never worn before: to emphasize his respect and loyalty amid the general disorder. There were tears in the young man's eyes as he kissed Javier's bald head. "Don't worry, Javier. It won't last forever. How's my father?"

"Not very well. The Marquis isn't exactly ill, but he's sad and depressed. He spends his whole time in the library, reading and writing. He's very low."

"Does he feel ill, Javier? Has he sent for the doctor?"

"He says nothing, seems lost in a dream, and will see no one. He doesn't utter more than a dozen words a day, even to me. Oh, it's so sad, so terrible!" Javier was crying and wiping away his tears with a dirty handkerchief. "They won't leave him alone. Yesterday they came to take away the tapestries from the great drawing room, and tomorrow they're coming to take the two El Greco's from the library. The Marquis doesn't even protest."

"Coming to take the El Greco's? But on what pretext?"

"They say it's immoral for one family to have the sole enjoyment of such works of art and that they're the heritage of the people. They want to start a museum, or something of the sort." Javier sniffed, blew his nose noisily, and shook his head.

Santiago felt sad at heart and so moved that he scarcely dared enter the library. "Don't weep, Javier. It will be all right in the end."

The old man pursed his lips, but his meaning escaped Santiago. "I'm living in terror. The day before yesterday they murdered the Count of Piedra Alta. They went to his house at night, pulled him out of bed, never even gave him time to put his trousers on, pushed him into a car, and yesterday his body was found two kilometers outside the town." Javier fell silent for a moment and then, in a voice broken with sobs, added: "I'm glad you've come. Since you're on their side . . ."

The old man did not complete his sentence. Santiago changed color and, without a word, went to the library door, knocked, and waited a few seconds; then, as there was no reply, he entered the room.

The Marquis de Leyes was sitting in a Louis XIII armchair beside the great hearth, on which, in spite of the appalling heat outside, some logs were burning. He did not move, made no gesture, but gazed at his son from the depth of his honest eyes. When he had kissed his father tenderly on the forehead, Santiago sat down silently opposite him.

He wondered why his father had a fire lit in the middle of July. Was he ill? Santiago looked at him attentively. The Marquis de Leyes had hardly changed, but dark rings under his eyes and two lines at the corners of his mouth were evidence of the trials he had undergone. The library was in shadow, the curtains half drawn; Santiago thought how handsome his father looked by the light of the flames. The old man was gazing steadily at a photograph of his wife which was standing on a table beside him. In his hands was a copy of the Bible. Santiago closed his eyes and remembered all the evenings he had spent in this room with his parents. Then he stopped thinking. His chest felt oppressed, his throat constricted. Was it the silence that made him feel so ill at ease? Or the heat?

The Marquis de Leyes was now staring at the flames leaping on the hearth. Suddenly he murmured: "I suppose lighting a fire in the middle of summer is rather unusual. Slightly mad, in fact."

Santiago scarcely recognized the veiled voice. It seemed to come from a long way off. The Marquis de Leyes spoke slowly, as if each word he uttered were being dragged out of him. He seemed to be talking to no one in particular.

"Nothing is so near madness as old age," he went on in the same indifferent tone.

There was another silence.

"Old age is the time of impossible desires and belated regrets. That is no doubt why the sages of the Orient destroyed all desire in themselves: at the same time they killed the haunting thought of growing old and dying. We Spaniards want too much. That's why we in Spain are perpetually haunted by death."

Santiago did not understand what his father was driving at. He seemed to be pursuing a private obsession.

The Marquis continued. "I have no more desires and am therefore no longer living. And, since I am no longer living, I am not afraid of death."

"You won't die, Father."

The Marquis de Leyes raised his eyes and looked attentively at his son, as if he were seeing him for the first time. Santiago blushed and lowered his head. His father no longer spoke the same language, and it was therefore vain to try to understand him.

"I shall not die, because I am already dead. The death of the body is nothing. It's the soul, the soul alone, which resists death." The old man stared at the fire once again. "My greatest desire was nothing but a childish fantasy. I wanted to win eternal life. One does not win paradise—one earns it." There was another silence. "I had misread the Bible. But who reads it aright?"

The old man opened the book in his hands and read in a voice quavering with emotion: " 'No man can serve two masters: for either he will hate the one, and love the other; or else he will hold to the one, and despise the other. Ye cannot serve God and mammon.' "

He fell silent for a moment. Santiago now saw what his father was driving at.

"I thought I could serve both. I placed my confidence in the Church, in sophists, in the friends of mammon, who told me that text required interpretation. It required to be lived, and not interpreted."

The Marquis de Leyes seemed exhausted. Sweat poured down his wrinkled forehead and cheeks. His white hair was soaking, as if he had taken a long walk in the rain.

He turned over a few pages and said loudly: "And yet the warnings are many, and definite!

'Blessed are the poor . . .' 'Woe unto you that are rich . . .' 'Blessed are ye that hunger now . . .' 'Woe unto you that are full . . .' "

The old man was weeping. He had thrown his head back, and his features were contracted with suffering.

"For sixty years I have been reading the gospels, to no purpose! I have understood nothing. It took the Revolution to force me to make the one Christian gesture I have made in my life, a gesture I have never had the courage to look on as even possible. No one can even contemplate such gestures now. The Church has conquered. Its theologians, its exegetists have pressed out the Divine Word, have emptied it of its truth and left nothing but an empty husk, dry as an old man's skin."

Santiago did not dare look at his father. He could not bear the sight of that pale face, covered with sweat and twisted with suffering and despair.

The Marquis de Leyes raised his right hand to his breast, then let it fall back with an air of discouragement. "I

153

thought I loved Christ and was close to Him. But it was an illusion!"

Suddenly, changing his tone, he said: "That good Javier has put on his gala suit to wait on me and thinks I'm suffering because I'm dispossessed. But the opposite is the truth! I have built a few model cottages and given the estate a church and a dispensary. I thought by doing these things I had merited paradise. I had got off cheaply, and these people have come to remind me of it."

In a deep voice the old man cried: "It's not my possessions I'm losing, but God! Do you understand, my son, they have torn my God from me! And I have nothing left! Not even hope! Can you understand, my son, that I shall die without hope?"

Santiago also had tears in his eyes. His hands and lips trembled. He understood.

"I repeated ready-made words and phrases. 'The passion of the Cross . . .' and it meant nothing to my mind, had no effect on me. I had a thousand good reasons with which to justify property. But how could reason and passion be the same thing? 'He that hath ears to hear, let him hear.' I saw nothing and heard nothing, yet everything had been shown me, everything had been told me."

"You have been just," Santiago could not help murmuring.

His father paused before answering. "We must not delude ourselves. A choice had to be made. One cannot serve two masters. I had chosen to stake my all on eternity and to put my trust in the word of God. I ought, therefore, to have followed my trust and my faith to their fulfillment. What is this faith that relies on shams and is nourished on pretexts? I had but to obey. It was as simple as that: obey to the fullest. Believe and obey. 'Whosoever he be of you that forsaketh not all that he hath, he cannot be my disciple. . . .' 'Go and sell that thou hast, and give to the poor, and thou shalt have treasure in heaven . . .' "

Then he went on with a cry of despair. "And I knew it all by heart! I have known those words by heart for fifty years, and my old peasants and servants have opened my eyes to my own wealth. I have had sixty years in which to work out my salvation, my son! Sixty years!"

"But who can carry his beliefs through to the end, Father?"

"What do those subtleties matter now? A faith that is not lived has no interest for me. It is an empty wine skin."

Santiago sat silent for a moment, then asked sadly: "But, then, who can be saved?"

"What does that matter to me? I should have taken care of my own salvation, and I have failed to achieve it. I am not an accountant of life eternal. What do numbers matter?"

The Marquis de Leyes had closed his eyes. He looked like a dying man.

"God is love," Santiago said automatically.

"And what greater proof of love could He have shown me than to die for me and then wait sixty years for me to make one single gesture towards Him? He has waited sixty years, my son. For sixty years He has called to me despairingly from the Cross and I have not made that one gesture that would lead me to Him."

"You had your family to feed. Life makes its demands. Who knows?"

"We must not deceive ourselves. I could have worked and fed you, too. One cannot deceive God. It's not worth trying. We can lie to ourselves to some extent, but what's the use of lying to God?"

"You loved Him and sought to serve Him. But you did not understand: God is mercy."

Santiago was aware of the poverty of his words, but could think of nothing else to say. Dumb with sorrowful astonishment he watched the tragic lacerations of conscience of the only just man he had ever known in his life.

"No, no, my son, I did not love Him! I loved myself, my specious virtue, and that detachment that came easily to me because I was rich. I had peace. I was a happy man. But it was not just *peace* I had to achieve, but *His* peace. I have sinned through pride. Only little children will enter into the Kingdom of Heaven."

There was another silence. Then in a veiled voice he said: "It can happen that the lover does not understand his beloved, but a real lover can never refuse his beloved anything. To love is to want to anticipate and go beyond the beloved's desires. Had I loved God, I could not have refused Him."

156

"You are now stripped of your possessions."

"It's too late, my son. God has left me."

"God cannot leave you."

"No, you are right. It is I who, by my lukewarmness, have chosen the party of God's enemies. I have mingled with the Scribes and Pharisees. God never condemns. Man chooses his own destiny." Then, in the tone of voice he might have used to say "alas," he said: "You have chosen the better part."

"I've left the Communist Party, Father."

"Parties do not interest God, for His kingdom is not of this world. A man is not the heir of a party, but of his own acts."

Then Santiago said: "I feel very far from God, too."

"That is not the problem. What is important is that you have been capable of leaving everything for Him."

"Not for Him."

"He is in His poor."

"I am far from the poor."

"As one is far from those one loves."

They sat for some time in a silence that might have been a desert.

"Do you think God is on our side, Father?" Santiago asked suddenly.

"On whose side?"

"On the side of those who are trying to achieve a better world."

The Marquis de Leyes looked severely at his son and said

157

scornfully: "What hypocrisy! Are you trying to make Christ a Marxist philosopher, an economist, or something of that sort? He belongs to no party. He glories in His poor. And when war breaks out, there will be poor in both camps."

After a pause he said: "No man will be judged by his ideas, but by his acts. An idea is nothing. But an act involves us completely in the face of God."

"Who can assume responsibility for all his acts? Our acts are contradictory, Father, and deny each other."

"There are only two kinds of acts, my son: those of love, and those of hatred. Those deriving from love, even human love, are always inspired by God. That is why Mary Magdalene was so close to Christ. Man has a terrible, a heart-rending need to love. And to love love is to love the principle of all love. Whereas acts deriving from hatred deny Him and are always wrong. There is no holy hate. All hatred comes from the Devil."

"Christ made one gesture of hatred," Santiago said. "He drove the money-changers out of the temple."

"He would do so again. Because it is they who prevent His poor from coming to Him. They sell even the Divine Word itself."

"The Church . . ."

"Never speak of the Church. The Church of God consists of those who receive His Word, keep it in their hearts, and translate it into acts of faith. And that Church has nothing whatever to do with the other."

Santiago smoothed his hair with an automatic gesture and murmured: "What can we do, then?"

"Nothing. There is nothing we can do. Wait and pray."

"Pray for what?"

"That His reign shall come."

Santiago closed his eyes, smiled bitterly, and said: "There is such a thing as history, and we have to take up our positions in it."

"History? We shall have no need to render an account of the march of history, but only of our own history. We are each one of us terribly alone and, in our total solitude, we must find our own salvation."

"But, Father, there's the proletariat and its suffering. We cannot abandon it."

"I don't know, my son. . . . I'm really too old to be able to take an interest in politics. But one thing is clear to me: in order to help the proletariat and contribute towards its liberation, you will increase the suffering of those who are not of the same opinion as yourself."

"One must take sides."

"If I still could, if it were not too late, I would take the side of God," said the old man in a broken voice.

"Which is the side of God?"

"That of love. History, you see, is written in tears and blood. God is with those who wipe away the tears and bind up the wounds."

"All the same, one cannot stand face to face with the suffering of the world and keep one's arms folded!"

"Political or military action does not solve the problem of suffering, my son. If you have to kill to bring about your Revolution, you will be a murderer nonetheless."

"The future—"

"The future, my son? We must not count on it. Death comes on us unawares, and it is better to come into the presence of God with clean hands than with hands stained with the blood of our brothers. Even if that blood was spilled in the most noble cause."

"How can one allow the innocent to be massacred before one's eyes without stirring a finger to help them?"

"That is 'the passion of the Cross.' One must accept all or nothing."

They fell silent. Suddenly Santiago cried in a despairing voice: "I want nothing to do with that God! I cannot accept poverty and hunger!"

"What can your revolt accomplish against life itself, my son?"

"I shall try to do my best to help the men who live in misery. I shall struggle with all my strength for a better and juster world."

The Marquis de Leyes replied slowly: "We only see one aspect of suffering, and this falsifies our judgment. There is nothing but sorrow on earth, my son. Nothing but sorrow. And that of the hungry is not perhaps the greatest. Men suffer from love, fear, pain, and despair. Sickness and death lie in wait for them. How can suffering be measured? Which is the greater suffering: that of a child crying from hunger, or that of a paralyzed child who also has not chosen his destiny? What suffering can be compared with that of a girl who has been abandoned by her lover and sits sobbing on a public bench? If you adopt the cause of suffering, you must do so completely."

"Is there no hope, then?"

The Marquis de Leyes looked sadly at his son. "There is no other hope but in the Cross."

They fell silent again.

"I cannot, Father! I cannot! I hate this God who allows human suffering to exist!"

"Who has done most for humanity, Santiago: Marx or St. Francis of Assisi? The law of God is that of love and it never makes victims."

"But will it change the world? Will it put an end to injustice?"

"I don't know, my son. I am as alone as you are and as despairing. One must believe in Him, love Him, and rely on Him. . . . One must work without hope. . . ."

Santiago got slowly to his feet, moved to one of the library windows, drew the curtains aside, and stood there motionless.

A raw, blinding light shone into the room.

The Marquis de Leyes, his face ravaged, rose painfully to his feet. In a low voice he said: "We have nothing left but to wait for death, which may not even come." Then he left the room.

Santiago made no reply. He was exhausted. The plain

stretched away in front of him. The laborers in the new co-operative were busy about their work.

4

MADRID heaved a sigh of relief. The streets ran with a strange crowd, made up of armed militiamen carrying old rifles, working-women delirious with joy, and undernourished children, who loved the whole hullabaloo. The capital was going to war as one goes to a village fair: with songs, laughter, wine, and a childish enthusiasm. Everyone was happy. The women waved clenched fists; the men played with their weapons, joking as they clambered into the trucks that were to take them to the front. No one thought of the danger and death that were slowly and stealthily approaching the festive city. After the agonizing weeks of tension, from the double weight of the heat and the imminent uprising, action at last seemed almost a liberation.

Loud-speakers shouted the latest news: the people of Barcelona were fighting desperately against the rebels and taking the Atarazanas barracks by assault. Montjuich was in Republican hands. The Madrid militiamen had repelled the Fascist columns threatening the capital. Then the announcer's voice shouted the cry that was taken up by eight hundred thousand voices: *"No pasaran!* They shall not pass!" *"No pasaran!"*

The Madrid populace had become aware of its own existence; it was amazed to find that it was an entity and had power. The poor had become the masters of the city and now smiled broadly at each other, happy in mutual recognition and their sense of solidarity. The air was full of cries and songs: the *"Internationale,"* the *"Marseillaise,"* the *"Caira."* Any hymn was good, as long as it was a hymn to liberty. The Madrileños sang them all, one after the other; the children from the workers' districts were delirious, darting from café to café, where the militiamen gave them drinks before leaving for the Sierra. It was a day of fraternity, of solidarity, and of simple heroism. The army and the Church had assembled their forces and were advancing inexorably. Madrid awaited them with song.

"There are perhaps no just wars," Carlos murmured. "But their struggle today is a holy one. You see, Santiago, the others are going to kill in the name of abstractions: order, Spain eternal, tradition. But these poor people are going to die to defend concrete things: their family, the liberty they have just hardly won, the right to rebel against hunger, the right to learn to read and write. . . ."

Santiago made no reply. The two friends were in a small office in the central headquarters of the U.G.T. A narrow window looked out on the street; from it they could see a few trucks loaded with militiamen armed with rifles. Around them women and children raised their fists and waved handkerchiefs, shouting the anarchist hymn at the top of their voices: *"Negras tormentas agitan las nubes."*

163

Carlos was leaning his forehead against the pane and looking down at the spectacle with excitement. He had placed one of his crutches against the wall, and his whole body leaned to the right. "You know, Santiago, it was worth losing a leg to see this. It's the hour of the poor and the disinherited. Look at them. Perhaps for the first time in their lives they feel they're free men. I regret nothing."

Santiago gave his friend a cigarette, lit one himself, and then asked, his voice sounding detached: "How did you come to join the Party, Carlos?"

"Come? I was, so to speak, born into it. I spent all my childhood and youth in Asturias. My father was a miner. It was a depressing village. It rained all the time. My father used to leave at six o'clock in the morning and come home at six o'clock at night. He worked eleven hours a day six thousand feet underground. My mother had to take in sewing. We rarely had enough to eat. It wasn't easy."

Carlos smiled sadly as if he were asking pardon for the banality of that poverty-stricken life. His eyes, normally so gay and restless, were veiled today by nostalgia.

"I remember the Sundays most of all," he said. "They left a lasting mark in my mind. They were wet and melancholy. The rain was thin and monotonous and seemed to fall reluctantly. We used to put on our best clothes and go to Mass. It was obligatory. A fat, unctuous priest talked to us of work . . . of the blessedness of labor! We sat uncomfortably in our poor, stiff clothes. The owner of the mine, who lived at Oviedo, used to attend Mass, accompanied by his wife and little daughter. They would arrive in their car, and the chauffeur would open the door for them. When we came out of church, the boss used to make the miners' children shake his little daughter's hand. She was a silly little thing, with fair hair and an absurd little mouth— like a girl from the Sacred Heart. It disgusted her to have to take our hands. But you have to be kind to the poor in order to go to heaven, don't you? So, she made the effort. But I don't mind telling you, it was a pretty painful experience. One Sunday she said 'How do you do?' to me. I was twelve or thirteen at the time. She was fourteen or fifteen. She stood between her parents, and was dressed in pink. I went up to her, shy and awkward in my Sunday clothes. My parents watched me anxiously. What an honor to shake the owner's daughter by the hand! When I got within a yard or two of her, I tried to make her laugh, but I must have been too nervous. I made a face that terrified the girl so much she began to cry. You might have thought it was the end of the world. My father smacked me. The owner's wife said I had put my tongue out at her. My parents were in despair."

Carlos fell silent for a moment. Outside, the trucks were leaving. The militiamen held their rifles above their heads. The women waved their handkerchiefs. Carlos went on talking. "On Sunday afternoons the men went to the local bar. They drank cider and beer. By five o'clock they were all drunk. They sang songs in chorus. If you have never lived in a mining village, you can have no idea of the effect

165

of those songs. They make a void in your soul. They're not songs of joy or of sorrow, they're worse: a sort of throbbing lamentation. There was a local band, too. We used to parade down the village street, playing military marches, with the rain coming down on our heads. The priest and his guests used to watch us go by. They thought we were 'delightful.' Besides, we were 'the good people of Spain'— sober, hard-working, hospitable, proud, and noble. There were any number of phrases available to disguise our poverty and hunger. We were always hungry."

Carlos fell silent and opened the window. The noise of the street reached them, and from the sidewalk they heard someone shouting over a loud-speaker in a grave voice: *"We know the tyranny of the order they wish to impose on us. Our flesh still bears its scars."*

Santiago instinctively looked at his friend's crutches. Carlos surprised his glance and smiled sadly.

"We wanted peace to enjoy the freedom we had won. We wanted to work in common to build a more just society. And they have declared war on us, denying us the right to become men. But we will face their artillery, their tanks, and their machine guns with our naked breasts and with the certainty that we have right and justice on our side. We are not afraid to die, for we have never really lived, and we shall die as free men."

Night was falling slowly over Madrid. The air grew fresher, light and soft as satin or as a woman's caress, filled with scents, laden with songs and cries. Santiago listened to the distant murmur of the city, the sound of cries suddenly cut short, and, nearer at hand, the grave voice expressing what each of them thought. The loud-speaker cried: "*No pasaran! No pasaran!*"

No one thought of eating or sleeping. Eight hundred thousand people—women, old men, children, invalids—were awaiting patiently the results of a battle in which well-trained divisions, with perfect equipment, led by experienced officers, were opposed to illiterate workers and peasants, who had never been taught to use their weapons. No one was afraid. Madrid was singing to allay its anxiety, and when silence fell, there was a distant rumble like a thunderstorm moving nearer or farther away.

Rifle shots could be heard on all sides. Fascist cars were dashing about the city, mowing down passers-by. Franco's Fifth Column was doing its worst. The trade unions had requisitioned private cars and were engaged in a man hunt, but the streets did not empty, and the people of Madrid seemed unconcerned about these street battles. They were even amused by them; they laughed and joked.

"My mother died of tuberculosis," Carlos said suddenly in a low voice. "My father could not have her properly looked after, for lack of money. There was no Social Assistance in those days, or anything like it. Then my father died. A minister came to attend the funeral of the sixteen miners who died with him. I was fifteen. The minister was an elegant man. He made a speech. Perhaps he went a little too far: the workers turned his car over and very nearly lynched him." He smiled. "It was my first revolutionary act."

He fell silent, lit a cigarette, threw his head back, and murmured: "I became a member of the Party at sixteen."

Children were going by beneath the window. They were singing the "*Marseillaise*" and laughing aloud.

"I can understand your concern and your apprehension, Santiago. You've always had enough to eat and you've always been able to buy the books you needed. You've come over to us out of a love of justice. You want a communism that is pure, noble, and perfect. But all these people, who may well become the victims of Franco's shells, have never had enough to eat and have never been able to buy a book. They are not perfect, and therefore the Party cannot be perfect.

"We carry within us and bear on our skins and faces the marks of misery and humiliation. Centuries of misery and humiliation. We may make mistakes. I shall be the first to deplore them. I would have liked a clean revolution, unstained with blood. But how can you expect these men, for whom no one has ever lifted a finger, to be concerned with justice now? They are splendid, and magnificent. For no one ever taught them heroism."

Carlos smiled in the dark room. The street lamps threw a faint light into the little office. The same grave voice was talking again over the loud-speakers.

"*Workers of Madrid! Women of Madrid! We ask you to think fraternally tonight of our comrades who have been shot by the Fascists during this first day of our struggle,*

*and also of our comrades who have fallen with their arms
in their hands.*"

"Only the proletariat knows what this struggle means,"
Carlos said. "They alone can know precisely how important it is. A person doesn't become a revolutionary, Santiago: he is born one. For these men going out to defend the
Government of the Republic, armed with old rifles, the
Revolution is not something outside themselves. It is part
of their very being, as thought is part of yours. That is why
you can judge dispassionately and even condemn their
struggle: it is not really a part of you. Intellectuals are
never true revolutionaries. They believe that a certain correspondence of ideas, a certain vision of the world is at
stake. But, in fact, the basic thing at stake is property. It's
as simple as that. There are just two camps: those who
have, and those who have not."

Carlos stopped talking. The door opened, and Ramírez
came in. He was dressed in khaki trousers and a blue shirt
and was armed with a pistol.

"Well?" Carlos asked.

"It's all right," Ramírez said. "Santiago has left the Party,
but he can very well go on being a member of the U.G.T.
We need every pair of hands."

"What's the news?"

"Barcelona, Valencia, and the whole east coast are with
us. The north is with Franco. He's threatening Madrid."

"We knew that already." Then in a casual tone Carlos
asked: "Will they get through?"

"They won't get through," Ramírez replied curtly.

There was a silence. Santiago had not said a word. In the dusk the three men felt, rather than saw, each other's presence. Ramírez asked: "Are you leaving for the front, Santiago?"

There was a pause, which seemed very long to all of them. The reply came at last. "No. I'm staying in Madrid."

"The fighting's not in Madrid."

"I don't want to fight."

There was an embarrassed silence.

"It doesn't matter, anyway. You can stay with the women. The city's theirs."

Santiago did not react to the insult. Ramírez left the room. Outside in the street the shouting and singing were still going on. The brakes of trucks, driven at full speed, squealed at the corners. Night had fallen over the city, and the air was cooler now under a sky overweighted with stars. The men and women of the militia, armed with rifles and cartridge belts, passed under the window, gathering in the first suspects: the hunting down of the Fascists was beginning. Farther away, in the Sierra, which Madrid felt to be so close, artillery was thundering without pause.

"You think I'm a coward, don't you?"

"I don't think you're anything. I'm ashamed, that's all."

"Ashamed of what?"

"Of having one too few legs. It's the first time I won't be at the side of the workers."

Santiago flushed and stammered: "I can't shed blood."

"I don't think that has much importance today. It's blood

we're defending, blood that will be shed if the Fascists win.
A lot of blood."

"I think men of peace will be wanted even in Madrid,"
Santiago murmured. "The Revolution is not just fighting.
It's reconstruction, above all. We need engineers, doctors,
and nurses, as well as soldiers."

Carlos turned to his friend, looked him in the eyes, smiled
with grave pity, and said in a gentle voice: "Santiago, you
can be sure I'm not criticising you. I know your worth. I'm
sorry for you."

"Why?"

"Because on this night of fraternity and solidarity you
are the most lonely of men."

"I've always been alone."

"No doubt. But never so alone as tonight. Am I wrong?"

"No."

"You can't serve both God and revolution, Santiago.
You have to make a choice. And you can't make up your
mind. It must be difficult to have to side with the whole of
human suffering."

"Very."

"No one can help you, Santiago."

"I know."

There was a long silence.

"What are you going to do?" Carlos asked at last.

Santiago hesitated and then replied, his voice deliberate:
"Pray. I must choose between faith in men or faith in God.
I cannot abandon God. I cannot."

"I understand."

The two friends left the trade-union office together. Carlos had difficulty in walking with his crutches. He was not yet used to them. Santiago looked at his friend, thinking that his whole life had been made up of hunger, humiliation, and fighting for liberty; and that now, at the age of barely twenty-five, he could move only with difficulty. He was quiet.

Several times militiamen asked them for their papers, and the two young men showed them their trade-union cards.

The street was still full of people. A few militiamen, who for various reasons had returned from the front, were surrounded by women and children asking them questions.

"They won't break through, I tell you! We may have no arms, but we've got guts," a boy was saying.

"You're right, my lad. There's not a man in Madrid who's not worth four of the bastards!" proudly declared a little black-clothed woman with a wrinkled face.

"Is it really true they've got tanks?" asked a child with a working-class accent.

5

MARIANITA had waited for Olny to get home so that they could go to the movies. She had waited for him without hope and she was not surprised when he did not come back at the expected hour. Then the delay had grown longer, and she had realized that if she were to go on living, she must hope. She stopped waiting then and began to hope; her hope became one with waiting, but was greater. On the second day Marianita rushed out into the street. She went to find Ramírez, who received her for a few minutes in a luxurious office and then sent her away, telling her he had better things to do than look for Olny. He said he could not understand how she could think of nothing but her trivial private life in the midst of such important events. Marianita listened to him in silence and made no answer; she had gone away sick.

There were times when she regretted the Zone. There, at least, she could have kept Olny. She loved him because he was himself, never analyzing or seeking reasons for the limitless love she bore him. Back there on the wasteland of the Zone they had known moments of huge happiness. They had been able to love in silence, build hopes for the future, dream together; but since they had come to the city, they had never been able to recover those moments of profound intimacy. They pretended to believe that nothing had changed, but sometimes felt embarrassed in each other's presence. Yet, they had everything necessary to their happiness: a house, a job. It was Olny himself who had changed. He had ceased being that big child with green eyes and golden, untidy hair, whom she had loved, and he had become a Communist. Marianita had witnessed helplessly his metamorphosis day by day. He came in at night from work, sat in the dining room, opened *The Workers' World*, and read it with voracious attention. Then at dinner he would use words Marianita did not understand; he would be carried away, launching into violent diatribes against "the bourgeois and reactionary forces," swearing and threatening. He no longer looked at the world with generous warmth, but with a bitterness that was often unjust. He had lost that sort of tender pity he had had for human beings, and could no longer tolerate those who did not hold the same opinions as himself—that is, those who were not Communists. For him the world was divided into two blocks: the Communists, on one side, and the bastards, on the other. All discussion was useless. Olny had reached the point of hating words, even when uttered in a gentle, friendly tone. He constantly repeated that the time for words was past and that only acts counted.

Marianita said nothing. It would have been useless to try to argue with her husband. What could she have said to him? Words were hard for her. She resigned herself to feeling intuitively, and she had a feeling he was wrong, that he was losing that spiritual candor she had always admired. He oversimplified things. Sometimes when he grew angry and threatening, she felt ill at ease and blushed; it was as though she had found him beating a dog or ill-treating a child. Injustice did not suit him.

But she suffered most from fear of losing him. She loved him; in her wretched life of poverty, Olny had been her one happiness, her one glowing light. She could not lose him. Her life would have no meaning without him. She had need of his glance, his smile, his grave, rather husky voice. With him she felt she could bear anything: hunger, poverty, dirt, blows. He was everything to her. Her love may not have been a very intelligent love; she neither knew nor cared. But she did know that she would be lost without him, that she would never recover from the disaster. That was why she was afraid of politics: she felt they were dangerous.

And, indeed, Olny thought more about the Revolution and the new society than he did about his young wife. He went out every night after supper to put up the Party posters. When he came home, he found Marianita sitting on a chair, a shawl about her shoulders. She looked at him sadly, seemed about to say something, thought better of it, and only smiled at him wearily. He would tell her about his work. He had become an expert in putting up posters and was proud of it; he had stuck them up on every wall in the capital, even in the most incredible places. The police had never managed to arrest him, for he had good legs and knew Madrid better than anyone. He always escaped and laughed gaily about it, and she forgave him everything, for she loved his laugh.

His absences became more and more frequent, and Marianita grew accustomed to waiting for him till two or three in the morning. She sat on her chair in a sort of dull trance, making superhuman efforts not to fall asleep.

175

As the summer advanced, she had had to learn to face her anxiety. Incidents were taking place more and more often and in almost every part of the capital. She had done her best to keep Olny from going out; now she could no longer wait and content herself with hoping. Santiago, whom she had gone to see when she left Ramírez, had told her not to leave the house. She had learned of Franco's rising and the news had left her frightened and helpless. She was afraid of all the hatred around her, and thought unhappily of the hours of tenderness and abandon she had known on the wasteland of the Zone.

Marianita started up. There was a sound of footsteps on the stairs. She held her breath, then sighed: it was only Santiago. She opened the door and looked the young man in the eyes. Santiago looked away, tried to smile, and failed. Then she was afraid and had to lean against the wall not to fall. There was a silence.

"Where did he die?" she asked.

Santiago opened his mouth to reply, then stopped. He was very pale. He pressed his eyelids with an automatic gesture and finally murmured: "Let's go in, Marianita. Sit down somewhere."

She obeyed, watching him silently.

Santiago did not know where to begin and seemed afraid of words. Face to face with Marianita's sorrow, he did not know what to do with his hands. He began walking up and down the room. Marianita had resumed her chair by the window. Santiago was afraid of this silence above all; he would have preferred to see her weep, hear her sob. Her tragic resignation was worse than all else. He nervously lit a cigarette; then in a shaking voice he said: "He's not dead, Marianita."

Her eyes grew a little brighter. He didn't know how to go on. He turned his back to her and put his burning forehead to the windowpane. "Not quite," he murmured.

"Wounded?"

He was expecting that question. He could have lied, but in any case she would soon learn the truth. It was better he should tell her himself. "Tortured," he said.

There was a silence. He was waiting for further questions, but none came. He turned to her. Marianita, her eyes wide, was staring at him. At last, unable to bear it any longer he broke the silence. "I searched for him everywhere. No one could give me news of him. This morning I learned that some militiamen had taken a house on the outskirts of Madrid by assault. Some twenty young Fascists had taken refuge there. When the militiamen broke in, they found . . ." He fell silent again for a moment. "The bodies were brought back to Madrid, to the San Fernando Hospital. I went to see . . ." He lit a cigarette from the stub of the other. His hands were shaking. "Olny was there," Santiago went on. "He's alive. The doctors think he'll survive. You can come and see him. Visitors are allowed."

Marianita made no movement. Suddenly she said: "They marked him?"

"No, Marianita, I promise you. His face is unmarked."

"It's his balls, huh?"

Santiago blushed. She was speaking like an automaton, a bitter smile at the corners of her mouth. He feared she might burst into laughter.

"Yes, that is—"

"Never can have sex again, eh? Burned off?"

Santiago wiped the sweat from his forehead. Marianita's deliberate vulgarity frightened him more than all the silences that had preceded it. He felt like weeping, and swallowed back his sobs. "Yes. He's become impotent."

"Electric current, wasn't it? I suppose they got a kick out of burning his hair off, too!"

Santiago bit his lips, crushed his cigarette out, and put his hands to his eyes again as if to efface the picture. He had come to the end of his strength. A strange sense of the absurd caught him by the throat. He wanted to scream. Outside, the same crowd that had been yelling its joy for the last three days was howling anthems. He was sick to his stomach.

Marianita got to her feet. Santiago nearly burst into sobs. He had never in his life seen anyone look as she did.

"Let's go," she said. "I'll take some food. The soup up there can't be worth much." She had suddenly become a resigned woman again. Moving back and forth between the rooms, she made up the bundle with the precise, mechanically tender gestures of every Spanish woman. Santiago took out another cigarette, but could not light it with his trembling hands. "I'm ready," she said. "You coming?"

He nodded, and they went out together.

The hospital was a big gray building with narrow windows. They went through the gate and entered a huge courtyard, square and stark. Ambulances were pulled up there, nurses, internes, and doctors busy around them. Mariana and Santiago went toward the right wing of the building. As they passed an ambulance with its rear doors open, they stopped as if struck by electric shock: inside, bleeding men piled one on another were wailing and screaming. A boy of sixteen or seventeen had managed with great effort to get his head out. His face ran with tears and blood. He was groaning feebly: "Mama . . . Mama . . . My little Mama . . . "

Marianita shuddered and clung to Santiago's arm; he stood rooted, suffocating. A nurse passed without looking at them, grumbling: "It just doesn't stop! They're falling like flies! We can't possibly handle them all! The doctor said we'd better start with the more critical cases. We'd better put the dying on the ground floor. In any case, half of them won't live through the night. . . ."

She was talking to a young medical student about twenty-five years old. He was a tall, thin, pale young man with brown hair and blue eyes. The nurse, small, dark, and very made-up, went to the ambulance and asked the interne to come over. They began taking the wounded boy out of the ambulance. The boy's screams grew louder; his face was contorted with pain, but pallid as marble. He cried: "Leave me alone! Leave me alone! Stop! Mama!"

His cries were inhuman, like those of a dog that had been run over. Santiago was trembling. Marianita turned her head away and burst into tears. Neither of them could move. Stupefaction and horror held them to the spot.

The wounded boy was placed on a stretcher. He must have trodden on a mine or been blown up by a grenade. His legs were a mass of raw flesh and blood. At the sight of the wounds, the interne turned pale and fled.

"Are you crazy?" cried the nurse. "We must take him to the operating room at once. If they don't amputate, he'll die. Come back, you fool! Stop acting like a girl!"

But the interne was out of earshot. She turned to Santiago and said firmly: "What are you doing there? Come give me a hand. Can't you see I'm alone?"

"I'm looking for—"

"You can look later. Come and help me."

Santiago went forward slowly. The wounded boy kept crying and calling for his mother. His screams grew weaker, sank to a sort of inarticulate groaning, and then began again, louder. Santiago lifted the stretcher, trying to avoid jerking the wounded boy. He could not take his eyes from the bloody, tear-drenched face. They carried the stretcher along corridors to the operating room. A doctor met them, raised the blanket from the boy's body, and said curtly: "We must amputate at once. Both legs."

The wounded boy made a superhuman effort, raised himself, burst into sobs, clutched Santiago's arm, and began shouting: "No! Don't amputate me! Don't amputate me! I want to see my mother. I must see my mother. I don't want it. Help me, don't let go of me!"

Two male nurses arrived. The boy was clinging to Santiago's arm with all his strength. Santiago was hypnotized by his eyes, by their expression beyond anything human; then with a nerveless gesture he broke his stare. The nurses were already taking the boy away. For a moment or two Santiago stood there motionless; tears poured down his face, and he saw that his coat was stained with blood. Then he walked slowly away from the operating rooms, back to Marianita in the courtyard.

He was thinking of nothing. He was stunned with anguish. In this grim, crumbling hospital, over the aspect of the Civil War which had begun amid singing and laughter, suffering rose and triumphed. He might have rebelled, might have accused the Fascists of having wanted this war and of having unleashed it. It was in part the truth. But there was another reality, before which words were powerless: the bloodstains on his coat. Santiago knew that in the Fascist hospitals other boys must be calling for their mothers, and he could hear nothing but these human, heartbreaking cries pounding through his mind.

The huge white ward had a row of beds down each side. Opposite the entrance door there was a crucifix above a clock. The heat was stifling, laden with the smell of ether and chloroform. Marianita walked slowly between the rows of white beds. She leaned toward each one to see better, for the patients were protected by mosquito nets. She felt the weight of the eyes of these men who had either just escaped or were condemned to death. From every bed came groans, or rattling breaths, or terrible silence. Suddenly she stopped and, with a quick gesture, pulled a mosquito net aside.

For a second or two she stood quite still. Olny tried to smile, but could only grimace; pain was written deeply across his livid face. She hurled herself on him, burst into sobs, kissed his hair and forehead, damp from the sweat of fever. She was trembling and muttering unintelligible words of love, clinging to him as if she could still protect him. He was weeping, too, and his handsome face, twisted by physical pain and covered with sweat and tears, was terrible. It was the first time she had ever seen him weep.

Santiago stood at the foot of the bed. He gazed at Marianita's black dress against the white sheets, heard her sobs and feverish whisperings, and watched his friend's tears flow.

War was showing its true face. Santiago suddenly understood the profound meaning of his father's words; indeed, no ideal, he thought, could bear the stain of blood. There were two kinds of men: those capable of dipping their hands in their brothers' blood to make history, and those who quietly wiped away the tears of the wounded to write the history of God. You had to choose between vengeance, humanly justified, and absurd, transcendent love. He was aghast. He turned his sad, glowing eyes from bed to bed and met all those other lusterless eyes. He felt tears welling, and had difficulty in forcing them back. He tried desperately to find some memory to cling to, the image of someone he loved, anything. He looked up and saw the crucifix. Then, after a moment's hesitation, he bowed his head. Santiago de Leyes had found peace.

"Is it true you left the Party?"

Marianita's voice sounded different. It was a second or two before Santiago realized she was talking to him. He hesitated and glanced despairingly at his friend. Olny met his eyes. Santiago hesitated, then murmured: "Yes, it is true."

There was a long silence. Then Marianita suddenly went to him and struck his face with all her force. Santiago turned pale, but did not move. Her fingers left red marks across his white face.

"Look! Look what you've done! Come and look, you scum!"

She pushed him toward the bed. Olny looked at his friend in hatred. Santiago said in a low voice: "Forgive me . . ."

"Are you being funny? Do you see what you've done?" Marianita was shouting at the top of her voice. Her thin shoulders shook with sobs; her face was ravaged by the terrible waiting of the last few days. "All that crap you

183

told him! And he believed you. You sent him to his death, but kept out of it yourself. You must be mad! He was all I had! D'you hear, you bastard! I had no one but him in the world. And what's going to happen to me now, answer me that? It's all your fault! He believed you, d'you understand? He's always believed you. You were educated, you could talk, you had the gift of gab. You looked kind. Him, he didn't know anything. You betrayed your friend. You let him down. You got cold feet and ran away. And how am I going to live now? What have I got left? Bastard! You're all bastards!"

She hit his face a second time. Santiago made no attempt to protect himself. He was weeping.

"They come to the Zone. They give you a lot of claptrap about the Revolution, the future, the world of tomorrow. They send the poor to their deaths, but they stay out of it themselves, all right! You're a murderer!"

Santiago opened his mouth, thought better of it, turned his back on Marianita, and went slowly to the door.

"That's right—clear out! Bastard! Traitor!"

Santiago felt utterly exhausted. He longed to lie down on a bed, close his eyes, and sleep. As he left the ward, his back bent, he heard a quavering voice cry: "Fascist!"

Santiago stopped and turned around. A man about thirty years old, with a drawn and dirty face and feverish eyes, was staring at him in hatred. Santiago stared back, but did not speak. The man's arm was gone.

. . .

More and more ambulances were driving into the court-yard. Nurses and doctors were running from one to another. There were no more beds available in the wards, and the wounded were lying on stretchers in the shade. Two or three hundred pale, dirty men were moaning, screaming, or breathing raucously. Santiago shivered. Where could he go? Where could he hide? A wounded man called him over and asked for a cigarette. Santiago gave him the pack and then left that hell of suffering and death, his heart crying, his throat tight. He moved away like an automaton, obsessed by the expressions on all those faces. Suddenly he could bear it no more and, hiding his face in his hands, turned toward the façade of a house and burst into sobs. He felt like a small child again, helpless in face of the flood of hatred washing over the world and scarring the people he loved. He wanted to lie down in the middle of the street and never move again. In rage he slammed his forehead again and again on the wall. Then a cry came to his lips, the cry every Spaniard utters when despair or death comes to him, when all else has failed him and he no longer knows to whom to turn: "Mama!"

His tears poured harder.

Close by, some young men were roaring a hymn to liberty. Girls were giggling embarrassedly among themselves. The heat had become even more stifling.

6

THE Marquis de Leyes closed his tired eyes for a moment, then opened them sadly on the fields of Castile which stretched out of sight. The sun was setting behind the Sierra; the earth was red and the mountains seemed unreal. Purple shadows spilled through the valleys. The old man was sitting alone in a book-lined room on the first floor. Some of the books were sumptuously bound; others, in paper covers, were dog-eared with use. The Marquis de Leyes called this room his "reading nest." For years this was the room he had used for reading, writing, or simply for dreaming. The Louis XVI furniture, the blue satin curtains, and the family portraits all gave it a quiet air of intimacy. The old man was sitting near the window at a desk laden with books and papers. By raising his head, he could look out at the red and desolate land.

But today the Marquis de Leyes was not reading. No book could give his mind the peace it craved.

Alone and sad, he was waiting. He had difficulty in comprehending all that was going on around him. Spaniards were killing each other. The land of Spain, which he loved so desperately, was being soaked in blood. Both sides claimed justice and right. But the Marquis had no opinions about the war. He felt like a rather disinterested spectator of a bloodthirsty and somewhat grotesque play. He had read much and thought much. For long years he had believed in the power of words; but today he had moved beyond them. "Men are killing each other because of words," he thought. His mouth wore a bitter, weary smile. Artillery thundered steadily in the distance. The Nationalists were besieging the old Castilian city and remorselessly tightening the vise in which they held it. They had aircraft, tanks, and well-trained troops; the Republicans were fighting with old-fashioned rifles. The Marquis de Leyes, who was a man of honor, would have felt sympathy for the weaker side had he not known that war never provides a solution to a conflict. With an automatic gesture he smoothed his hair, which had turned quite white. His back was bowed, his features drawn; he looked like a very old man, though he was barely sixty. He could no longer stand upright and his walk had become a shuffle. The Marquis was no longer of the living. He was alone, surrounded by the books he had loved, but they were of no use to him now. He had entered that zone of silence which precedes death. He had neither desires nor hopes any more. All about him men were stirring restlessly, taking sides, making speeches, but he no longer believed in speeches. He knew the essential lay elsewhere and was inexpressible. He was concerned only with God; and he was thinking that God had given him sixty years in which to become a better man and that he had made no use of all that time. "None," he murmured.

187

He had set out to become a civilized and cultivated man, and had perhaps succeeded. But though he had studied Plato, Saint Augustine, Descartes, Nietzsche, Hegel, and Marx, he felt as lonely and helpless as any illiterate peasant. He was very conscious of the utter uselessness of culture. "Words," he repeated with contempt. Those millions of little symbols contained in those thousands of volumes he had read, devoured even, had lost all meaning for him in this decisive hour. Words had prevented him from obeying, prevented him from becoming a saint. He would have liked to die in peace, close to God, but, as it was too late, he must prepare to die as a proud and lonely knight.

He got to his feet and crossed the room slowly to the far window that looked toward the city. The sky had now grown dark, and the first stars were beginning to appear. The earth was slowly sinking into the cold sleep of the night. Above the city the glow of fires tore the darkness apart. For the last three days the German Junkers had been sowing death. Whole streets were on fire; four-hundred-year-old palaces had fallen a prey to the flames; the civilization of old Spain was being annihilated. "All civilizations are destroyed sooner or later," the Marquis de Leyes thought. And he added aloud: "In centuries to come tourists will gaze at a heap of ruins. 'Here was the Escorial, the ancient Pantheon of the Kings of Spain,' they will be told."

He stood there motionless. The sky was red over the city and black over the countryside.

"What culture can vanquish flames, bombs, and death?" he thought.

And the Marquis de Leyes asked himself the question only because he thought he knew the answer: a humane culture. Such a culture, which would transform mankind and help it to become better, would be safe from destruction. But he had no illusions; he was aware of all the forces arrayed against the advent of such a culture. The world would continue to burn and crumble; he had no doubt of it.

He stared down at his long-fingered hands and smiled; then he threw his head back and closed his eyes.

For nearly a week fifty thousand men had been awaiting a miracle, which would not occur. Day and night the Fascist guns and planes had been spraying constant fear and death. The Republicans died where they stood. It was a furious and desperate battle, as the Fascists continued to advance. The whole city was in flames. The hospitals were full of wounded women and children. An immense wail, hoarse and paining, rose to the sky from the martyred city.

The Marquis de Leyes could no longer even weep. When the Fascist bombardment had begun, he had stood aghast at the window, telling himself that this was a scene from the end of the world. But soon he had realized that the sight would be a daily one; that one by one the citics of his land would become a prey to the flames. Then he had lost interest. Bitterly he began to wait for the end of the bombardment as well as his own end, which he hoped was near. It was not so much that he wished to die, but that he felt incapable of surviving so much insanity.

The bombing had begun at dawn on a Monday, when fifteen Junkers flew over the city. Men, women, and children had rushed into the streets, waving handkerchiefs. They had never seen so many aircraft before and did not guess their mission of death.

The sky was green, patched with rose. The steeples of the churches and the clock towers of the convents were etched against the uncertain light of dawn. The earth was coming majestically to life. Then in the peace of the hour the first Junker let loose its string of bombs; their whistling tore into the quiet of the morning. The whole city rocked and crumbled. After the first explosions, there were a few seconds of profound and astonished silence. No one could understand what had happened. Then, suddenly, there was panic. The air was full of the screams of the wounded, the sobs of children, the shrieks of women, the groans of the dying. The panic-stricken crowd ran in circles. Women fell to their knees, their arms outstretched in the form of a cross. Whole streets were on fire; huge buildings crumpled; there was a smell of burning human flesh. For more than an hour the ancient capital of Spain[5] helplessly endured the agony. And before they left, the Junkers strafed the population as it fled in terror into the country-side. By nine o'clock in the morning all was silence. A terrible silence: the silence of cemeteries. The score of this first bombing came to more than four hundred dead and six hundred wounded. The Nationalists published a laconic communiqué. "Our air force has made a successful raid of reprisal behind the enemy lines. All our aircraft have returned safely."

[5] Valladolid was the capital of Spain before Madrid.

An hour after the end of the bombardment the first refugees reached the doors of the manor: old women dressed in black, children wide-eyed with terror, mothers who had lost their children. They had walked the seven kilometers from the city to the domain.

The Marquis had lodged the refugees on the ground floor of the house and had spent more than forty-eight hours feeding the children and tending the wounded.

Then the waiting began. He had taken refuge in this first-floor room to await the end. The Fascist artillery and air power were systematically destroying the city. More and more refugees streamed into the manor: old men, women, children. They were innocent victims, understanding nothing of what had happened to them, come to seek safety in this austere house lying amid the thick belt of its centuries-old trees. They had done nothing but hope to become freer men in a more just society. The shells and bombs had destroyed their hopes. They were broken.

There was a knock at the door. The Marquis was still standing by the window. He was gazing at the column of fire rising from the martyred city to the sky.

"Come in."

Standing there was a young man of about twenty-eight, with a long, pale face, deep-set, dark eyes, full lips, and a short, straight nose. He was wearing a militia uniform, but he had on *espadrilles;* and he was armed with a pistol. As the Marquis made no move, the young man crossed the room.

191

"Comrade . . ." he began in a low but firm voice.

The Marquis de Leyes turned slowly and looked at the stranger in weariness.

The young man flushed, lowered his eyes, and continued: "Señor Marquis . . ."

There was a silence. The young militiaman's hands attracted the old man's gaze. They were long and slender. "Artist's hands," he thought. "What did you do before all this?" he asked suddenly. And with a gesture of his hand he indicated the glow of the fires against the dark sky.

"I am a pianist."

The old aristocrat made no answer, but his face changed.

The young militiaman noticed his expression and asked: "Does it surprise you to see me fighting with the workers?"

For a moment there was a light in the Marquis's eyes. He replied in his sad, hoarse voice: "Why should it surprise me? I was wondering merely what you must be feeling at this sight."

The young man did not reply at once. He felt the nervous tension relax. He went slowly to the window and looked out. Beyond the black barrier of the trees, he could almost envision the city. The sky was red above it. They could hear the noise of explosions, muffled by distance. It was a fine, starry night.

The two men stood in silence, in wordless understanding. Suddenly the old man asked: "Did you come to tell me something?"

"The Republican Committee has asked me to thank you for the help you have given to the refugees. Our cause is

lost. The Fascists will be here tomorrow morning at dawn.
The Committee asks you to protect, in so far as you can,
the lives of those who have sought refuge and safety in
your house."

The room was dark; the only light came from the moon
and the reflection of the fires. The two men could hardly
see each other. The old man crossed the room with his slow
step and lit a low lamp of Chinese porcelain. Then he sank
into an armchair and motioned to the young man to sit
down. "And what are you going to do now?" There was
a strong tenderness in his voice.

"Rest a little. Then . . ." With a gesture of resignation
the young man put his hand to his pistol.

There was another silence.

"What's your name?"

"Serafín Álvarez."

"You must be tired, Serafín. A man, particularly if he is
an artist, should not die tired and dirty. You must have a
bath, and you will find suits to choose from and clean linen
in the cupboard in the bathroom. The clothes belonged to
my son." The old man added, with a quaver in his voice:
"He was about your size."

Serafín looked up in surprise. "Was?"

"We can talk of people only in the past tense now. We
are part of the past ourselves."

"Perhaps. I don't know."

"No, you don't know. You are young. Lucidity is the
exclusive property of old age. I know."

"Have you no hope at all of seeing him again? After all,

tomorrow you will be liberated. They're your people coming. You have reason to hope."

"My people? *Mine?*"

Serafín smiled sadly. "I understand," he said.

The old man shook his head. "No, you don't understand. For your people are not mine, either. I am alone."

"But injustice and crime—these shells and bombs. The city is full of disemboweled women, the charred bodies of children . . ."

"You have chosen to suffer only one part of the injustice and the pain. And it is proper that it should be so. But I, Serafín, I feel every crime, those you have committed, too. And I am alone."

Serafín felt a lump in his throat. He cried: "You are a good man."

The old man looked at him with compassion. "Even if I am, of what use has my virtue been? Has it prevented butchery? Has it opened the eyes of those who drop bombs or shoot women and children? Good? What good is it?"

Serafín did not know what to say. He smoothed his dark hair. The old man got to his feet and signaled to the young man to follow him. The Marquis de Leyes had become the master of the house again and spoke politely now. "I hope the water will be hot. I am so sorry to put you to the trouble of running your own bath. Nearly all my servants have left me long ago. When you are dressed, you will find me in this other room. We will dine alone together. There's a piano in the room. I hope it is not too much out of tune."

194

Serafín lowered his eyes.

"You have the whole night before you," the Marquis added in his slow, weary voice. "Don't be in a hurry to die."

The two men dined alone in a room whose walls were covered with Louis XV wainscoting. The Marquis de Leyes had had a little table set near the hearth, on which a few logs were slowly burning. The red velvet curtains were drawn. Serafín, now that his hair was brushed and he was freshly shaved and properly dressed, looked like a new man. The old man had changed his clothes, too, and was now wearing a dark blue suit. His features seemed more drawn than ever; his white hair softened the outline of his face, which might have been cast in bronze; his large dark eyes were heavy with melancholy. He sat upright, his head held high. Serafín watched him covertly and could not help but admire him. He loved him already, and the idea that he would never see him again made him pensive and sad. Javier, still wearing livery, did his best and served the dinner with even a little too much ceremony.

Outside, the distant noise of the bombardment had ceased. The night was a void, peopled only by the thoughts of suffering men.

Time seemed to have halted its murderous course. Serafín was happy. He knew the night must come to an end, nonetheless, and that the next day was close at hand. He felt an overwhelming, an almost voluptuous joy in each minute of life which remained to him. Never could he have imagined that his last hours would be spent in such a house with so exceptional a man. It was a sweet, melancholy respite in a world of silence and death.

"It's strange," said Serafín aloud. "I would never have thought an aristocrat could be like you. Those I happened to meet before the war were rather—"

"Stupid and pretentious," the Marquis finished. "We did not know our own country," the old man went on tonelessly. "We lived by myths because we had lost all contact with the people. Do you want to know the real malady of the Spanish aristocracy? Boredom. It no longer knows what to do, how to feel, or what it stands for. It's a very difficult thing to be what one is, you know."

There was a silence. Then Serafín asked: "Do you think the social class to which you belong can still make sense in the modern world?"

The old man looked at him keenly. " 'The modern world,' 'social class'—what do they mean? And why should I believe you? There is no modern world. There is a world, that's all."

The Marquis sat in silence for a moment or two, as if absorbed in his thoughts. Then he said: "There will be an aristocracy everywhere and always. Even in the Soviet Union. But one must define the term. It is not my title, nor my patent of nobility, yellowed with time, which makes me an aristocrat, but simply the consciousness that I have of the reality of my country, of its historic destiny. To be a Spaniard is to be an aristocrat."

He made a gesture of lassitude.

"To be a Spaniard, conscious of what our country stands for, what it means in relation to the world, and to believe in the destiny of Spain—yes, all that is very difficult!"

Serafín was thinking that these words were no doubt the language of fascism. But the idea he had conceived of fascism had no relationship with this old man, who, in the midst of chaos, calmly asserted his faith in his country.

"It is in the name of the historic destiny of Spain that the worst injustices have been committed," Serafín could not help remarking.

The Marquis smiled bitterly. "I know. That's why I say that it is very difficult to be a Spaniard."

He fell silent, gazed attentively at his hands, rubbed them together, then put them to his eyes as if he wished to wipe away his fatigue. Then he went on in an even voice: "Atrocities have been committed in the name of Christianity. In the name of socialism and a new world thousands of innocent people have been and still are being massacred. And yet, you, an artist—and I'm not judging you—continue to put your faith in the Communist Party."

The Marquis paused again and then said: "Your argument has no validity, or very little. One must be honest, Serafín. Even if only on the eve of one's death."

The old man looked into the young pianist's eyes and continued in an almost solemn voice. "You know now as well as I do that it is as difficult to be a good Spaniard as it is to be a good Christian or a good Socialist." He closed his eyes. "There is only one real aristocrat alive today, one true grandee of Spain, and his name is Miguel de Unamuno." Then, as if talking to himself, he said: "I had to see my country a prey to flames in order to become aware of its true reality. I had to see the people of Spain suffer and weep in order to discover them and become conscious of the love I bear them."

"And do you think those who will be in power tomorrow will have a more accurate awareness of what Spain is than we have?"

The Marquis's smile was disillusioned. "We are alone. No, they do not know the real Spain. They love its past. They have enclosed it in myths: Isabella the Catholic, Charles V, Philip II, the Empire. They turn their backs on the reality."

"But then—where is Spain?"

The old man looked at his hands with concentration, then replied: "In us."

There was a long silence. It was the Marquis who broke it. "Will you have a liqueur?"

"No, thank you."

Serafín got up and sat down at the piano. His long fingers caressed the keyboard. He smiled shyly and excused himself. "It's so long since I touched a piano!"

The Marquis made no reply. He made himself comfortable in an armchair, closed his eyes, and gave himself up to the music.

Serafín played Falla's *Fantasia Baetica*. The music, infused with the colors, sounds, and smells of the south, evoked, in its sad, voluptuous, syncopated rhythm, the profound and mysterious poetry of Andalusian nights.

Then he played the melodies of Turina and Albéniz. The Marquis sat motionless; he listened with a strange melancholy at heart. Suddenly they heard the rattle of machine guns close at hand. A violent explosion shook the house, making the pictures and *bibelots* quiver. Serafín slowly closed the piano and asked in a firm voice: "What's the time?"

"Ten minutes past five."

The young pianist smiled. "They're here," he said.

The Marquis got to his feet. The two men looked at each other with emotion. Then they silently shook hands.

"Thank you for this evening," Serafín murmured.

"Thank you. You *were* a great artist."

There was a short silence, then a sound of footsteps in the park. A machine gun was firing bursts almost under the windows. The women were screaming on the ground floor. "The Moors! The Moors!"

"I will leave you alone now," the Marquis said finally. "I must go and calm them."

He left the room. Hardly had he closed the door when he heard the sharp noise of an explosion, then the softer sound of a body falling.

The Marquis started, but did not turn his head.

The suicide of the young pianist with whom he had spent the night was the ultimate horror.

He walked along the corridor, reached the great staircase, and slowly descended it. Huddled together were some fifty women and children, staring in terror at the front door.

The Marquis said in a firm voice: "Have no fear. The war is over for you. You are under my protection."

As he was speaking, the door slowly opened and the first Moor appeared, armed with a submachine gun. He was wearing a khaki uniform and boots and a dirty turban on his head. He had coarse features, and his eyes were bloodshot.

The Marquis saw him and smiled at him. "Don't worry," he said to the peasants, "you have no need to be afraid. You are now under the protection of the Nationalist army."

By now two more Moors had come into the house. The old man said: "Welcome to you. This is my house and you will find neither arms nor enemies in it. Merely women and children."

One of the soldiers smiled contemptuously. Without warning he fired at the old man point-blank.

For a moment the Marquis appeared not to understand what had happened. He staggered, opened his mouth as if to speak again, and a gush of blood flowed from it.

Then he fell and turned over and over like an unstrung puppet before coming to rest on his stomach with his arms extended.

Appalled by the scene, the refugees held their breath.

The Moors turned their weapons on them. One of the women rushed forward and cried, her voice broken by sobs: "Don't shoot! Don't shoot!"

The submachine guns stuttered. The bodies fell slowly, one on another.

As the Nationalist troops continued their advance, an immense fire lit up the sky. The Marquis de Leyes's house was burning. Black clouds of smoke ballooned over the façade, and huge flames spurted up toward the roof. The fire roared, and the first floor fell in with an appalling crash. Then the roof cracked, and the flames shot upward through the gaping holes. The nearest cypresses were soon on fire, too.

7

THE people of Madrid had settled down to war. After the enthusiasm and joy of the first days, there was stunned horror, then resignation.

Three months had elapsed. Autumn had come; the trees in the Retiro massed gold and copper now. The wind from the Guadarrama was already cold as it swept through the streets of the capital. Yet, in these silent streets, patrolled by armed bands, there were long motionless queues. Black-clothed women, shod with *espadrilles*, waited patiently for hours in the futile hope of buying a few lentils, some bread, or a can of condensed milk. There were famished faces in every district of the city: old women with wrin-

kled skins, young women with dull eyes. There were long
resigned queues everywhere. The shop doors remained ob-
stinately closed; but no one went away. They were waiting
for a miracle to happen. Night and day the Madrileños
waited for the most prodigious of miracles: something to
eat.

For the inhabitants of Madrid suffered more from hunger than from the Fascist aircraft that came to spread fear
and death two or three times a day.

In October Olny left the hospital and went home. Marianita nursed him with tenderness and devotion, but they
avoided each other's eyes and rarely spoke. Each was living
in the loneliness of his sorrow and of the destruction of
his future. They could find no words with which to com-
municate, so they remained silent, absorbed in their own
thoughts and their common memories, which it would
have been vain to try to share again. Life seemed to have
lost all meaning for them. They never spoke of the past or
of their love. Yet, it was not dead; it had changed in nature.
Marianita knew her husband was suffering and she lavished
on him the silent, tender cherishing of a devoted woman.
As for him, he did not know what was happening to him.
It was not only his mutilations that made him suffer, but
the throbbing memory of those days in the hospital when
he had come face to face with the tears, the blood, and
the death of his comrades.

He had joined the Party because he had wanted a better
world, because he had known poverty, endless hunger, and

social ostracism. Then he had seen that: mutilated bodies, faces disfigured forever. He could make no connection between the classless Utopian world and that other world of the hospital, slow agonies and heartbreaking groans. It did no good to tell himself the Republicans had neither desired nor begun the war; his mind was still full of the sights of the hospital ward and the stifled cries that sounded through the long hours of the night.

Olny stretched his hand out in the dark for his pack of cigarettes on the bedside table. He tried not to make a noise or awaken Marianita, who the evening before had long been out in the cold and the rain, standing in line at the baker's. He struck a match, and the sudden flare of light made him blink. He reopened his eyes slowly, lit the cigarette, and before he put the match out, glanced at her lying beside him.

Her eyes were wide open. Her long brown hair made a dark patch on the white pillow; he gazed at her in silence. Suddenly he felt his heart constrict and quickly put out the match: Marianita was weeping. Olny gently raised her head and slipped his left arm under her neck, caressing it with the tips of his fingers. "Don't cry," he murmured. "You mustn't cry."

He did not know what to say. Then he added tenderly: "All the same, I'm lucky. You saw the poor guys in the hospital. . . . I'm alive. You mustn't cry. I'm here. Don't."

Marianita grew quiet. And then, in a voice broken with

stifled sobs, she asked: "Do you believe there's a God?"

Olny hesitated before replying. He, too, had thought about the question, lying in his hospital bed. "I don't know, Marianita. It's too complicated. I don't think there is."

"I need Him. Silly, isn't it? But all the mess: the dead, the kids screaming . . ." She paused, looked for her handkerchief under the pillow, sniffed a few times, and went on sadly: "There must be a God. Otherwise, what would we be doing here?"

There was another silence. Olny could think of nothing to say. He, too, hoped with all his heart and mind that there was a God. He needed to assure himself that all was not lost; that the hunger for love and justice they carried within them would one day be filled. But he felt discouraged. Where was God? How could you find Him amid the crashing of bombs and the cries of innocent victims?

"I must get up," said Marianita in a different voice. "I may find some chick peas. You haven't eaten for two days."

"It's still early. Not even day yet. There's no point in getting frozen for nothing. It's cold outside."

"It's already five o'clock. I bet fifty women have been freezing for more than an hour. I'm never the first."

She got up in silence, began dressing, and went into the kitchen.

She stood motionless for a moment or two by the stove. Her face was tired and discouraged. Four months had made of this girl, who had come trembling to love, a tired and exhausted woman. And yet, all hope was not dead in her. From time to time she caressed her stomach with a touch of love. Within her warm body another life was awaiting its hour. Marianita dreamed despairingly of her son, wondered in anguish what would become of him. She would have liked her child's eyes to open on a happy world at peace. But this little life, nourished in her own hunger, would have made acquaintance with misery and suffering even before its birth. His first sleep would doubtless be lulled by the racket of explosions and wailing sirens. She clenched her teeth, forced back her tears, and shrugged her shoulders in resignation: there was nothing she could do about it.

Marianita stopped thinking of her unborn son and began heating some water. She did her hair, washed her face and hands, and dressed, and then wondered what she could put into the boiling water. There was nothing left. She shrugged her shoulders, opened the cupboard, and took out a few stale crusts of bread. With these and some garlic she could make a soup.

"Poor kid!" she said aloud. She was thinking of her son again. For Marianita knew there would not be enough soup for both her husband and herself. She would lie to him as usual, saying she had already eaten in the kitchen.

When it was ready, she filled a soup plate, took a spoon, and went into the bedroom. Olny was up and dressed. He had parted the curtains and opened the window.

Day was breaking; the sky was pale and the air transparent. A light breeze was shaking the branches in the old garden. Copper-colored leaves were falling majestically, after hesitating for a while suspended between earth and sky. The streets were empty. Two militiamen, armed with pistols, passed beneath the window and went on their way, laughing.

"Eat. It's hot."

Olny turned to her, smiled, and thanked her with a nod of the head. She avoided looking at him, for hunger made her giddy and she was afraid of betraying herself. Olny took the plate in both hands, sat on the bed, and began slowly drinking the soup. Marianita pretended to be looking out of the window at the trees and lawns of the Retiro. But she was obsessed by the noise the spoon made against the plate. Sweat poured from her forehead and down her sides from her armpits. She felt she might faint, and pressed her burning forehead against the ice-cold windowpane, covered with frost.

Olny stopped eating and looked at her anxiously. "Why aren't you eating?" he asked.

"I've already eaten. Don't worry."

"Where did you eat?"

She shrugged her shoulders. "I tell you I've eaten."

Olny got to his feet, went to her, and looked into her eyes. "Don't lie."

Marianita no longer had the strength to lie. She burst into tears.

He turned his head away. "Why didn't you say anything?"

She blew her nose noisily and muttered between two sobs: "It doesn't matter."

"Yes, it does."

He bent his head, kissed her on the forehead, and said in a determined voice: "That's all over now. We'll get food, I promise you."

Marianita looked at him anxiously. "What are you going to do?"

"Nothing."

She clung to him and said wearily: "Don't do anything silly. It's better to die of hunger. You mustn't."

"Don't worry, Marianita. I'll do as the others do. Why should we be hungry while the others are filling their stomachs? Why should we, eh? I'm a revolutionary, too. I've done my share. So . . . ?" He was silent a moment, then added in a gentler voice: "We have to think of the baby. He hasn't done anything. We can't let him die of hunger."

He felt the point had gone home. Marianita wiped away her tears and asked calmly: "What are you going to do?"

"I'm going to find Comrade Ramírez. We'll have a talk. I'll bet he's got food, all right. You see, a political commissar has to eat to serve the people!"

"Be careful, Olny. They're quite capable of shooting you. Only last night they came looking for someone in here. The man on the second floor, the one who played the cello."

"Why?"

"Fascist. It seems he'd hidden a priest. They take them away in cars and they're never heard of again. They liquidate them in the East Cemetery. They call it the *paseo*."

The young man smiled in bitter disgust. "Don't worry. Comrade Ramírez can't liquidate me. I'm a hero. Don't forget that. All the papers had my picture on the front page. Besides, Ramírez is scared of me. He knows that I'd kill him in a minute. He's a damn fool."

"All the same, be careful."

"I promise."

Marianita fetched a basket and tied a scarf around her head.

"Are you going out?"

"I'm going to stand in line."

"You won't need to any more."

"One never knows."

"As you like. I'll come with you."

They left the flat and went down the stairs. They had reached the first floor landing, when the sirens began waking the tenants with their waves of sound. Olny took Marianita's arm. "We'll go down to the cellar."

"It's not worth it," she said. "I hate being shut in. If we've got to die, I'd rather it happened in the open air."

"No one likes it. Let's go down all the same."

Doors were banging. An old woman jostled past them. She was tiny, and her face was wrinkled, her hair white, her eyes afraid. She seemed nearly blind and was muttering unintelligibly. Olny heard "My God, my God!"

Then the neighbor from their floor arrived with other tenants. A stout man with a kindly air was helping his wife, a small, thin, fair woman with big eyes and the pale complexion of an invalid. The man was wearing a gray overcoat over his striped pajamas; the woman had on a pink nightdress and a fur coat. She smiled at Olny, who smiled back.

They all gathered in a small, dark cellar, in which a furnace stood.

Olny stood. Marianita crouched silently at his feet. The old grandmother told her beads, her head nodding and trembling; she muttered endlessly. At Olny's right stood the man whose wife seemed to be an invalid. She was shivering, and he could hear her teeth chattering in the silence. She was sitting on a chair, her husband holding one of her hands between his own. He leaned down to her. "Are you all right, Alicia?"

"Yes . . . a little cold, that's all." Her voice was sad and musical.

Olny took a pack of cigarettes from his pocket and offered the man one. He accepted, smiled, and said in a dull voice: "They're earlier today. They usually let you sleep till eight o'clock."

Olny nodded in agreement. Then no one spoke. They suddenly heard the noise of aircraft engines in the silence. The noise came slowly closer. The silence in the cellar grew heavy. The man in pajamas stroked his wife's hair with a tender, protective gesture. The sick woman shivered. The old grandmother said her beads faster and faster.

Suddenly they heard the first whistlings of bombs, followed by the explosions. The old grandmother began whimpering. "Santa Maria del Pilar! Murderers! Killing women and children! Santa Teresa del Ávila, pray for us."

Olny lit another cigarette and took Marianita's cold, moist hands between his own. He kissed them tenderly. The sick woman had a fit of coughing. They waited, silent and patient, for death to choose among the thousands of women and children who were awaiting it in fear like themselves.

The sound of the aircraft engines grew louder and louder. Olny held his breath. The silence had become more oppressive yet. The man in pajamas muttered in a strange voice: "They're right above us."

A long, shrill scream tore through the silence. It was not a whistle, but like a gull's cry. With an appalling roar everything seemed to crumble around them. Olny was knocked off his feet and thrown to the floor with the rest. He had difficulty in grasping what was happening. At first there was a terrible silence in the cellar. Then the old grandmother began shouting for help. Olny got to his feet, enveloped in a cloud of dust; he could see nothing around him. Stabbed suddenly with fear, he began shouting at the top of his voice: "Mariana! Mariana!"

She rushed sobbing into his arms. Their lips sought each other despairingly. Olny's eyes filled with tears, his strong hands caressed Marianita's face and body desperately, as if to assure himself that she was whole; he was muttering broken words and phrases. They had found each other again on the far side of pain and death, and were not ashamed of their tears. There were cries and sobbing all about them.

"Alicia! Alicia!"

"Pablo, Pablo, where are you?"

"Santa Teresa del Ávila!"

They were all suddenly talking the simple language of love. Their words were basic, naked, and direct; they had no pride or false shame left; they wept, embraced, clung to each other. For they had been raised from the dead.

The sirens sounded the all clear, and they slowly left the cellar that might have been their tomb. They were dazzled by the light outside. The sun was already high, and the sky was blue.

Marianita and Olny went out into the street. A terrible sight greeted them. The next building had collapsed. Only the façade was still standing, its doors and windows gaping, the ruins smoking. There were two trucks parked by the pavement, charred bodies heaped in them in a mass of mangled flesh and bone. Wardens were rushing and stumbling about, in blue uniforms with Red Cross armbands. Firemen hosed the smoke-blackened stones, desperately trying to limit the disaster. A thick ring of onlookers gathered, shifting and stretching to see each new casualty. Murmurs swelled loud; some women were crying and blowing their noses.

Marianita leaned her head against Olny's shoulder. He

stroked her quietly, his eyes on the wreckage. There was a sudden silence, and all eyes turned to an emaciated young man with a smudged, sweating face, wearing a blue warden's uniform and carrying the body of a child in his arms. As he came slowly forward, they could see his drawn face, his black-encircled eyes, and his hollow cheeks. It was as if he were carrying some fragile burden he wanted everyone to see. He was staggering like a drunken man. The child's head had been crushed. His face was unrecognizable. But his small legs were visible, as were his feet shod in tiny shoes.

Standing next to Olny, a woman with gray hair and a wrinkled face suddenly became hysterical and began screaming: "Murderers! Criminals!" She burst into sobs, and a silence fell over the crowd.

Marianita muttered: "It's not he, it's not he!"

Nor did Olny want to admit that the emaciated young man with the feverish eyes and uncertain gait was Santiago de Leyes. And yet, when he had put the child's body with the others in the truck and turned toward them, no further doubt was possible: it was their friend. But was it he, or was it only his shadow? He did not see them.

Olny kissed his wife and went off. He walked quickly. When he had gone some three hundred yards, he stopped, looked up at the sky in anger, and cursed it.

8

COMRADE Ramírez was sitting comfortably behind his desk. In front of him on the wall were portraits of Marx and Stalin. On his left was a big window that looked out on the street.

Ramírez was happy. The war filled him with satisfaction. Yet, he was not a wicked man and he might well have been affected by the sight of the bodies of women and children. But his optimism rebounded immediately. For, dialectically speaking, and taking the future into account, this butchery could not help but serve the interests of the Party and therefore those of the proletariat. Moreover, it gave the workers the opportunity to get rid of all the Fascists in the capital. On Ramírez's desk lay long lists of suspects awaiting his signature.

He glanced at the list: "The Count of Pella, the Marquis of Altofuegos, the Duke of Los Fallos . . ." "Nothing but aristocrats," thought Ramírez, and his long, thin face lit up for a few seconds with a contemptuous smile. Then he looked up and thought with confidence of the future. The population had come to the end of its strength and nervous resilience. The daily bombings and the cruel hunger would teach the Spanish people what fascism was. And it was a good thing that they should learn to hate fascism, for the hatred would translate itself into action. The Spanish people were beginning to understand that if they wanted to win the war, they must fight fascism with its own weapons. To one discipline another must be opposed: to the unity of the Nationalist camp, the unity of the other camp. "The Anarchists are losing ground." The thought made Ramírez smile. For, though he had nothing but contempt for aristocrats and bourgeois, he hated with his whole heart those parties, so-called of the Left, which did nothing but sow confusion in the mind of the proletariat.

Perhaps the moment for getting rid of them was at hand. Ramírez dreamed of the day when the Communists would be strong enough to organize a St. Bartholomew's Day. There could be no doubt about that, and the directives from the Central Committee of the Russian Communist Party were explicit: Trotskyites, Anarchists, and other parasites of the Revolution must be mercilessly liquidated. Those people wished to be, and indeed called themselves, humane! As if the triumph of socialism could be a humane business!

Ramírez got to his feet, stretched himself, lit a cigarette, opened the window, and threw his match out into the street. Children were playing on the opposite sidewalk, carrying imaginary guns on their shoulders and shooting each other.

"Bang, bang . . ."

"Rat-tat-tat-tat . . ."

A brown-haired little boy was pretending to be a

bomber plane and, arms outstretched, dove at the enemy. But a fighter was already coming to intercept him, and the battle was on.

Ramírez looked at the scene with emotion. He listened and could hear the rumbling of artillery in the distance. Everything was going well. The Revolution was pursuing its glorious advance toward a better tomorrow and a future built in the image of the U.S.S.R. At the moment all the forces of the Left were fighting against fascism; when that battle was won, the Communists could undertake the real Revolution at last—their own. Then the world would burst into a thousand pieces. Free men would be able to sing a hymn of joy and build together a just and classless society. Of course, people would have to be killed to achieve this goal—many people, all the enemies of the Revolution. And they were numerous. Comrade Ramírez thought of the last speech delivered by the Secretary General of the Russian Communist Party, Stalin, and his eyes filled with tears. Under the aegis of such a leader, the victory of socialism could not be in doubt.

"*Hola*, Comrade! Perez's wife is outside. I told her to wait."

After his long revery, Ramírez had difficulty in making contact with reality again. He had been standing by the window, absorbed in his thoughts and memories. Nothing had changed. Outside, the children were still playing. The guns rumbled in the distance.

"What does she want?" Ramírez asked.

"She's crying."

"Send her in."

A thin little woman with a bowed back, a drawn face, and sad eyes came in. She was wearing a threadbare blue dress and *espadrilles*.

"Sit down, Comrade."

The woman obeyed, took a dirty handkerchief from her pocket, and wiped her eyes.

"As you know, Comrade, the people are hungry. Women are standing in line at the food shops." Ramírez's voice was severe and peremptory, the tone he always adopted for official business. The woman had begun crying again. Her thin shoulders heaved. Ramírez, who was standing behind her, could see only a back shaken with sobs, and hair that was turning white. She said nothing. From time to time she merely muttered: "I was hungry. . . . I was hungry."

"We're all hungry, Comrade. Your husband, who's fighting for liberty and democracy, is hungry, too. It's no excuse. You have deceived the Party, which placed its trust in you."

Señora Perez was the wife of an old militant Communist. She had a child of five months, but she could not feed him, for there was no milk in Madrid. She had applied to Ramírez, who sent her a few bottles each week. Yet the child continued to waste away. It had just been discovered that it was the mother who drank the milk.

And now she sat there, sobbing and ashamed, face to face with this official personage of whom she was afraid. She wondered whether she would be shot.

"I gave you the extra ration of milk to feed your child. The son of a Communist is the future hope of the Party. It is our children who will build the socialism of tomorrow. Comrade Stalin himself, in a speech made to the Praesidium, encouraged Soviet mothers to—"

"Aren't you a little bit off your rocker?"

Ramírez looked around. Olny had come in silently and was standing by the door, his legs apart, his hands in his pockets.

"Comrade, this woman has been letting her child die of hunger and drinking the milk the Party gave her. She has—"

"She has nothing at all. . . ." Olny advanced slowly toward him. Ramírez disgusted him. He wanted to hit him. "She's hungry, that's all. Have you ever been hungry, Comrade bastard?"

Ramírez turned pale. "I forbid you—"

"What? You forbid what? You make me laugh! This poor woman's crying. Don't you see she's ashamed? Don't you see she's trembling with self-disgust? Don't you realize a mother must be literally dying of hunger before she's capable of drinking her child's milk?" Olny stood face to face with Ramírez, his back turned to the mother, whose sobs grew louder and louder. "Did you ever have a mother?"

Ramírez flushed. "Yes," he said.

"I'd never know it. Because if you had, you wouldn't dare bully this woman. And speeches, too! Who do you think you are? I knew you when you were down-and-out and were alway insulting the bourgeois, and you're more of a bastard than they are. A thousand times more!"

Olny raised his voice. Santiago's face was still before his eyes, and, because it had shaken him, he felt the need to shout and relieve his feelings on someone. He turned to the mother. "Don't cry! Do you know what I saw downstairs? Cartons full of cans of food: rice, milk, jam. And do you know who it's all for? It's for these bastards who take the bread out of your mouths! And then they dare shout and make speeches!"

"Those cartons—" Ramírez began.

"What about those cartons? I suppose they're for the orphans! Who do you take me for? I know you. Political commissar! A commissar of bastards! Is this your Revolution? Standing behind a desk and abusing a starving woman? Why don't you go and abuse the others, eh? Why? You disgust me! You lousy rotten bastard—you're full of crap!"

Ramírez said nothing. His teeth were clenched. He dared not have Olny arrested, for he had become a sort of hero of the Revolution. All the newspapers of the capital had published photographs of him and the account of the torture he had undergone. It was better to wait. But in his heart of hearts Ramírez swore to liquidate him.

There was a silence. Ramírez said to the woman: "Leave us. We've got things to discuss."

The woman got up without a word. Her eyes were weeping and smiling at once.

"You were wrong to insult me in front of her," Ramírez said when she had left the office. "By behaving like that you weaken the Party. We must maintain order and discipline in our ranks if we want to win this war. You're not a good Communist."

Olny looked Ramírez in the eyes, his expression one of disgust, and in a low voice he said: "No. I'm not a good Communist. I joined the Party because I'd been born in the gutter and I believed what you said. I've worked for you, I've been tortured for you, because Santiago was with you and because he was clean. Now I know why he left you. You're a lot of bastards."

Ramírez said nothing. He thought the time had not yet come.

Olny went up to his old comrade. Their faces were almost touching. "I saw plenty of them in the Zone, but never one like you. Never! You're not even a man. If you were a man, I'd break your jaw for you. You're just a weak punk."

Ramírez felt stifled. His hands were trembling. He wondered what would happen if he shot Olny point-blank, but he dared not do it. "What did you come here for?" he asked.

"To beg." Olny moved away from Ramírez. "I've come

about food. Mariana is expecting a child. We're dying of hunger. I want the child to live. . . . Because I can't give her another."

Ramírez smiled. He now knew how to get rid of Olny. He waited to hear what more he had to say.

"I've done my bit like the rest. I'm a revolutionary, too. So, I want my share. Why should you keep food, blankets, clothes, even confiscated radios for yourselves? I want cartons, too."

"Of course," Ramírez said calmly. "You're right. It's only fair. I'll give you an order. You can have two packages a week like the other comrades. But, of course, I shall have to be able to justify them. Considering your state of health, and your wife's, I can't send you to the front. Nevertheless, you could go to San Isidro. There you'll be with a few other comrades whose job is to escort the Fascists condemned to death by the Revolutionary Tribunals."

As he spoke, Ramírez had sat down behind his desk and written a few words on a piece of paper, which he handed to Olny. "Here's your order. With this and your Party card you can get what you need. Go to San Isidro tonight. The comrades there know what to do and will explain it to you."

Olny took the order, read it, folded it carefully, and put it in his pocket. Then he said in a hoarse voice: "I don't know what kind of dirty trick you're up to. But I warn you: I'll find you and kill you. Good-by."

"Good-by."

9

OLNY left Marianita to go to the San Isidro cemetery. The windless night was cold, the sky very high and dark. The stars were like diamonds on black velvet. There was no one in the streets except a few armed militiamen in requisitioned cars. Olny walked through the silence with a rapid, decisive step. Ruins and shattered houses, ill-lit by a wan moon, appeared out of the dark to remind him that wartime nights had no resemblance to those of peace. He lit a cigarette, drew a long first puff, and hurried on. He seemed to be living in a sort of stupefied silence. The war made less sense to him than ever. He would have liked to go back and begin everything all over again, but it was too late. Life had played him false, as it had his parents. He had dreamed of a just and fraternal world in which children could grow up in happiness: a world without a Zone. And now he was surrounded by ruins, charred corpses, and mutilated children. "It's not my fault," he muttered. "It's not my fault. I didn't want it. Santiago should have told me and explained things." But he was not quite sure about what it was that Santiago should have explained. How could one explain the corpse of a child? What justification could one find for the tears of a mother who had lost her son? There were no words to explain the sufferings of the innocent.

Olny reached the wall that circled the cemetery. Shadowy cypress trees stood out black against the night. He hesitated before going through the gate. Without knowing why, he had a strange feeling of uneasiness at the idea of spending all his nights behind this wall, with abandoned tombs for sole surroundings. He tried to smile, but could not manage it. It was as though he were moving toward a rendezvous with fate. He felt that he should flee while there was still time, that he should do something about it—but what? He was too weary, too disheartened. And then, too, there was Marianita and the child on the way. Olny went in.

A long alley opened before him. The cypresses stood a dignified guard. To left and right he could see the silhouettes of the tombs by the pale light of the moon. Some, of white marble, glittered in the night; the more humble were barely visible. The crosses had been torn down and trampled underfoot; they lay scattered and derelict over the ground. Some of the tombs had been violated, and there were piles of skeletons lying about, while more recent corpses had not yet been buried. The air was foul with the nauseating reek of decomposition.

Olny came to a halt: what should he do now? His eyes felt heavy, and his legs were trembling. Cold sweat trickled down his face. His hair was drenched; he ran his hand over it again and again. He could see nothing but the violated tombs and the piles of corpses under the pallid autumn moon.

He walked on slowly. There was a stifling sensation in

his throat. He felt like falling to his knees, bursting into tears, and praying. But to whom would he pray? Suddenly he started back; he had stepped on a skeleton that crumbled under his foot. After a panicked moment, he controlled himself and went on. Finally he came to a stop by a heap of corpses stripped of their clothing and piled one on top of the other, like grotesque, absurd marionettes. Olny bent down, held his breath, and stared wide-eyed at each of them in turn. Most of them were men; some must have been in prison, for their heads were shaved. There were a few women among them; he could tell only by their long hair. Their eyes, dilated with horror, stared up at the immensity of the night. One of them had been finished off by blows from a rifle butt. Her purple face grimaced, under its black contusions and hideous wounds, and her hands were swollen. They must have trampled on her.

Olny straightened up with difficulty. His hands were trembling. Shudders were running down his spine, and his eyes were wet with tears. He was aware of an overwhelming exhaustion.

"Hands up! What are you doing here? Looking for a relative? Comrades, there's a Fascist in the cemetery!"

The voice rang out strong and determined. Olny put his hands up. There were other voices behind him. He was afraid and tried to cry out, but his voice was strangled in his throat. He made a desperate effort to speak, but his body was shaken with long shudders and no sound came. For some moments, so long that time seemed to stop in its course, Olny thought he was going to be killed. He told himself he did not want to die, that he was on their side, that they had no right to kill him. He thought of Marianita, closed his eyes, made another attempt to speak, and could not.

"Turn around."

Olny obeyed. Three militiamen armed with rifles were standing there. They were wearing Russian hats and boots. The man who had spoken first and seemed to be their chief was strong and tall. His nose was crushed like a boxer's and his features were coarse. Had it not been for his uniform, he might have been taken for a convict.

With some difficulty Olny managed to mutter tonelessly "I've come here on duty. I'm a member of the Party."

The militiaman with the criminal face laughed. "You should have said so! We could have shot you by mistake. Don't you realize that?" He laughed again.

Olny heaved a sigh of relief and followed the three men. They went toward a small red brick house at the entrance to the cemetery. The room they entered was unfurnished and had whitewashed walls. There were camp beds in the corners for the sentries, and a coal stove in the middle of the room, with two wooden benches by it. Olny handed his papers to the leader of the group, who examined them carefully. Then he was given a uniform similar to those the other three militiamen were wearing.

"You can turn in now. The trucks never get here till four in the morning. Make the most of it and get some sleep."

224

Olny put on his uniform and went and lay on one of the beds. His neighbor was a very young man, barely twenty years old, blue-eyed and thick-nosed, with a pouting lower lip and fair hair.

"Are you asleep?" the boy asked.

Olny opened his eyes. They were alone in the corner, their beds almost touching. If they talked in low voices, the others, sleeping at the other end of the room, would not be able to hear them. "No, I'm not asleep," Olny replied.

"What's your name?"

"Olny."

"Mine's Perico. I come from Vallecas. Where do you come from?"

"From the Zone."

There was a silence. At last Perico said in a low voice: "You don't like this, either?"

"What?"

"The dead."

"No, I don't like the dead."

Perico spoke in a sad voice, a little like a child telling his mother of his night fears. "It was terrible in the beginning. I'd never seen anyone die, or killed anyone. It's awful hearing them scream when they're going to die. Especially when they're women. I'm not used to it yet."

Olny thought he could not have understood him aright and asked: "Do you kill people? Here?"

"Of course. You'll do it, too. That's our job. All those

dead outside, we did it. They bring them here in trucks, about fifty or sixty every night, and we shoot them with machine guns. Yesterday there was an eight-year-old child. He was the son of a count, apparently. The child was crying and calling for his mother. I fired at the others, but I couldn't fire at the child."

Olny thought he was going to faint. He wanted to shout for help. He told himself it was not possible, that he must have heard wrong. Spaniards could not do things like that. Then he closed his eyes, for he already knew that even Spaniards were capable of killing women and children.

"Why haven't you run away?" Olny asked.

"Where to? They watch us. One of my friends tried to get to an embassy, but they caught him and shot him. It's like that: you kill or you get killed. You've got no choice."

"But why do they shoot them?"

"It seems they're Fascists. For the most part they're aristocrats." In a voice hoarse with anguish the young man added: "It's the women that are so awful. It's not quite so bad with the men. But it's terrible shooting the women. Then you have to strip their clothes off and finish off those who aren't dead. Sometimes you hear them screaming from under the heap."

"But why don't they bury them? Why do they leave them lying about like that?"

"It'd be impossible to bury them all. Every few days we pour petrol over them and burn them."

Olny fell silent. He had no courage to ask for more information. He had only one desire: to sleep, to find rest. He told himself he was already a potential murderer. His sleep tumbled with appalling nightmares.

IO

STOPPING at each flight to get his breath, Santiago de Leyes climbed the stairs to his room. He had spent the whole day clearing rubble, recovering bodies, piling them in trucks, and finding lodgings for the bombed-out. Then he had gone to visit Francisco, Olny's little brother, as he did every Thursday. The boy had run weeping into his arms. He, too, was afraid. Santiago had placed him in a private school as a boarder. The child seemed happy, had forgotten the Zone and the trumpet, but had begun learning the violin. His master said he had an outstanding musical gift.

"Who knows?" Santiago thought. "Perhaps he'll become a great musician." The idea made him smile. It seemed to him at once sublime and absurd that a child should be able to learn to play the violin in the midst of this universal madness of hatred and destruction.

Santiago hesitated a moment before going into his room. The door was open. He was not surprised, for he never locked it; but it meant he had a visitor, and the mere thought of having to talk to someone made him feel tired.

It was Carlos. Santiago was relieved and delighted to see his friend again. He was sitting on the sofa, reading a magazine, and before him, on the low table, was a half-empty glass. Santiago looked at it questioningly.

"Sherry," Carlos explained with a smile. "I managed to get a couple of bottles and came to drink them with you."

Santiago smiled. The two friends had not even greeted each other. They met as if they had only just parted.

Without a word, Santiago took his blue coat off, poured water into a basin, and began carefully washing his face and hands. The freshness of the water against his burning face soothed him. Carlos watched. Suddenly he asked: "Does what you're doing give you a good conscience?"

Santiago realized that Carlos was referring to his civil-defense work, and hesitated before answering. After a long pause, he murmured, as he dried his face: "You can't have everything."

"What do you mean, everything?"

"Life and a good conscience."

Carlos made no reply, took a sip of sherry, and lit a cigarette. Santiago had taken a white shirt from a drawer and was concentrating on selecting a tie. He had no idea as to why he wanted to put a tie on or what color he wanted it to be.

"Are you going out for a walk or something?" Carlos asked.

"Can one ever tell?"

Carlos grasped the allusion, smiled bitterly, and went on in a level voice: "You're right—can one ever tell? A human life no longer has much importance. Any fool can accuse you of fascism and put you up against a wall. That's what revolution is." Carlos inhaled his cigarette slowly and added: "Do you know what I've come here in search of tonight?"

"Yes."

As if he had not heard the answer, Carlos went on: "Friendship. That's what I've come to find. I wanted to see you, talk to you, and empty a bottle with you. Me, the zealous Communist and militant, I felt so lonely I had to come in search of you. To belong to the Communist Party and yet to feel lonely is a sort of contradiction in terms, isn't it?"

Santiago turned off the ceiling light and lit a small table lamp. Then he sat down in an armchair facing his friend. "Everything is a contradiction," he said in a weary voice.

There was a pause. Carlos suddenly got to his feet and went to the window. In a low, almost furious voice, he said: "Don't you realize what a couple of fools we are? We're behaving as if we were tough, talking quietly, trying to find the answers, when we're both petrified. Yes, we're afraid! We're afraid of pain, dying, everything! We're not men, Santiago, we're children. What we really want is to cry and call our mothers. Do you realize we're no better than a couple of kids—we've been playing with fire and now things have gotten out of hand. Do you realize that it doesn't help to talk any more? We're murderers. We deliberately prepared all this!"

He gestured toward Madrid lying in the darkness.

Santiago wondered what had happened to Carlos. He looked at him anxiously, trying to guess what sights or happenings had driven him to reconsider his convictions. He waited impatiently for what more he might have to say.

" 'Contradictions, loneliness'—they're nothing but phrases! Like 'the future of the world,' the 'happy tomorrows,' the 'links of brotherhood.' It's all nonsense! Words, just words that lead to bloodshed. We're mad, Santiago. I'm sure we're mad. We're guilty of the sin of pride. We believed in ideas, words, and slogans, and forgot that this kind of game always ends badly."

Carlos stopped speaking, went over to Santiago, and realized he was weeping. "Forgive me. I didn't want to upset you, really. I'm outraged, that's all!"

"Don't worry! I'm just tired. We're all exhausted."

Carlos sat down again. His eyes glowed in the soft light that barely illuminated his face. He filled his glass again and emptied it at a gulp.

Santiago did not move. He felt as if his head were bursting. He wondered what Carlos really wanted to say to him.

"Do you know what I saw this evening?"

"No."

"Women crowded in trucks being taken to the outskirts of Madrid. Do you know what they were going to do with them?"

"Yes."

Carlos went on: "There's no hope, because fascism is no better. Nothing makes sense any more."

"Yes." Santiago's voice seemed to come from a long way off. "Yes. There's always Christ."

"And everything that has been done in His name?"

Santiago looked at his friend with tears in his eyes. "One must live with the poor and for the poor, and love them because they are made in His image. One must try to become the light and the salt of the earth." As if he had just made some superhuman effort, Santiago murmured in a broken voice: "One must pray."

Carlos got up and went to the window. He stood there silent and motionless for a few moments. Santiago sat in his chair, with his head in his hands. It was some minutes before Carlos made up his mind to break the silence.

"We're being very romantic." He might have been saying "Alas!"

"Not romantic—exhausted."

"It's the same thing. The others aren't wasting their time weeping tonight. They're cleaning their weapons and preparing to meet the Fascist columns marching on the capital. Do you know that General Franco has declared he'll be in Madrid tomorrow? The trade unions have armed the people. We may be living our last hours of democracy. It's sad to think they're being stained by crime and blood."

Carlos threw his head back and went on in a low voice, as if he were talking to himself. "Only a week ago I would have given anything in the world for the extermination of the Nazi-Franco divisions. Today I no longer wish for anything. For I know that even if we win, there will be injustice still!"

Carlos spun one of his crutches and added in a strangled voice: "We're two poor idealists. We don't know how to *act*. We think too much. We can't live our ideas to their ultimate conclusions. Perhaps it's the most difficult thing for a man to do: to live his ideas."

"It's not our ideas we should have lived, but our life." Santiago's voice sounded hoarse.

"Our life? But what life?" Carlos asked.

"The humble life. Life as it is, made up of insignificant actions, small pleasures, pains, and difficulties. The life of work, love, and death. Daily life."

Carlos leaned his crutch against the wall and asked suddenly: "How often have you read *Don Quixote?*"

Santiago looked at his friend in surprise, as if trying to make out the object of his question. "Fairly often."

"There's nothing so pathetic in the whole world of literature as that poor madman's last speech when he recovers his reason and questions the whole tendency of his life, when he begins to doubt his most noble and generous actions." With a bitter smile Carlos added: "I would never have thought I should one day have to compare myself to Don Quixote. We too have been fighting windmills." Suddenly he broke into a nervous laugh, recovered himself, and added in a tone of false gaiety: "Enough of this cheap philosophizing! I came to tell you good-by."

"Good-by?"

"Yes. I'm leaving for the front tonight to defend Liberty, Democracy, and Justice! All the capital letters, in fact."

Santiago asked no questions. He knew his friend would say all he had to say, that he had come simply for that purpose: to get it off his chest.

"Above all, I'm going in order to get killed. I feel quite certain I'm going to die. And oddly enough, death does not frighten me. But life? How can we go on living after seeing what we have?"

He paused again, turned to Santiago, and concluded in a voice full of emotion. "Will you believe me, Santiago, when I tell you that at this last hour I still believe in liberty, in justice, and in fraternity? That fascism still seems to me to represent absolute evil, and that I have not lost the hope that men will one day be capable of constructing a better world? That my despair is greatest because I placed all my hopes in the Party and that the Party has betrayed us? Can you believe that?"

Santiago stood up. The two friends were face to face. Santiago placed his hands on his friend's shoulders and replied in a sad voice: "Yes, Carlos, I believe you. I still hope, too."

"Thank you. I must tell you one thing more: you are the human being whom I love and admire most in the world. I regret that, unlike you, I have no religion."

"But you have, Carlos. You are very close to Christ. I can assure you of that. You were hungry and thirsty for justice and you will be satisfied. He has promised it."

"I have never known how to pray."

"You have made the whole of your life one long prayer, a battle against lying and injustice. That is prayer: to follow in His steps."

"Good-by."

"Good-by, Carlos. I hope we shall meet again soon."

The two friends embraced. Carlos left the room. Santiago heard the sound of his crutches on the stairs. Then he fell to his knees.

"Lord, I know not whether the path I have chosen is the right one. I am sure of nothing. But I love You. I know that You exist, for without You the world would have no sense. I ask You to grant me the courage to die well. Have mercy upon me. . . ."

II

SANTIAGO woke up with a start. Had he been dreaming? Sweat was pouring from his forehead. The window was open and he shivered in the cold night. The battle raged round Madrid; cannons and gun-flashes lit up the horizon. Santiago wondered whether the Republicans were still holding out or whether the front had collapsed. He had no time to seek the answer. There was a violent knocking at the door of his room. He tried to get up, but could not. His legs were trembling—he was afraid. Ever since July he had been living in terror of the moment when they would come to arrest him in the middle of the night. His sleep was always broken by nightmares. But tonight, he had surrendered to his fatigue and the violent knocking at the door caught him by surprise in the middle of a wonderful dream. He had been revisiting the old monastery where, as a child, he had gone at twilight to listen to the monks singing vespers. His mother was beside him, stroking his hair and kissing his forehead. The high, vibrant tenors sounded above the deep bass voices.

> *"Qui tollis peccata mundi,*
> *Dona nobis pacem."*

They echoed among the old stones of the empty church; the bass voices sounded among the columns of the abandoned nave, and the tenors rang out in the heights of the vault. It was a great, dolorous prayer, which rose to heaven, imploring peace. The little Santiago—for he saw himself as a child again, with curly hair and dressed in a sailor suit—wept and prayed. He asked God to give men peace: His peace.

"Open!"

The knocking redoubled.

235

Santiago slowly returned to reality. "Who is it?" he asked.

"The F.A.I."

Santiago got painfully out of bed and went slowly to open the door. There were two militiamen outside, rifles in their hands, hate in their eyes. One of them was small and dark and had black, gleaming, slit eyes like an Oriental's. The other was big, with a red face and gray eyes, and looked like a peaceful bourgeois.

"Santiago de Leyes?" asked the militiaman with the slit eyes.

"Yes."

"Come with us."

Santiago said nothing. He was so tired he lacked even the strength to speak. For a few seconds he stood there motionless, not quite knowing what to do.

"Hurry up," said the broad militiaman, threatening Santiago with his rifle.

"I'm ready." And then after a slight hesitation he asked: "Can I get a coat?"

The two militiamen looked at each other. "Hurry up," the short dark one muttered.

Santiago switched on a table lamp and looked sadly around the room in which he had lived so many months. Everything was in its proper place: the armchairs, the desk, the piano in the corner, the prints on the walls. He took a coat from the cupboard and, turning the light out, left the room and went slowly down the stairs. He felt the cold touch of steel in his back.

• • •

After ten days in a cell in the basement of the central police station, alone with his thoughts and memories, Santiago heard the news of his transfer with relief. He had not been brought before the People's Tribunal, or subjected to any form of interrogation. Officially he was listed as "a suspect, at the disposition of the Director General of Police." It was a fairly vague definition, but Santiago had no illusions about the fate that awaited him and knew that Comrade Ramírez would see that he did not come out of prison alive. He was ready to die. But this waiting for death, these long nights in which he dared not close his eyes for fear of being awakened sharply, these dawns whose silence was shattered by rifle shots, had finally exhausted him. His pallor, the dark rings around his eyes, and his two weeks' beard made him unrecognizable. He was frighteningly thin; when he got up for the daily soup ration—there was only one, at midday—he seemed a skeleton.

Santiago sat in a corner all day, near the thick-barred window, and gazed intently at his empty bowl. Hunger made him giddy. At times he felt like screaming and banging his head against the wall, but he knew it would be useless.

He suffered more from thirst even than from hunger. A pint of water was issued to the prisoners once a day. This was not enough for men in their condition. Santiago's throat was dry and his lips were cracked; he had scarcely enough saliva to moisten them.

At night the silence of the prison was rent by the cries

and groans of the tortured: electric shocks, the water torture, a glaring light in the eyes. They were not really cries any more; they were harrowing howls. Santiago tried to stop his ears, to distract his attention, to think of something else. But it was futile. The screams of men in unbearable physical suffering dominated everything else. It became an obsession. There was nothing in the world but these groans and desperate cries that the stones could not muffle. And when silence fell for a few minutes, he waited, his heart beating, for the appalling concert to begin again. It went on till dawn. As soon as the sky started to turn pale green and rose, the shootings began in the courtyard. The firing finally shattered the prisoners' nerves. Some snapped suddenly and began screaming; the militiamen went into the cells and silenced them with rifle butts.

Santiago was no longer capable of consecutive thought. His lips moved continuously. He prayed day and night. The prayers he had learned in childhood brought him nearer to the God he loved so despairingly. He no longer knew why he prayed or for whom he prayed. But it seemed to him that these words, repeated so often, held him in permanent contact with Him who had suffered hunger and thirst, loneliness and desertion before himself. In his misery he could not tell whether he had always acted rightly. He was no longer certain of anything, but lacked the courage to reconsider his life in its entirety. He offered it to God with all its good and all its evil. Disgust was his main emotion. Like Carlos, he still believed in freedom and justice and had no desire for a Fascist victory. He felt deep anguish for the future of his country and of the workers. But he had done what he could and now he placed himself in God's hands. Perhaps all was not lost. Night was slowly falling over Spain; but somewhere, perhaps, the men of the future already existed, and they would be capable of making that humane and bloodless revolution of which he had dreamed. They would learn the lessons of all the errors that had been committed and would know how to attach greater importance to human life and the freedom of individuals.

Santiago's hopes were no longer precise; his dream of justice had no particular form. The Fascist rising and the Civil War had taught him to beware of ideologies. He felt he must pray for all men so that they might become capable of accomplishing within themselves, within their own hearts, to begin with, the most total of revolutions. Only men who were deeply humane and had a profound respect for their fellows could make this kind of a revolution. For, indeed, from outside, the present war appeared to be a comparatively simple historical fact; observers could take sides with one or the other camp in accordance with their own tendencies or interests. For some the Fascists appeared as pitiless, heartless executioners who massacred women and children; for others these same Fascists appeared as the conscience of the country. Judgments just as contradictory were being made about the Republicans. But the reality was something else. There were men of good will in both camps, men who had been overwhelmed by events, but who aspired to one thing only: to live in peace. And yet there was nothing but bloodshed everywhere.

Santiago's calvary was coming to its end. That very evening he was to be transferred to another prison, and he knew it was the last stage before the end. Thousands of innocent men were in prison without trial, men who had committed no crime other than that of being nobly born, of practising their religion, or of having a relative in the Nationalist ranks. Any pretext was good enough.

Santiago neither judged nor condemned his executioners. He understood the state of nerves of this population suffering terrible hunger, incessant bombing, seeing everywhere the fearsome shadow of fascism. "It's the war. Their nerves are worn out. One must try to understand them."

His last day in the cell at the central police station seemed to him longer than the preceding ones. But night came at last, and the air turned cooler. The sky grew pale. The cell door opened, and Santiago went out.

He joined about fifty men, haggard and pale; their eyes were shadowed and their steps uncertain. Among them were two grandees of Spain, two priests, three diplomats, and a few officers. The grandees of Spain looked at Santiago with infinite contempt. He bowed his head; but their hatred left him indifferent. He had come to the end of his strength, felt drunk with fatigue and dazzled by the evening light. The militiamen went up and down the ranks, counting the prisoners, but seemed unsure of themselves and had to begin all over again several times. One of the grandees said: "Poor fellows! They can't even count. Should we help them?"

Santiago looked up and felt like saying that if the militiamen could not add, it was because they had never been allowed to go to school. But he was so tired he remained silent.

At last the prisoners were led out of the gate. A police wagon stood ready. On the pavement were a crowd of working-women, who screamed insults and threats at them.

"Bastards! Fascists!"

"Kill them!"

"What's the use of feeding that trash?"

"Sons of bitches!"

Stones and an array of other things rained down on them. Santiago prayed. He had only one longing: to find rest somewhere. The truck set off amid a chorus of yells. Santiago looked for the last time at the streets of the city he loved so deeply: they were filled with Communist flags, with ruins, and with black-clothed women standing hopeless guard before the bakers' shops.

12

NINETY prisoners were crowded into a square room with bare walls. The door had a Judas through which could be seen a long corridor and at the end a barred window overlooking a huge square courtyard. The prisoners were led into the courtyard once a day. They walked up and down, grew acquainted, and exchanged their impressions. For the most part they were aristocrats, priests, soldiers, or civil servants. None knew on what charge he had been arrested, for they had not been brought before a court. They were all violently pro-Franco and hated their executioners from the bottom of their hearts; they were hated in return. The prison regime was savagely cruel: the prisoners received no parcels or letters, their food was disgusting and sparse, the guards bullied and insulted them constantly.

As at the central police station, the prisoners suffered most from waiting and from the uncertainty of what the morrow might bring forth. They were all obsessed with the fear that the prison might be taken by assault; outside they clung close to the walls, for militiamen and working-women often fired at them from neighboring balconies. Other prisons had been stormed and the prisoners massacred. Self-appointed orators harangued the crowds in the streets and invited them to exterminate "the reactionary Fascist scum." And the populace, exhausted by their privations and the Nationalist bombing, was ready to commit any violence. The prisoners waited, fear in their hearts, for the storming of the prison which would mean death to them. Some faced the prospect of death with calm and dignity. They felt nothing but loathing and contempt for the populace and the militia; others gave way to the darkest despair; a few went on hoping.

Santiago was ignored by his fellow prisoners. The day he arrived an old friend of his father's came up to him and slapped his face without a word.

He was a man of about eighty, with white hair and gentle eyes, who still walked upright, never complained, and was always by himself. His wife and only daughter had been shot at the beginning of the Civil War. He was now awaiting his turn.

Santiago had made no attempt to defend or protect himself. He sat on his straw mattress, his head between his hands; only his lips went on living. He had no fear of dying. He lived in a sort of interior silence that he dared not break.

He often thought of his father and felt he should not have abandoned the lonely old man, but should have helped him run his estate, and made his love for him apparent by his acts. Then he shrugged his shoulders; it was too late for remorse or attempts to justify himself now. A life cannot be erected on the edge of death.

The nights were appalling. The prisoners could not

sleep. They knew that men were often taken out to be shot in the middle of the night, and their hearts failed them at the thought of being awakened by their executioners. They lay on their straw mattresses, staring at the single electric bulb that gave them light, till dawn and thought with sorrow of the past. Sometimes one of the priests recited his rosary, and the prisoners made the responses. In this antechamber of death, the words took on a new meaning. As they repeated the prayers they had recited so often and so automatically, tears came to their eyes. They lived the empty, lusterless past over again, that past they had wasted, and made plans for the future, determined to become better men, more concerned with the disinherited. They saw their lives in a new light, but, in their heart of hearts, somehow knew that even if they escaped death, they would be neither better nor worse, that the world would claim them again, and that they would forget their good intentions.

That night everything was as usual. The heavy silence was broken only by the cries of the guards doing their rounds.

"Post one, all's well!"

"Post two, all's well!"

Their voices were multiplied by the echo. Far off, they could hear the rumble of the battle slowly approaching Madrid. Some of the prisoners claimed that the Fascists had taken the North Station and would be at the Puerta del Sol within forty-eight hours.

"They can't kill us all!" one cried.

"Particularly since we're not the only ones," added another. "All the prisons in the capital are spilling over. They're even crowding hostages into the monasteries."

"And if the Reds hold out?" someone asked anxiously.

"They won't hold out. They've got no arms," snapped a third.

"I'm sure they won't leave us alive. When they know they've lost, they'll set fire to the prison," a pessimist said.

"Impossible. International opinion would turn against them, and these people are very anxious to appear civilized abroad," said a third, who always had a knowledgeable air.

In fact, none of them knew anything, even how close Franco's troops were to Madrid. They had so often taken their wishes for fact that they no longer put faith in news, even when it came from outside. They waited, battling patiently with their one enemy: time. Having no future, living only in the past, they yet looked on each extra minute they succeeded in wresting from life as an immense victory. Each hour might be their last. Wondering every evening, agonized, whether they would see the dawn, they sighed with relief each morning and felt as if they had added ten years to their life's span.

Santiago had no hope. Even if the Republicans did not kill him, he would not escape the Fascists. He was a renegade in the eyes of both camps. One side took exception to his name, his origins, and his pacifism; the other, to his ideas. He had nothing to hope from anyone. But death did not frighten him. Even if he had been told to leave the prison freely and begin his life again, he would have hesitated. Living was too complicated a business. He would have had to choose again and Santiago no longer felt strong enough to make a choice. At times he envied the poor, the wretched, and the simple-minded, who were not given a choice. But was that certain? Perhaps Olny at that very moment was faced with a choice that would decide the rest of his life. Every man sooner or later had to make such a choice.

He closed his eyes. He had been sleeping almost constantly for three days. His work as a warden during the last two months had left him exhausted, and his sojourn in the basement of the central police station had weakened him further. For him prison was a rest. He spent his days lying on his mat, sleeping or dreaming, and got up only at mealtimes and for exercise. No one spoke to him, and it was better this way. He had no wish to talk and desired nothing but the greatest rest of all: death.

The night was cold. Santiago shivered, curled up like a cat, and tried to protect himself with the thin, worn blanket of the prison administration. Someone coughed. In a corner one of the priests was repeating the words of the absolution in a low voice. Santiago heard *"Te absolvo"*; then silence fell once more. He felt comfortable. There was probably a freezing wind outside. Santiago thought of the men fighting in the trenches under the rain, of the humble women in lines at food shops. The thought saddened him. Then he let his imagination run wild. . . . He dreamed he was loved by a tender and devoted young woman, with fair hair and blue eyes. They spent their evenings by the fireside, reading aloud the poems of Alfred de Vigny and Gongora. They listened to the soft sound of the rain in the city's streets and were happy. Their children—they had three—were playing on the floor at their feet. There was no such thing as evil. People were contented; life was good; there was no poverty.

Someone touched Santiago's shoulder, and he started.

"Did I frighten you? I'm sorry. I thought you were awake."

"I was awake, Father. I was dreaming."

It was the priest who had spent the evening confessing the prisoners. Around sixty years old, he was bald and had an aquiline nose, thin lips, a jutting chin, and dark, anxious eyes; his small hands were fat, and his voice was high and a little ridiculous. "Am I disturbing you?" he asked. Without waiting for a reply, he said: "I wanted to talk to you. But don't think that I've come to you in the hope of trying to make you confess. I know you're a Communist and I deduce from that fact that you're an atheist, too. Besides, you never join us when we are saying our prayers. I've merely come to you as a friend."

"I'm not an atheist, Father."

The old priest looked at him anxiously. "You're not an atheist? You believe in Jesus Christ and in the Holy Virgin?"

"I don't know, Father. I've never asked myself whether I believe in God. I love Him."

"But so do I, my son. I left everything to serve Him and

preach His Word." The priest seemed somewhat abashed, and continued in an anxious voice: "I love God, too. I, too. You must believe me. But I don't understand how you can love God and be a Communist. The Communists are excommunicated, you know that?"

Santiago was lying on his back; the old priest sat down on the mattress. He was wearing a striped gray suit and seemed ill at ease in these strange clothes.

"I'm not a Communist, Father."

"I've been told that, too. They say you repudiated the Party. Is that why you've been arrested?"

"I don't think so."

The priest paused. His adam's apple moved quickly up and down in his throat. He touched his bald head two or three times, opened his mouth as if to speak, but changed his mind.

Santiago watched him out of the corner of his eye. He could see that the priest was afraid, and he had come seeking comfort. But Santiago felt so tired he had not the energy to say the few calming words the priest hoped for.

"May I ask you a question?"

"Of course."

"Will you answer me sincerely?"

"As sincerely as I can, Father."

The priest hesitated, then said in a different voice: "Are you not afraid of dying?"

"Sincerely, I don't think so."

"That's what I thought. But are you not afraid of being afraid?"

"I know I'll be afraid. But it will be a physical fear, an organic reaction. My mind is at peace. Only my body will refuse to die. Do you understand me?"

"Perfectly."

There was a long silence. The other prisoners were asleep. In the distance a clock struck three.

The priest lowered his head and said in a quavering voice: "I am very much afraid." He looked anxiously at Santiago. "Do you despise me?"

"Why should I despise you? I've been frightened, too, in my life."

The priest seemed relieved. "You've been afraid?"

"Of life, for instance."

"You're joking, aren't you?"

"No."

There was another pause.

"How can one be afraid of life?" the priest asked at length. "Life is the Kingdom of Light, and Death that of the Shadows. It's the temporary triumph of the Devil."

"Do you think so?"

"Christ was afraid of dying, my son."

"You may be right, Father. That is what most people think. As for me, I've found life very difficult and have never thought that it consisted of light."

"It was a metaphor. I know well that illness exists, and poverty. I have always thought of the poor, you know. In my parish there were many miserable families, who lived in caves. I often went to visit them and I reminded the rich of their duty to think of their less privileged brothers. I

249

may even say, and without vanity, that I gave much of my meager stipend in charity. I have always cared for the poor. And I don't know why, after that, they should have put me in prison and burned down my church. I don't hold them all responsible, you know. I'm inclined to believe it's due to a handful of hotheads. Don't you agree with me?"

"No."

The priest gazed at Santiago with curiosity. "Do you think they were right to burn down the churches and massacre the priests?"

"No one is ever altogether right, Father. I understand them, that's all."

The priest smiled. "You're not much of a churchman, I see."

"No."

"Were you as a child?"

"When you're a child, you merely think of God."

"I meant: did you go to Mass? Did you make your first Communion?"

"Yes."

"Do you never think of the church to which you went as a child, and of the priest who taught you your catechism?"

"Yes. I often think of nature, too. It's the same thing."

The priest did not reply at once. "Do you know that God is with His Church who is His mystical spouse?"

"I don't believe it."

"Why?"

"Because, Father, I think that God is with those who

weep, with those who are hungry, with those who suffer, and with those who doubt and seek Him. If He were in the Vatican, I should no longer believe in Him, and you would not be afraid of dying."

The priest said sadly: "I am a bad priest. I have never had the courage to face life. I was a strange boy, you know. I should never have gone to the seminary."

There was an embarrassed silence.

"Do you believe in the saints?"

Santiago smiled: he was expecting that question. "Yes, Father. I believe in them."

"And you don't believe in the church which produces them?"

"I have faith in certain medicines, Father. Does it follow that I must have faith in the druggists who sell them?"

"You're unjust."

"I know, Father. Forgive me. I'm exhausted. For some time past, you see, I have had to face much more important problems than that one. So your Church . . ." Santiago closed his eyes and added in a gentle voice: "I believe one can work out one's salvation anywhere, as well within the Church as outside it."

"I see."

The priest bowed his head. His eyes were red, his features drawn. "Do you think they'll shoot me?" he asked at last in a level voice.

"You? I don't know, Father. They'll certainly shoot me."

"Do you think they might release me? I have never

meddled in politics, and I have nothing to reproach myself with."

"Perhaps they'll release you. They can't kill us all!" With a smile Santiago added: "You don't look dangerous."

The priest relaxed and smiled, too. "Is there anything I can do for you, my son?"

"I don't think so. . . . Unless . . ."

"Don't hesitate. I promise that if I get out of here alive I shall do everything in my power to help you. I admire you very much. That may seem odd to you, but you're the sort of man who inspires confidence and whom one wants to love."

Santiago smiled. "Thank you, Father. I'll tell you what it's about. I've taken charge of a ten-year-old boy and put him in school as a boarder. He's my godson. When Franco has won, the money I put down for his education will be worthless, and the child might possibly be sent home. I should like to prevent that."

Santiago paused before saying in a weary voice: "To guard against such an eventuality, I have buried a few gold ingots. You could dig them up and take care of the boy till he comes of age. He's learning to play the violin." With a sad smile he added: "He may become a virtuoso."

The priest took Santiago's right hand between his own and said, much moved: "Thank you, my son, for putting your trust in me. I promise to look after the boy's future as if he were my own brother's son. Thank you."

Santiago searched in his pockets and handed the priest a

carefully folded piece of paper. "You'll find all the necessary information here: the boy's name and the place where the ingots are hidden."

The old priest got to his feet, took the paper, and ended the conversation by saying only: "Good night, my son. May God be with you!"

"Good night, Father."

It was some time before Santiago fell asleep. The guns were thundering close to the city as the battle drew slowly nearer to Madrid.

13

CARLOS was sitting in the bottom of a trench. His face was mud-stained and dirty with fatigue. The rain was trickling down his back, soaking his greatcoat. Shells were whistling overhead as the Fascist artillery, at the far end of the Casa del Campo, aimed more and more accurately. The Fascist forward infantry was barely four hundred yards from the Republican trenches. Carlos bit his lips, wiped the sweat from his forehead, and muttered: "Damn this rain! I'm soaked to the bone."

"So what? Did you expect luxury in the trenches? As far as I'm concerned I've never known anything else *but* this kind of lousy life."

"Shut up, Loto."

"S'pose I don't want to?"

"Shut up all the same."

Loto laughed and went on digging. He was dressed in a khaki uniform that was too big for him and a steel helmet that came down over his eyes. "What the hell did these fucking soldiers dress me up like this for? I can't see a goddam thing."

The boy threw his spade down, took his helmet off, and smoothed his curly hair. A machine gun rattled. The bullets tore through the air and made the mud spurt. Loto threw himself flat on his stomach in a puddle and put his helmet on again. "Shit! Why can't they quit firing! They could cut it out at least till our hole is finished. It's not fair."

"How do you know what's fair and what isn't?" asked a thin man with a month-old beard.

"I know as much about it as you do, you jerk. Besides, I wasn't talking to you."

"All right, kid."

The last speaker was a stout man with a red face and gray eyes—a lieutenant. His helmet had slipped to the back of his head. Loto turned to him, put his hands on his hips, and said: "Leave me alone, you fat bastard! Dig—you might lose some weight. Otherwise the militia-women may hack you into bits and turn you into sausages."

The men burst out laughing. They were sitting on the ground in the bottom of the trench and smoking butts, passing them from one to the other. Some were asleep. An

Andalusian with velvet-dark eyes and a thin face was softly playing a guitar.

Loto went and sat beside him. Carlos put his crutches on the ground and sat down opposite the Andalusian.

"Do you think they'll attack?" the Andalusian asked, still playing.

"What do you mean, attack? You don't think they've come all this way to listen to you playing a symphony, do you? You kill me."

The soldiers were all looking at Loto and laughing.

"If they attack, we've had it," said the guitar player in a level voice.

"Had it, had it! Don't exaggerate!" cried Loto. "Why should we have had it? We've got arms, haven't we? We'll hold on without you, you flute player!"

"At Guadarrama . . ." the Andalusian began.

"Guadarrama is not Madrid, chum. We're men here. I'm telling you: the boys from Madrid never surrender."

"And where do you come from?" the stout lieutenant asked.

The men roared. They knew that Loto came from Murcia.

"The land of sausages, fatty. And the guys where I come from aren't pigs."

"Obviously—they have nothing to eat."

"All right, and what did your mother eat? Flour, eh?"

But the answer was lost. A Fascist shell exploded a few yards from the trench, raising a fountain of mud.

There was a silence. Loto had turned pale. The Andalusian put down his guitar and lit a cigarette. "They've got artillery and tanks," he said, his voice still level.

"And we've got guts," Loto replied.

"That's not enough," the guitarist retorted indifferently.

"It'll do for now."

"At Guadarrama we had heavy machine guns. Yet, in spite of them—"

"Shut up! We all know that story of Guadarrama!" cried the lieutenant. "This is Madrid."

The Andalusian shrugged his shoulders, picked up his guitar, and began playing softly again.

The rain was falling thick and fast. The men shivered in the wind. They sat huddled together in the bottom of the trench, waiting patiently in the mud. In the faint light of early dawn the city behind them was hidden by rain and mist. At regular intervals the Nationalist shells screamed over their heads to burst behind them. No one spoke, except to make an occasional joke. Most of the men had been fighting continuously for over a month in the snows of the Sierra, outnumbered ten to one, only to fall back to Madrid. The Fascist attack was imminent now, and here they were, trying to gather their strength before the decisive battle.

Carlos lit a cigarette and handed the pack around. Someone asked: "Can I take the last?"

Carlos nodded.

The lieutenant came and sat on the ground beside him. "Do you think they'll attack?"

256

"Of course they will," Carlos replied.

"Have they got tanks?"

"Probably."

The lieutenant swore, straightened his helmet, and murmured: "How can we hold on? We've got only four machine guns in the sector, and the men are exhausted. If there was any chance of reinforcements, it would be different."

"I hear the unions have been handing out arms during the night."

"It doesn't make sense. We can't fire at tanks with old hunting rifles."

"What else can we do? There are heavy guns in Madrid, and they'll give us supporting fire."

"But what about the tanks?"

There was a silence. Carlos shivered. He was soaked through.

The lieutenant seemed thoughtful and finally asked: "At what time do you think they'll attack?"

"Not before tonight. They'll send the Moors in and try to make a breach. Then they'll advance in strength."

"What can we do?" the lieutenant asked. "What can we do about it? The men can't do any more. Look at them."

The men were sleeping in the mud, huddled into a mound to protect themselves from the cold. Loto had fallen asleep in a corner. They lay there, dirty, exhausted, and already defeated. The rain poured down on them.

"What on earth can I do with them?" the lieutenant asked.

"Make war."

"War! It's easy enough to say! You don't know what the retreat was like. It was way below zero up there, and the snow was up to our knees. They can do no more."

Carlos fell silent. During the last forty-eight hours he had seen the exhausted men arrive. He could guess what their life had been like in the Sierra during these last weeks. "They'll hold on," he said without conviction.

"Do you really think so?"

"I hope so."

The lieutenant got to his feet. "Come and have a look."

Carlos got up, too. They walked a few yards down the trench. The sentries were at their posts. In front of them the ground stretched away, open and slightly rolling, toward the trees of the Casa del Campo. Still farther away, on the horizon, was a low hill from which Madrid could be seen.

"They've put their guns up there," the lieutenant said.

Carlos nodded.

"Do you think they'll make their attack here?"

"Surely," Carlos replied. "They've got the trees of the Casa del Campo for cover. It's too open everywhere else."

"What would you do?"

Carlos thought for a minute or two. "Have a few flares handy and place your heavy machine guns so that they can sweep all this ground. When their artillery begins firing, ready your men and let the Moors advance. Don't open fire till they're two hundred yards from the trenches."

"Suppose I don't see them?"

"You can send up flares."

"It's an idea."

There was a pause. Carlos added: "Send a message to the gunners. There's no point in their firing at the Fascist batteries. They're certain to be well protected. It'd be better to cut off the Moors' retreat and prevent their regrouping."

The lieutenant smiled. "You're quite a tactician."

"Not much of one."

"What did you do in civilian life?"

"I was a student."

"The son of a bourgeois?"

"No, a miner."

"Forgive me. Have a cigarette?"

"Thanks."

The lieutenant struck a match, but the wind put it out. Carlos took the box, opened his coat, bent down, and managed to light the cigarette. Then the lieutenant lit his, inhaled a first puff deeply, and went on with his questions. "An Anarchist?"

"I was a Communist."

"You were? And what are you now?"

"A Republican."

"That's pretty vague."

"Yes."

They were talking in low voices.

"Why aren't you an Anarchist?" the lieutenant asked.

"I don't know. I've never thought about it."

"The Communists are all bastards."

"Not all."

"The Communist leaders are all bastards."

"Not all."

The rain was still falling.

"Why did you leave the Party? Were you disappointed in it?"

"I couldn't fight dictatorship and approve dictatorship at one and the same time. It seemed rather silly."

"You were right. I'm for liberty, too." The lieutenant paused again and then repeated: "You did well."

Carlos made no comment. His political past left him indifferent. He never even thought of it now. Since he had been at the front he had recovered that atmosphere of enthusiasm and simple comradeship he had known in his youth in the Asturias. The soldiers of the Republic bore no resemblance to the men behind the lines. They were sincere, decent, and generous, and what they were fighting for was clear to them. They asked themselves no questions, had no time to doubt or become cruel. They were conscious of what was at stake in the war: fascism was the worst of ills, and it must be defeated. The problem began and ended there. For these men, exhausted by battle, the present was fused with the future. They did not seek to know whether the society of the future would be Communist, Anarchist, or Socialist; they were content to fight furiously so that it might not be Fascist. A Republican victory was their sole hope and aim.

Besides, politics were rarely in question at the front. Anarchists, Socialists, Liberals, and Communists fraternized and died together. If they talked politics, it was generally by way of a joke. Only the Communists had their reservations.

Carlos found renewed hope. Like his comrades, he had but one object on this cold and wet November day: to repel the Fascist attack and save Madrid.

The lieutenant went on: "I must admit I know nothing about soldiering. They made me a lieutenant because when I did my military service thirty years ago I ended up as a sergeant. Since then I've never had a rifle in my hands. Being in command's not easy. Besides, the guys don't obey orders. There's no discipline in our ranks. You saw how the boy answered me back. What should I do? Get angry? I'm not a professional soldier and I've always been an antimilitarist. To be antimilitarist and be made a lieutenant is rather funny."

"Don't worry too much about discipline," Carlos said. "The important thing is that they should fight, and you know you can count on them for that. That's the essential."

"You're right."

The Fascist batteries opened fire. The shells were passing very high above their heads.

"What are they shooting at?"

"Madrid," Carlos replied indifferently.

The lieutenant changed color and swore. "Do you really think they're firing on the city?"

"Turn around and look."

"The lousy bastards!"

"That's their tactics: to demoralize the enemy's rear lines."

"Rear lines! There are women and children and invalids there! And the hospitals are full of wounded."

"They know that very well."

"Oh, the bastards!" the lieutenant repeated, turning pale.

Tall columns of flame rose from the capital into the sky. Formations of Fascist bombers flew over the Republican trenches on their way to the city. The lieutenant fell silent and clenched his teeth. From time to time he swore or muttered: "What bastards!"

Carlos slid down to the bottom of the trench and closed his eyes. He would have liked to sleep for a while, but the lieutenant sat down beside him.

"What bastards they are! When we make mistakes we've got some excuse: we've been exploited and maltreated for centuries. We haven't been taught. But they're really bastards!"

"Yes."

"Do you want to sleep?"

"Yes."

"Shall I leave you?"

"Yes."

The lieutenant got to his feet and moved away, walking bent over. His helmet prevented his seeing, and he tripped over several sleepers, who swore at him. Carlos lay down in the mud. The rain was falling with dense, monotonous regularity. The surrounding country was melancholy. There were muffled explosions in the city. A guttural voice shouted through the loud-speakers: *"Spaniards, people of Madrid! You are fighting us in vain. We are not your enemies. You have been taken in by lies. . . ."*

"Make him shut up, for God's sake!"

"We know that record!"

"Shut up, you son of a bitch!" a militiaman shouted.

"That's enough!" another yelled.

"We know that you do not agree with your Communist ministers who obey the directives of Moscow."

From the Republican trenches the sound of the *"Internationale"* from a loud-speaker drowned the guttural voice and the noise of the bombardment.

"How the hell can you get any sleep! The pigs won't give you any peace! They'll certainly win the battle for noise, anyhow. What sons of bitches!"

Carlos opened his eyes. It was Loto. The boy was sitting in a puddle. He had turned up the collar of his greatcoat and was crouching against the side of the trench to shelter from the rain.

"To hell with it! What weather! Even God's sticking his nose in! They must spend all their time burning candles to Him! He's sold out to Franco, too!"

"It's raining on both sides."

"Yes, that's true! Maybe He's not sold out to them, after all."

Loto put his hands in his pockets. His back shook as he

shivered, and his teeth chattered. His dirty face made him look even younger than he really was.

"How old are you, Loto?" Carlos asked.

"Fifteen and a half."

"Why don't you go home?"

"Why don't you?"

"I'm a man."

"And what am I?"

"A child."

"Really? . . . You want to see them?"

Carlos smiled and got up. "Do you want a cigarette?"

"Thanks."

Loto lit his cigarette. His hands were trembling. Carlos guessed the boy was afraid. He said in a gentle voice: "You're not old enough to die, Loto! You're young."

"Do you think the planes are dropping candy apples? I'd rather die here." The boy's voice was serious now.

"There are cellars in Madrid."

"So what? If I've got to die, I'd like to kill a few of the bastards first."

Carlos was silent a moment. He couldn't see the boy's face. They were both bent double.

"Why do you hate the Fascists?"

"I don't hate them. But I prefer our people."

"Why?"

"I don't know. . . . I come from the Zone. Before, when the Fascists were in power, you couldn't say or do anything; you could only die in silence. Things are not much better perhaps with Republicans, but you can at least yell about it, and go on strike. You can *do* something. I'm all for being able to yell. When things don't go right, you have to be able to kick about it."

Carlos made no reply.

The Fascists were still bombarding the city. Above the trenches the Republican loud-speakers were shouting hymns to liberty; the Nationalists were broadcasting the "Cara al Sol." [6] The soldiers were sleeping in their holes. The rain was still pouring down.

Toward eight o'clock at night the Fascist artillery grew quiet. The wind had fallen; the sky had cleared.

Their hearts beating, the Republicans were waiting behind their parapets for the Nationalist attack. All was silent in Franco's camp. The hours passed slow and monotonous.

Carlos grimly clutched his rifle as sweat poured down his forehead. He could hear the beating of his heart through the silent waiting. Someone struck a match, and the sudden burst of flame tore into the darkness for a few seconds. No one uttered a word.

Loto was doing his best not to tremble, but his legs buckled under him. His throat was dry, and his eyelids felt heavy; his teeth chattered.

"Perhaps they won't attack after all," the stout lieutenant muttered.

[6] The first words of the Falangist song.

Carlos put his finger to his mouth and listened. "Send up a flare," he whispered.

The lieutenant looked at him in surprise "Why?"

"I've got a feeling they're coming."

"Who?"

"The Moors."

"Are you mad?"

"I don't think so."

"We would have heard them."

"They crawl very silently. That's their speciality."

"And if you're wrong?"

"You can have me shot," Carlos whispered.

The lieutenant hesitated for a second or two, then went off, bent double. Carlos wiped the sweat from his forehead. Loto edged closer to him.

Suddenly the flare tore through the night, rose into the heavens, burst into light, hung there, and fell slowly, illuminating the terrain. The machine guns went immediately into action. The Moors dashed forward, yelling. The Republicans were firing at practically point-blank range. Then the Fascist artillery opened up. The noise soon became deafening. Mingled with the sound of exploding shells, the rattle of machine guns, the cries of the advancing Moors, and the screaming of the wounded, was the noise of engines in the sky. It was as if the earth were bursting open. More flares lit up the battlefield, covered with corpses. Reinforcements were coming up to support the attackers; the Republican machine guns swept the terrain and mowed them down. The Nationalist shells were falling closer and closer to the trenches. The air smelled of powder, fire, and burning flesh. Soon two of the Republican machine guns were reduced to silence. The Moors and Franco's legionaries came shouting into the attack. It was a human wave. Carlos stopped firing only to reload his magazine. Loto had forgotten his fear and was uttering little grunts of joy each time his aim was accurate. As for Carlos, he didn't even bother to aim; he fired into the mass. The German Junkers dropped their first bombs, and the earth trembled.

"We're going to be overrun!" the lieutenant shouted into Carlos's ear.

"Telephone headquarters. Ask for artillery support."

"They've got aircraft!" the lieutenant shouted.

"So I see."

"But where the hell are our fighters?"

More waves came into the attack against the Republicans' trenches. The Moors, whose numbers were steadily increasing, were advancing closer and closer. Carlos was shuddering and firing continuously. The two machine guns still in action had only a limited field of fire. Carlos could now see the faces of the attackers, for they were barely fifty yards from him. A third machine gun was put out of action. In some sectors hand-to-hand fighting with bayonets was already going on. The bottom of the trench was full of dead and wounded. The earth was red with blood, and the Junkers, skimming the ground, strafed the Republicans. . . .

·   ·   ·

And then, suddenly, there was a miracle. The Republican artillery opened up. Fighters flew into action, attacking the Fascist Junkers head on. Thousands of men, armed with old sporting guns, swarmed to the trenches. The Moors retreated. The whole population of Madrid had come out to defend their city. They were fighting with whatever they could find, fighting with a furious obstinacy.

The Republicans howled with joy, embraced each other, threw their helmets into the air. They could not restrain their pride. Madrid had held out. The nameless, the ragged, the illiterate, the disinherited, had won the most astonishing of victories. Ill-armed and ill-organized, they had repelled disciplined battalions equipped with modern weapons.

Carlos smiled with happiness. Loto was jumping with joy and screaming at the fleeting enemy.

"Cowards, shits, bastards!"

Someone began singing the *"Internationale,"* and from all the Republican trenches hoarse, weary voices rose in the hymn of liberty.

Suddenly Loto staggered and fell. Carlos rushed to the boy, but he was already dead. Carlos could not grasp what had happened. He took off his greatcoat, threw it over the boy's body, and looked miserably about him. A stray bullet must have hit the boy in the middle of the forehead, for there was a big black hole from which the blood oozed. His comrades had noticed nothing. They were still singing and dancing. Carlos trembled, helpless in the face of this meaningless death. His eyes were wet with tears. He thought of how stupid it was. He felt suddenly as if some-one had punched him on the shoulder, and he tried to turn around. Then he realized he had been wounded himself. Everything swam before his eyes. He tried to cling for support to the edge of the trench, but could not manage. He slid and fell. His mind grew cloudy. As if in a dream, he heard voices singing and shouting. He made an effort to get up, but could not.

It was only at dawn that the deaths of Carlos and the boy were noticed. The stout lieutenant was much moved.

14

IT HAD snowed gently on Madrid. The city was white; the sky was laden with stars. A full moon made the snow sparkle in the cold, intoxicating air. Everything was silent. There had been no bombing that day and there probably would be none that night. It was Christmas.

The people of Madrid were celebrating this first wartime Christmas with sorrow. There would be no midnight Mass and no turon.[7] But, because it was Christmas, families gath-ered nevertheless to dine and sing together. In many

[7] A sort of nougat which Spaniards eat a great deal of at Christmas.

homes there were faces missing, vacant chairs about the table. It would also be a night of silence and meditation, of forgiveness and forgetfulness. No one would think of the war, except to mourn those absent, some of whom might never return.

Olny had celebrated Christmas with Marianita, with a chicken and champagne. They had gotten a package three days before.

It was already late at night. Olny liked hearing the snow crunch beneath his feet in the empty streets. All was peace. He was going to the cemetery, though he thought he might just as well have stayed at home. No one would be shot on Christmas night.

Olny had become used to his duties. He avoided thinking of them and tried to forget in the morning what he had seen the night before. Sometimes he felt like killing himself. But he told himself he had no right to do it, since he had a wife and a child on the way. He never looked at his victims. He would have shot anyone with the same indifference and the same disgust. It had become a means of making a living, like anything else, and he had no choice. Marianita, thanks to the food parcels from the trade union, had put on weight and recovered her health. Olny refused to surrender to remorse, telling himself that it was not he who condemned his victims to death, and that if he did not shoot them, someone else would do it in his place and would get the food packages.

He had no hope or illusions left. The fate of the Revolution and even that of the Republic left him indifferent. He despised both himself and the men who organized these massacres. He loathed everything and everybody. He would have shot Republicans just as willingly, as long as it brought him the same advantages. He avoided thinking of his past and what he might have become had he stayed in the Zone.

He reached the cemetery and went to the red brick house. His comrades were asleep. Olny went to bed, too. But he could not sleep. He kept wondering what sense there was in the sort of life he led. There was nothing in it to be proud of. How he regretted the Zone now! He would have liked to go back and begin all over again. He understood his parents better now and told himself that, in the end, fate always played cruelly with men.

There was the sound of a truck outside. Olny got up, took his keys, and grumbled to himself. "Even at Christmas! They could give us a little peace!"

He opened the gates. The truck drove in and stopped.

"Oh, it's you, is it?" It was Ramírez. He held out his hand. Olny silently refused to take it, and spat.

"It'll be over quickly tonight," Ramírez said. "There are only fifteen of them. Wake your comrades."

Olny nodded and went into the house to wake them. They got up muttering and complaining. Perico was still half asleep; but the cold air outdoors woke them up. With Ramírez there were five of them, armed with submachine guns. They shouldered their arms and surrounded the truck. Ramírez opened the rear door of the truck and said: "Come on, all of you! With your hands up!"

Olny knew the form by heart. He was sleepy and simply wanted to get it over with as quickly as possible.

The prisoners got out of the truck, their arms raised above their heads. Among them were an old man with white hair, who tried to hold himself upright, and an officer with a cold, disdainful expression. . . . Suddenly Olny felt faint. A long shudder shivered down his back: Santiago de Leyes emerged from the truck.

He recognized Olny. They stood face to face, as if petrified. Olny was trembling. He wanted to explain to his friend that it was not his fault, that he had not wanted this, that he was only a pawn in the game and that he would have liked to die in his place. Santiago smiled gently, his gaze warm and affectionate. Olny's agony paralyzed him. He tried to signal to his friend, but he could not move his hand.

"March!"

The prisoners walked in single file up the long cypress-bordered avenue. Santiago was the last. Olny was close to him. The two friends were almost touching.

"I've got to save him," Olny thought. "My God, he can't die. I have to save him. Perform a miracle, dear God. Just one, a little one. Then I'll believe in You."

Santiago stumbled, and Olny put out a hand to steady him.

"Thank you," said the young aristocrat.

Olny's eyes were stabbed with tears. He wanted to cry

out, to call for help; he hoped still. This thing could not happen: Santiago could not die like this. He drew near to his friend and murmured in a voice broken with sobs: "I love you. It's not my fault. I didn't know."

Santiago smiled and replied: "I know, Olny. I love you, too. Kiss Mariana for me. Don't cry." He added a few words Olny could not hear. ". . . fascism . . . It is worse!"

Olny thought he was going mad. His head whirled. The prisoners had reached the end of the alley and now they stood side by side, their backs to a ditch in which bodies were already heaped.

The submachine guns spluttered. Unconsciously, by a sort of automatic reflex, Olny had pressed his trigger. The bodies bounded into the air before falling into the ditch. A few seconds later all was over.

"Are you coming?" Ramírez asked. "I've brought some champagne."

The militiamen went off. Olny heard them laughing as they walked away. Alone and aghast, his eyes dilated, he stood by the grave in which some forty corpses were piled one on another. He no longer tried to hold back his tears, they poured down his face and his shoulders were twisted with sobs. He leaned over the ditch and looked down. Santiago's body lay at the bottom. Olny sobbed and shouted, hit his head against the ground, muttered incoherent words, beat his breast, cried for help.

The moon burst through the clouds and illuminated the scene.

·   ·   ·

Three years have gone by. General Franco has won the war. His troops marched down the Castellana, where a delirious crowd cheered them.

Ramírez got out of Madrid in time. He is living in France now.

Olny has gone back to the Zone with Marianita; their son is nearly four years old. The children of the Zone say Olny has gone mad. He spends his days in bars and beats his wife regularly.

The Zone has not been much affected by the war.

A Note on the Author

Michel del Castillo was born in Madrid on August 3, 1933. His father was French and his mother was a Spanish journalist whose Republicanism forced them to flee Franco Spain. In France the boy and his mother were interned as political refugees in a concentration camp in Lozère. When the Nazis entered this territory, Michel del Castillo was separated from his mother and taken to Germany, where he spent the rest of the war. At the end of the war Michel del Castillo was sent back to Spain, only to be placed for several years in an orphanage and delinquents' home. After his escape from that institution, he spent two years in a Jesuit school in Ubeda.

Upon leaving the school, he worked for some months as a laborer in a factory near Barcelona and then, after his twentieth birthday, made his way to Paris, where he was admitted to the Sorbonne and began to write *Child of Our Time*.

Michel del Castillo resides now in Paris, where he wrote *The Disinherited*.

A Note on the Type

THE TEXT *of this book was set on the Linotype in Janson, a recutting made direct from the type cast from matrices long thought to have been made by Anton Janson, a Dutchman who was a practising type-founder in Leipzig during the years 1668-1687. However, it has been conclusively demonstrated that these types are actually the work of Nicholas Kis (1650-1702) a Hungarian who learned his trade most probably from the master Dutch type-founder Dirk Voskens. The type is an excellent example of the influential and sturdy Dutch types that prevailed in England prior to the development by William Caslon (1692-1766) of his own incomparable designs, which he evolved from these Dutch faces. The Dutch in their turn had been influenced by Claude Garamond (1510-1561) in France. The general tone of the Janson, however, is darker than Garamond and has a sturdiness and substance quite different from its predecessors. This book was composed, printed, and bound by H. Wolff, New York. The paper was manufactured by P. H. Glatfelter Co., Spring Grove, Penn. Typography and binding based on designs by George Salter.*